COLLEEN SNYDER

RECKONING

Colleen Snyder

DEDICATION

To the readers who may one day read these words and think, "I
resemble that remark."
God be with you.

MONDAY

Radio static. "Commander, we reconned over the ridge. I think there's a problem."

Return static. "What problem?"

"There's a lake, yes, ma'am. But there's a lodge with cabins."

Silence. "Say again?"

"A lodge."

"Tell me exactly what you're seeing."

"The highway runs north-south. There's a west turn-off. Runs a mile back to the lake. Lodge sits on the north end of the water. Cabins are west. Dirt road circles around in front of them. Volleyball, basketball courts. Couple of firepits. No, it does not look deserted."

Silence. Long silence. Cursing. More silence. "We will have to get creative, then."

"How creative?"

"We're here to train in stealth, camouflage, recon, and surveillance. Maybe we get real-world experience."

"Whatever you say, Commander."

"Leave two of your troops there. I want eyes on the area at all times."

"Yes, ma'am."

MONDAY AFTERNOON

"Your dad's home."

Sam jumped up from his desk, grabbed his mitt and baseball, and raced to the kitchen. He wiggled and did little hops. Sheltie and Missy barked and danced at the door. Sam heard Dad's hand on the doorknob, turning it slowly, slowly, increasing the dogs' agitation and excitement. They growled and fought to be first in line to greet Dad. The door opened, and they swarmed their master. Sam bounced from foot to foot until the dogs were loved and hugged and kissed and rewarded. Only after they raced to the living room with dog bones in their mouths did he step forward and throw his arms around his dad. "Hi!"

Dad untangled himself. "Hey." He stepped around Sam and moved into the kitchen, where Mom waited. She made as if to kiss him, but he blew raspberries in her face. Then he laughed. Sam could see the hurt in his mom's eyes.

Dad did, too, because he turned away. "Can't anyone take a joke in this house? You look for things to get mad at."

Mom's voice didn't sound mad. Quiet but not mad. "How was your day?"

"Don't ask. Same as always. They're looking for a reason to get rid of me. I know they are."

Dad walked into the bedroom. Sam knew better than to follow. He waited in the living room. Dad came out, dressed in sweatpants and a t-shirt. "Cokie, the new girl? She's trying to get me fired."

"What happened?" Mom walked into the dining room so she could see and hear him.

"I've been joking around with her. Playing, you know? I like to sneak up behind and scare her. The first couple times I did it, she laughed. Then she started getting mad about it. Told me to stop."

Mom said, "But you didn't."

Dad threw a pillow onto the couch. Hard. "It's a joke. No one can take a joke anymore. She told Abbott she would file a harassment complaint against me. Abbott called me in. I apologized, but I'm done. I'll go in, do my job, and then leave. I'm not talking to anyone." He tossed a handful of mini-bones onto the floor to get the dogs off the couch. Sheltie and Missy fought over who got the most and the last. Dad laughed.

Mom wiped her hands on the dishtowel she held. "Did Abbott say anything to Jeff or Erin?"

"I don't care if he did. Erin's never liked me. I made a crack about him and his wife being a fudge-striped cookie once. I think he holds it against me." Dad closed the living room curtains. And the dining room curtains. He liked it dark in the house. That way, the neighbors couldn't look in the windows and see what they might want to steal.

Sam sat on the floor to wait for the conversation to end. Why would Uncle Erin be upset with Dad? And why would Dad say mean things about Aunt Vy? They weren't really his aunt and uncle, of course. Erin worked as Dad's boss at Trinity Builders and had married Vy. But they always acted like family. And Vy was cool. Yeah, she might not be white, but Mom said it didn't matter what skin color you had. It mattered what you did. What you had in your heart. And Vy's heart was always full of love.

Mom's voice softened. "Erin loves the Lord. He doesn't hold grudges."

Dad dropped onto the couch and turned on the TV. He sneered, "'Erin loves the Lord.' Like I don't? You never take my side, do you?"

Mom didn't say anything. Sam's heart dropped. He stood and walked to stand in front of his dad. "Can we go throw the ball, Dad? You said we would when you got home."

"I've got a headache. Maybe later. After I get up."

Sam bit his lip. "I've got a game tomorrow afternoon. Can you come watch?"

"You know I have to work. I don't get to take time off just because I want to. Why do you have to play baseball, anyhow? I don't like baseball. Why can't you play football?"

Mom reminded Dad, "They don't have football this time of year. He could play soccer."

"I hate soccer. It's like watching paint dry. Guys running up and down the field and nothing happening." He flipped the channels. "Where are Wendy and Brutus?"

Wendy and Brutus. His big brother and sister. Wendy was eighteen. Brutus was nineteen. Ten years older than Sam.

Sometimes Brutus didn't want him around. Sometimes he did. *I like it when he does. It's fun.*

"They have an activity at church tonight." Mom leaned against the wall.

Dad snorted. "They spend more time there than they do at home. Always something."

"They have friends there. What are you complaining about? You don't drive them."

"I've seen some of their 'friends.' I don't like them."

Dad turned the channel to a movie. Dad liked movies Mom didn't. Movies about people kissing and rolling around in beds. Sometimes they didn't have clothes on. Sam sat down in front of the couch. "Can I watch with you?"

Mom's eyes narrowed. "I think—"

Dad cut her off. "Sure, buddy." He stuck his tongue out at Mom. "At least someone wants to sit with me." He rubbed the top of Sam's head. "You love me, don't you, Sam?"

"Yes, Dad. I love you."

Dad jeered at Mom. "See? At least there's one in this house who does."

She turned away. "Dinner will be ready at six."

"What did you fix?" He grinned at Sam, and then mouthed, *"Watch this."*

"Chicken."

"I don't want chicken. I had chicken for lunch. Fix something else." His face crinkled with silent laughter.

Mom walked into the kitchen and called over her shoulder. "What do you want?"

"What have you got?" Dad rubbed Sheltie's head. Missy snapped at her. Sheltie snapped back. Dad laughed and pushed them away from his side.

Sam heard the refrigerator open. Mom called, "We still have roast beef."

"Nah. Your leftovers are always dry."

"I can make an omelet." Sam heard Mom moving things around on the shelves.

"You have any fish?" Dad grinned at Sam.

"It's not thawed."

"Thaw it. I'll wait." Dad pulled the pillow over his head. "Wake

4

me up when it's ready."

Sam leaned against the couch.

TUESDAY

Tuesday evening, Collin Farrell slipped into an empty chair directly behind Pam and Tom Quince. The meeting—an informational session—had already started. She'd been delayed by the triplets. Again. Joshua wanted to play cars. Caleb wanted to play with the building blocks instead. A fight ensued. Their sister, Talitha, wanted to read books to her brothers, but they wouldn't sit still. Fact of life with four-year-olds.

Jeff Farrell, her husband, faced the assembled Trinity Builders senior management team, their wives, husbands, and significant others. "This will be our 'dry run.' If we can pull it off with you, we believe we can pull it off company-wide."

Jeff pulled up a slide projected on the large screen in the front of the room. "Read, and then ask questions. One, no, this does not count against your regular vacation. Two, yes, consider it mandatory. It's five days, people. Your normal work week. So maybe it's abnormal, but considering some of our weeks, well…" Jeff trailed off, and then smiled. "Call it an investment in Trinity Builders. You do better when we do better, right?"

Collin groaned inwardly. I told you not to use that line. Oh, Jeff.

Her husband continued his presentation. "The company is paying for everything. You're guests at our family lake and lodge here in Ohio. Farrell Acres." Someone groaned. Probably her brother, Erin. Jeff laughed. "Yeah, we're working on a better name. Maybe we'll make it a contest. Best entry wins another free week."

Maybe not the best incentive, my love.

Jeff put up another slide. "We'll have activities for those who want to participate. Quiet times for those who don't. Call it enforced relaxation."

Someone asked, "WiFi?"

"Nope. And no company cellphones allowed. We can't keep you from bringing your own, but I warn you, reception is of the, 'Can you hear me now?' sort. We have a landline for emergencies. The number is in the information we sent you."

More questions. More answers. More laughter. Snacks were served. Collin slipped out at eight-thirty to relieve the babysitter. Their adult son, Rob, had volunteered to watch the triplets. As part of the Trinity company, he'd been on the planning team for the retreat, which excused him from attending the meeting. In exchange for staying with his siblings, Rob got to raid the refrigerator. *Rob insists he gets the better end of the deal. I'm not going to argue with him. Love him, but not argue with him.* Never.

WEDNESDAY

Sam pulled his baseball jersey on over his shirt. His mom's phone rang. He slipped out of his room and tip-toed down the hall to listen. He held his breath so she wouldn't hear him.

Mom answered. She had it on speakerphone. She might be working on sewing. Someone from her work paid her to make pillows from old cheerleading uniforms. Mom liked sewing things. She made all his Halloween costumes. He needed to think about what he wanted to be this year. There were still three months until trick-or-treat, but Mom had to have time to sew everything. And find all the parts he sometimes needed. She was really good at finding things.

"Hello, Tom."

"Tell Sam I'm not going to make it to the game."

"You promised me. Now he's going to be disappointed." Sam sagged against the wall. His stomach began to hurt. "You always leave me to deal with everything."

"Yeah, well, tell him I have a headache. You'll have to take him yourself."

"It's a doubleheader. You could make the second game." Sam perked up. *Maybe?*

Dad's voice tensed. "I said I'm not coming. I've got a headache. I'm coming home, and you'll have to take him. Bye." Dad hung up.

Sam snuck back to his room and hung his head. *He never comes. He goes to all of Brutus's games. And Wendy's. He must hate me.* He grabbed his mitt and threw it on the floor.

Mom walked into his room. She had her sewing scissors in her hand. She laid them on his chest of drawers, and then gave him a hug. "I'm sorry, Sam. Your dad won't be coming to your game. He's got a bad headache. You don't want him to come when he doesn't feel good, do you?"

Sam's face burned. "He goes fishing when he doesn't feel good. Why can't he come to my game?"

Mom hugged his shoulders. "I don't know, Sam. I'm sorry. I'll have to take you again, and we'll go out after for dinner. Your choice. Dad can fend for himself."

Sam gave her a single nod. He loved Mom, but she couldn't replace Dad.

Mom sighed. "Guess I better get back to work." She left the room.

She forgot her scissors. He picked them up, jerked his jersey over his head, and slashed it to shreds. Sam stuffed the remains between the mattress and the box springs. And then he put the scissors back where Mom left them. He sat on the bed, kicking the floor. *Dad hates me. He hates me. He hates me.* Tears filled his eyes. *I hate him.* Sam buried his head in his pillow and wept.

* * *

After midnight, Sam slipped down the hall from his bedroom to the kitchen. On the way, he picked up Dad's cigarette lighter from the ashtray in the family room. Sam flicked the lighter. The spark ignited the butane. A one-inch blaze jumped in his hand. What should he burn? Sam held the flame under the edge of the kitchen counter.

A dark shadow formed on the rolled edge of the laminate work surface. Sam moved the lighter to make a second mark. Would Dad notice? Would he ask about it?

Sam pulled the lighter back. The two black columns stained the edge of the counter. Sam's heart hurt. Dad would say they were just dirt marks. Maybe something that had been there for a long time. Dad wouldn't care.

Sam twirled around and flicked the lighter again. The hem of the flimsy café curtains caught fire. Sam pounded them out in panic. *No! I don't want to hurt anyone. I just want him to notice me.*

Sam slipped quietly through the family room and put the lighter back in the ashtray where he found it, and then tip-toed to his room and crawled into bed. He hugged his pillow, burying his face.

Please. Love me, too. Please. He cried himself to sleep.

A shadowy figure stole through the family room. It stopped and picked up the lighter. Gliding into the kitchen, the figure flicked the flame to life. It held it under the curtains. The shadow watched the blaze consume half the curtain before extinguishing it with an oven mitt. Satisfied, the shadow crept into the bathroom where Sam's jeans lay. It stuffed the lighter into a pocket and replaced the jeans on the floor. And then it slid to the back of the house and closed the bedroom door.

THURSDAY

Thursday night, Jeff Farrell closed the office door at Trinity Builders behind him. "Quitting time. I thought it'd never get here."

Tom Quince swung his pack over his shoulder. "Comes this time every day."

"Some days, it takes longer." Jeff juggled his backpack, briefcase, and his lunch box. Ponies. The triplets picked it out for him for his birthday. *Real men carry pink ponies. The boys chose the ponies, Tee chose the color. I'll carry it proudly.*

Erin Winger, Jeff's brother-in-law, rocked along on his arm crutches. "I agree with Jeff. This has been a long week. I want to be out of here by noon tomorrow. I've got packing to do for the retreat." The men headed down the hall to the elevator and freedom.

Tom stopped and stared at Erin. "You're married, right?"

Erin frowned. "Yeah. So?" They started walking again. Erin leaned into an open office. "Go home. It'll be there tomorrow." A desk drawer closed in reply.

"So it's the wife's job. Your job is to pack the fishing gear and be ready to leave."

Erin clucked disapproval. "Do *not* let my wife hear you say such things. We work as a team. We pack as a team. And do everything else the same way."

Jeff nodded. The men reached the elevator. "Yeah, Collin is of the same mind. She's packing the kids' clothes, but I pack the rest."

Jeff pushed the button for the ground floor.

As they waited for the doors to open, Tom waved a hand dismissively in the air. "Hen-pecked. You need to train your wives better."

Erin raised his eyebrows. "Vy and I have our relationship working just fine, thank you. I respect her, she respects me, we do things together. Parity. Peace."

The elevator door dinged open. The three men entered, turned, and faced forward. Tom continued his goading. "Pam respects me. She does what I say. I'm the head of the house like God appointed. You can only have one boss." The elevator dropped from the seventh floor. Going down.

Jeff cleared his throat. "Um, I think we're a team." He indicated the three occupants of the elevator by circling his finger. "Sometimes Erin takes the lead. Sometimes you do, Tom, and sometimes I do. We work together. No one is the head all the time. We work to each other's strengths."

Tom shrugged. "Maybe in business. Home is home. It's a man's castle, right? The place where everything runs smooth as glass because I am the head."

Erin's jaw dropped. "And you've been married how long?"

"Twenty years."

Erin cast his eyes sideways to his brother-in-law. Jeff rolled his eyes covertly so Tom couldn't see. Tom rocked back and forth on his heels. "Jeff, I could use some help tomorrow. Sam wants to stay with the triplets. It would really help me if I could bring him over about seven, and he stayed with you and the family overnight."

Jeff stared at the floor. "I don't know, Tom. We do have a lot of packing to get done."

"You're not leaving until Sunday, anyhow, right? You'd never leave before church. So it's one night. Help me out, man."

Jeff breathed out sharply. "Let me check with Collin." He reached for his phone.

Tom pointed at him and laughed. "I prove my point. You're hen-pecked, both of you. You always have to check with higher headquarters. Why can't you just say, 'Yes,' and it be okay?"

Jeff punched in the speed dial to home. "Because I love and respect Collin too much to drop something like this on her without asking." He held the phone to his ear. *No, I will not put it on speaker phone, Tom, though I know you want me to.* "Collin, milady. Tom, Erin, and I are leaving work. Tom wants to know if Sam can come over and spend Friday night. Tomorrow, yeah."

He listened, and then directed his comment to Tom. "As long as you pick him up by noon on Saturday. The trio is going to a birthday party at one."

"Can't Sam just go with them? What's one more kid?" Tom shrugged to make his point.

Jeff shook his head. He didn't wait for Collin to weigh in. "It's not about one more kid. It's a four-year-old turning five party. Sam would be miserable."

"Meh, he can adjust."

Jeff repeated, "You have to pick him up at noon, Tom. It's the arrangement."

Tom scowled. "If that's the best you can do for a friend, I guess it'll have to work. Just means I'll have to stop what I'm doing to come get him."

Jeff nodded. "Sorry about the interruption to your time. It's all we can do." He returned to Collin on the phone. "Thanks, dear. I'll see you in an hour." He ended the call.

Erin glanced at Tom. "What are you working on?"

"Brakes on the Cavalier. They need to be changed and bled."

"You want some help? I can…"

Tom cut him off. "No, you can't. I need someone who can crawl under the car." He clapped Erin on the shoulder and laughed. "No offense, Tin Man, but you're not the most nimble. And I heard if someone gives you a wrench, you'll try to hurt yourself with it. I'll be fine."

Erin chuckled. Jeff watched his eyes and saw the spark of hurt pass through them. Quick spark. Tom laughed. "It's a joke, man. Don't people have a sense of humor anymore?"

Jeff decided to change the subject. "You think we can get a volleyball game going next week? We'll modify the rules. No limit on the number of people on the court, and the first team to one hundred wins."

Erin grinned. "I can get behind a game with those rules."

Tom frowned. "Volleyball. I swear, all you people want to do is froth up the lake and chase the fish away. I'll never get any serious fishing done. If you're not splashing up the shores, you'll be out pulling rafts or skiers. Man can't have any quiet time. I've half a mind not to go."

The elevator stopped at the fifth floor and took on two more passengers. Jeff suggested, "We could easily make a no-wake zone specifically for fishing. Have designated quiet hours for swimming and fishing only."

Tom tossed his head. "I guess. I'd get all the crappy hours, though, wouldn't I?"

Erin chimed in. "You could have four or five in the morning 'til about ten. And then again from about eight to eleven in the evening. How do those hours sound?"

Tom considered it. "I don't know. If it's the best I'm going to get, I'll have to take it, I suppose." He tilted his head and raised one eyebrow, shooting a look at Jeff and Erin. "Don't you need to check with the bosses before you make this decision?"

Jeff shook his head. "Not this."

Erin agreed. "Not for this. It'll be fine."

Jeff added, "The main thing is for you to come. It's semi-mandatory, right? Trial run for senior management and their teams. If it works, we can have the whole company. Come enjoy yourself."

Tom all but jeered. "Having the company pay for it is the best part."

Jeff shrugged. "As long as we can, we will."

The elevator stopped on the first floor. All the bodies disembarked. Tom headed to the garage. "I need to call Pam. I'll see you later, Jeff. And thanks a million."

Jeff waved and said nothing. He put his hand on Erin's shoulder. "Don't take it personally. Tom…"

Erin continued, "… is Tom. It's who he is. Who he'll always be. I'm used to it."

"You and Vy want to ride up to the lake with us?

Erin hesitated. "We'll pass. It'll be quieter in the car. I'm sure we'll have plenty of time alone with members of the trio this week. Time for reading books and coloring pictures and asking questions about nature." He smiled. "I'll take a couple hours of peace first."

"Coward."

"You got it." Erin pursed his lips. "You have any idea what Rob wants to talk to me about?"

Jeff smiled. "Rob's twenty-four. He's thinking about life. And I think he had some questions you and Vy could answer for him."

"Did he ever get his genealogy DNA test back?"

Jeff and Erin walked out of the building and onto the street. They headed to the parking lot. "It didn't help much. A lot of what he already knew. Lots of mixed parentages, from all over Africa, Somalia, Turkey, The South Sea Islands, you name it. He's also got Polynesian, French, Guyana… Rob is a man of the world. But what he's not is Anglo-Saxon."

Erin unlocked the car door. "He's a man of color. He likely wants to talk to Vy and me about relationships."

The men slid into the car. Erin positioned to drive. "Vy is a woman of color. I'm about as white as they come. He wants to know how we make it work. Bet?"

Jeff shook his head. "No bet. I'm sure you're right." He paused. "What will you tell him?"

Erin smiled. "Find a woman as wonderful and fantastic as Vy. And then there'll be no problem."

Jeff shook his head. "I'm sure it will be a lot of help." He didn't bother to hide the good-natured sarcasm.

"It worked for me. No, we have advice. And counsel. And scripture. What we don't have is the woman God has for him. Her, he has to find for himself." Erin grinned.

"Maybe he already has, which is why he wants to talk." Jeff raised an eyebrow.

Erin started the car and pointed it towards home. "We'll have to wait and see. Won't we?"

Jeff's phone buzzed. He looked at the caller ID. "Tom. So soon?" He answered. "Hey. Everything okay?"

"Yeah. I'm going to be in late tomorrow. Probably around eleven. Pam has an appointment I need to attend. Women." Jeff heard the eye-roll over the phone.

"Anything serious?" Anything this quick can't be good.

"Depends on who you ask. She thinks it is. I think it's a lot of female hysteria over a minor incident."

Jeff exchanged glances with Erin. Erin shrugged and shook his head. Jeff said, "Okay. If there's anything you need, let me know."

"A million bucks."

"Sorry. Can't help you."

"I see how you are." The call ended.

Erin pulled into traffic, and then scowled. "Tom being Tom. I wonder when we'll get the full story?"

"We'll get it from Pam or not at all."

"Truth, bro."

They rode the remainder of the way home in silence.

FRIDAY

Tom and Sam arrived at six-thirty Friday night, with the Farrells in the middle of dinner. Tom stuck his head in the door. "I catch you eating?"

Collin grimaced. Jeff smiled and muttered so only she could hear him. "Do not let him get to you."

Collin put on a happy face. "Yes, but come on in. We've got plenty for everyone. Soup beans and cornbread."

Tom laughed. "Good. My timing is getting better." He pulled Sam into the room and pointed to the cabinet beside the sink. "Plates are over there, boy. Eat up. Your Aunt Collin makes the best food. Even if you can't tell what it is."

Sam's eyes dropped to the floor. No light shone in them. Collin studied him a moment, then offered, "You don't have to eat if you're not hungry, Sam. Or I can get you something…."

The boy looked up and interrupted her. "No, this is fine. Honest. Thank you for letting me eat dinner with you." Sam got a bowl out of the cabinet and carried it to the table. He broke a piece of cornbread into chunks and ladled white beans over the top.

The trio remained seated but bumped up and down with excitement. "Sam's here! Sam's here!"

He grinned. "Hey, guys. Good to see you."

Joshua asked, "You have a new game to teach us this time?"

Caleb asked, "Like you did last time?"

Sam sat next to Joshua and nodded. "Yeah, I do. After we eat and help your mom with the dishes."

Talitha's eyes seemed shy. Hesitant. "Can I play, too, this time?"

This time? Wasn't she allowed to play before?

Stay out of it. Children need to work out their own battles.

But she's only four. And they were here at her house.
Doesn't matter. Do not interfere.

Collin snapped out of her internal debate and turned to Tom. "I'm sorry about tomorrow, but Sam has to be picked up by noon."

Tom shrugged. "That's what Jeff said. I'll make sure Pam gets the message. She'll be here."

Collin cocked her head. "Pam? Isn't she working tomorrow? Mandatory overtime or something?" Collin filled a glass with milk for Sam and handed it to him.

Tom sneered. "They can't order her to work overtime. It's stupid. I told her before. She'll leave work in time to come get Sam. If they say anything about it, she'll quit."

Collin's eyes flared. "Quit? She's been working there eighteen years. She told me she had to be there twenty to be fully vested in the stock-sharing plan. If she quits, she'll lose it all." Collin's foot tapped under the table.

"Let them try to fire her. Or take her benefits away. I'll raise such a fuss they'll regret they ever did anything. She'll own the place by the time I'm finished with them." Tom waved his hand in the air.

Jeff held up his hand. "Um, I'd think twice or maybe three times before you start a battle with Poe, Lyman, and Wolery. They practice law for a living, you know."

Tom laughed. "I'm not scared of them. They think they know everything. They don't know me." He shoved Sam's shoulder. "Be good." And then he walked out the door, closing it behind him.

Collin looked at the floor, shaking her head. Jeff touched her hand. "We'll keep it in prayer."

Sam eyed Jeff. "Dad says prayer doesn't do anything. It's just an excuse people make when they don't want to help you." He shoveled in a spoonful of the bean and cornbread mix.

Collin's insides twisted. She breathed slowly. "In my experience as a believer in Jesus, prayer is talking to my Heavenly Father, no different than talking to you. Except He knows all the answers and can do something about the problems. That's why I pray. And your dad is right. Sometimes we don't know the answers to everything. When I don't, I ask the One Who does."

Sam chewed and then mumbled, "Dad used to believe, too. But he doesn't anymore. He says God can answer the little things through nature, but not the big things."

Collin cocked her head. "Like what?"

"Oh, God can fix a cut because that's how He made our bodies. But He can't fix a problem I have at school."

Collin looked at Jeff. Jeff pushed back from the table. "Maybe this week at the lake, we'll have time to talk about this with you and your dad."

Sam shrugged. "Maybe." He finished his bowl. The trio finished, placed their bowls on the counter by the sink, showed Sam where to put his, and then rushed to the back to show Sam the new room arrangements. Joshua and Caleb now shared a room. Talitha had her own. The playroom had been converted to the guest room, and the main bedroom remained the same.

Jeff kissed Collin. "Excellent dinner, milady. Why don't I clean the kitchen, and you can pack the trio's clothes?"

"Sounds like a plan." Collin and Jeff rose from the table and cleared the rest of the serving dishes, the more breakable glasses, and anything pointy and sharp.

Jeff nodded. "Sounds like a good plan. Otherwise, your male offspring will have no underwear, no matching socks, and only the shorts and shirts they're wearing for the entire week."

Collin grinned. "And our female will have a suitcase full of books, dolls, and doll clothes, but nothing she can wear, either."

Jeff gave an exaggerated sigh. "One of these years…"

Collin moved off down the hallway to the boys' bedroom. Caleb and Joshua sat outside the door on the floor. The door was closed. Collin stared from boy to boy. "Where's Sam?"

"He wanted to play with Tee first. He wants to teach us to play doctor, and the girl goes first."

Collin flung the door open. Sam stood in front of Talitha, holding her arm. Talitha argued vehemently, "I don't want to play doctor, Sam."

Collin quivered. She swallowed hard, swallowed again. "Sam. We have a rule. If someone doesn't want to play, they don't have to play. Doesn't matter what it is. Let her go."

Sam dropped Tee's arm. "I only asked her because she said she wanted to learn a new game."

"That's fine. But she doesn't want to play doctor, so she doesn't have to. I don't think it's a game her brothers need to play, either. Why don't you get the electric Simon Says, and see who can follow

21

it the longest?" Collin forced herself to smile. *Breathe. Smile. Breathe.*

Caleb jumped up and down. "Yeah! It's a fun game."

Sam nodded. "I'll be Simon and tell you what to do."

Collin shook her head. "The game is Simon. It calls a color or number or shape, and you have to touch it before the buzzer goes off."

Joshua caught Sam's arm. "It's really fun, Sam. And it's hard. We'll show you."

Sam called, "I get to go first. I'm biggest." Caleb dove in the closet to retrieve the box with the game.

Collin added one last rule. "The bedroom door stays open. Got it?"

Three small voices called, "Yes, Mommy." Only after a hesitated second did Sam agree. "Yes, ma'am."

"Good." Collin grabbed a pile of clothes from the dresser, and took them to the kitchen. She set them on the table, and then walked into Jeff's chest.

"Hold me." Her face burned. Her knees wanted to buckle.

Jeff set down the dirty plate on the counter, wrapped his arms around Collin. She buried her head into his shoulder. "Oh, Jeff."

"What is it? What happened?" He did not let go of her.

Collin couldn't stop shaking. She waited until her body relaxed before she looked into Jeff's eyes. "Sam… wanted to play…doctor…with Tee. Just the two of them."

She felt his arms tighten around her. His eyes narrowed. His jaw clenched. He breathed in through his nose. In. Out. In. Out. "Did he touch her?"

"No. I interrupted them first. She's fine. I told them to play Simon Says. With the door open."

Jeff nodded. Collin felt his muscles remain taut. "I'll have a talk with him."

"He's nine, Jeff. And he's not our child. I don't know what to do."

Jeff relaxed slightly. Only slightly. "I hear you." He paused. "Lord, direct us. Our words, our actions, our thoughts. Show us what You want us to do. This is hard, Lord. Guard us. Guard our children. Guard Sam."

Collin finished. "Amen." She hugged her husband. "Thanks."

"You're welcome. Thanks for holding me back."

"What do we do now? Nothing happened." Collin regained her sense of equilibrium.

"Because you intervened. I'll talk to Tom tomorrow afternoon. See if I can get through to him." Jeff released Collin from his arms and took a step back.

"I'll talk to Pam. Maybe she'll listen."

"Yeah." Jeff looked at the clock. "I'll finish here, and then get the boys and Tee in their pajamas. They'll need to go to bed early if they're going to the party tomorrow."

"Right."

Collin drifted back towards the hallway, listening intently to the tone of the voices from the boys' room. The door stood wide open. A sigh whistled across her teeth. *I need to relax. I can't be on edge all night.*

Can't I?

No, you can't. Tee will be fine. She sleeps with her door closed. We'll sleep with ours open. Tonight. Just tonight. She dismissed the vision of sleeping across her daughter's door like a watchdog.

Watchdog, huh? Gretchen can sleep in Tee's room tonight. The boys have Sam. Tee can have Gretchen. The German Shepherd would keep the littlest Farrell safe. And enjoy doing it.

* * *

The remainder of the evening went without incident. Jeff couldn't help keeping an extra eye on Sam. The boy did nothing suspicious. Nor did he seem to favor Talitha in any way. The four played like kids do, fought like kids do, made up like kids do, and generally had a good time. No one argued about bedtime. Sam would sleep in the boys' room on the fold-out bed. Jeff reversed the bedtime prep order, however. "Brush your teeth. Say goodnight, and then go to your rooms and get your pajamas on. We'll come in and say prayers after you're in bed."

Talitha seemed happy to have Gretchen sleeping in her room. But, "She snores, Daddy."

"I know, honey. But she cuddles so good."

Talitha wrapped her arms around the dog's neck. "Yes, she does. Thank you for letting her sleep with me." Gretchen washed Tee's face with her tongue. The girl giggled.

"You're welcome, little one. Kiss your brothers goodnight."

The words were out before Jeff could second-think them. Tee raced down the hall to her brothers' room. Jeff hustled to stay up with her. He watched closely as Tee hugged all three boys, Sam included. Nothing amiss in the return. Jeff breathed easier for the moment. *Stop. He's a boy. A nine-year-old boy, not a street stalker. Grace. Give grace.* Jeff tousled each boy's hair as he hugged them. "We'll see you all in the morning."

Jeff and Collin watched the children head to their respective rooms. Collin slid her arm around Jeff's waist. "I know why you switched the order. You didn't want Sam seeing Tee in her pajamas, did you?"

Jeff shrugged. "I'm not sure what I want at this point. I don't want to treat him like a stalker. But I want to be careful, for Tee's sake. Does that make me a bad parent?"

"No. Not at all. There's a balance here. We just have to find it."

Jeff frowned. "Well, when you find it, let me know."

"After you tell me." Jeff kissed the top of Collin's head. They went to say prayers with the children. And for themselves.

SATURDAY

Collin woke the children at eight. She instructed the boys, "Get dressed and then come eat breakfast. Put on some grubby clothes."

She gave Tee the same instructions adding, "Put your bathing suit on under your clothes."

Talitha's eyes widened to saucers. "Are we going swimming?"

"No, but put your suit on anyhow. You'll see. And don't tell your brothers or Sam you're wearing your suit. We'll keep it a secret."

Talitha nodded and pulled out her bathing suit. She put the one-piece suit on, and then pulled her shirt and shorts over it. "There, Mommy. Now it's a secret."

Collin smiled. "Good girl. Let's eat breakfast."

As soon as the pancakes, eggs, and bacon had been consumed, Collin announced, "I'm going to set up the sprinkler and sliding mat. You can play in the backyard until it's time to get cleaned up for the party."

Happy dances all around. Well, Sam didn't dance, but he did join the cheering. Collin left the screen door open so she could see and hear the revelry from the back. She stripped the covers off Sam's bed, only to find the sheets wet. Collin found his pajamas kicked behind the bathroom door. *Poor Sam.* She would not make a big deal of it. Instead, she gathered the bedclothes and his pajamas and set them to wash while she continued packing.

The idea for the retreat had been a joint brainstorm. Just a good time to be had by all. If it went well, they'd try having the entire company. No fights, no commotion. Fun.

Let's hope it stays that way.

Jeff came in from the garage wiping his hands on an oily rag. "You want me to get the backpacks from the attic?" He leaned against the doorframe.

Collin's jaw dropped. "Of course. Yours are all things overhead. I get the basement. Remember?" *Ever since the "monkey in the attic" incident.*

Jeff grinned. "Just checking." He glanced outside, gesturing to the kids with his head. "How's it going?"

"So far, so good. Nothing to worry about." Laughter filled the ear waves. Nothing sweeter than children laughing. Gretchen added her voice to the confusion. Keeping the kids in line, no doubt.

"Good." Jeff snuck a kiss, washed his hands, and then disappeared to retrieve the packs from the attic. Collin could hear him bumping around overhead. She continued folding and counting underwear piles, pajama piles, shorts, and shirts…all for the trio. As she patted down the last shirt, she listened to voices yelling outside.

"I get to tell you what game to play. I'm the biggest one here. You have to do what I say."

Collin started to move, stopped, breathed out, and then went back to her business. The trio would have to learn. Learning in the safety of their own home would be a good place. *Right?*

"Let's see who can get the wettest. Tee, you go first. Stand under the hose."

"I don't want to go first."

"You do what I say, or you can't play."

Again, Collin started towards the back. Again, she stopped.

Caleb shouted, "We want Tee to play. Mommy says we don't make people do things. We ask them. If they don't want to, it's okay."

Sam's voice lost its volume. But Collin still heard him. "That's stupid. People should have to do what you say. What good is it to be the boss if no one follows you?"

Joshua chimed in. "But we want to be the boss sometimes, too."

"If you don't want to be wettest, take your clothes off. Then you won't end up wet."

Collin's eyes lost focus. She stood up and walked to the door. As she reached it, Talitha asserted, "No. Mommy says girls don't take their clothes off outside. And boys should only take their shirts off if they spill something nasty." Collin watched out the door to see

26

what Sam's response would be. She could see him standing in the backyard near the slip-slide surface. Gretchen danced and pranced and slid along in the water. Blades of grass covered the mat along the edges. Soapsuds covered the grass along the edges. Shoes sat in a pile under the picnic table. Oversize plastic bats and soft rubber balls were strewn about the yard.

"Your mom has too many rules." Sam stomped over to the bench and flopped down. He yanked his shirt off and slammed it on the grass. "There. I took it off. Because I wanted to. See? I can do what I want to."

Now. But carefully. Collin counted to five and then called out, "Hey, people. Anyone want a snack?"

Bodies crowded to the back door. Collin eyed Sam. "It's okay to leave your shirt off for a few minutes. But any longer, you risk getting sunburned. And you could ruin your time at the lake."

Sam nodded. "Yes, ma'am. A few more minutes. It made me cold."

"Wet clothes can do that. I have some brownies and juice for you all. Go sit at the picnic table, and I'll bring it out."

The group obeyed. Collin carried a tray out with small dishes and napkins. Each plate had a double-decker chocolate-frosted brownie. "You've got about another half-hour to play, and then you'll need to get cleaned up." She passed around juice packets and then smiled. "Sam, your mom should be coming at noon, and the trio has a birthday party to go to. It's for a little girl in their class, and there won't be children your age for you to hang with."

Sam cocked his head. "Mom's coming?"

"Yes. Around noon. It's what we arranged yesterday." *Why do you look surprised, Sam?*

Sam shrugged. "Dad said he'd see me this evening after I got home. Mom had to work, but she would pick me up after she got done at four." He picked up the brownie and shoved half of it into his mouth. Frosting smeared up his cheek.

Collin's eyes widened. "Oh, really? I must have heard wrong, then." *Someone did.* "Well, you get cleaned up when the trio does. I'll talk to Jeff."

She walked to the garage. Jeff worked to strap the kayaks on top of the van. He looked up as Collin approached. "I know the look. We have a problem. What?"

"Sam. According to him, his mom is coming for him after she gets off work at four."

Jeff's eyes narrowed. "She is, is she?" Jeff fished his phone out of his pocket and punched in a number.

The call went straight to a recording. "Sorry, the number you have called is switched off or unavailable. Please try again later." The line went dead. Jeff tapped another number. Same result.

Collin watched her husband breathe in and out slowly. He scowled. "What do you want to do? Call Pam?"

Collin nodded. "I'll leave a message. She can't take personal calls during work, but she always checks her phone at lunch." Collin slipped her phone out of her back pocket. She scrolled up the contact information, and then dialed.

"Sorry, the number you have called is switched off or unavailable. Please try again later."

Collin closed her eyes. "That was deliberate. It sounds like the phones were placed in airplane mode. Now what? I can't take Sam to the party. He'll be bored out of his mind. And I hate party crashing." She leaned against the body of the van.

Jeff sighed. "I'll take him out somewhere. Maybe we can try the new Bounce Palace. See if it's suitable for the trio." Jeff coupled the last bungee in place, pulled on it, pulled on the kayak, and then stepped away.

"I'm sorry, Jeff. I know—"

"Don't apologize. It's not your fault. Tom and I will have a long talk about this, however." Jeff's face darkened. "And a few other issues."

Collin debated. *Tell? Don't tell? Is it really a big deal?* "Sam tried to get Talitha to take off her shirt. He wanted her to get soaked down, and when she said no, he suggested she take off her clothes."

Jeff closed his eyes and hung his head. "I've had it. I'm done." He dropped the bungee cords he held. "I'm going to get cleaned up and take him out."

Collin laid a hand on his arm. "I hope you mean as in taking him out someplace."

Jeff chuckled. "Yeah, that did come out wrong, didn't it?"

"A little." Together they walked back into the house. Collin went to the backyard and sat at the picnic table with the children. She motioned to Sam's shirt. "You don't have to put it on, but lay it over your shoulders, so you don't get burned."

"Yes, ma'am." Sam complied without complaint.

Collin waited until the snacks were gone and the juice consumed. The children stacked their plates and rolled-up foil pouches on the tray. Collin instructed, "Okay, we laid out clothes for the party last night. Go wash up and get dressed. Sam, put on some dry clothes. Jeff said he's got a surprise for you."

Sam's face lit up. "Really? A surprise? For me?"

Collin laughed. "Unless you want to hang around a bunch of four and five-year-olds all afternoon."

"No, ma'am. What kind of surprise?"

"You'll see. Now, everyone in the house."

Four bodies raced to be first in the door. Collin followed behind with the tray and trash. She eavesdropped on the conversations. But she heard nothing suspicious. The boys came out dressed appropriately in clean shirts and khaki shorts. So did Talitha. Collin sighed. *Thank You, Lord.* Jeff emerged from the bedroom about the same time. Collin passed Sam off to Jeff, loaded her trio into her van, and headed to the party. At least she could come off high alert for a couple of hours. *Poor Sam. Poor Pam. And give Jeff the words he needs to talk to Tom. Sam needs help. Now. Please, Lord. In Your will.*

* * *

Jeff put an arm around Sam's shoulders. "How about we go check out the Bounce Palace and see what it's like?"

Sam's eyes filled his face. "Honest? Really?"

"Why not? We've got time to fill. Be much more fun than being with a bunch of screaming five-year-olds."

Sam wiggled and beamed. "Yes, it will! Wow. The Bounce Palace? I've wanted to go. I keep asking Dad, but Mom told me he says he's got better things to do than watching me hop around like a monkey." The boy shifted from one foot to another, ready to go.

Jeff directed the boy to the garage and the second van. "Like what?"

"Like sleeping on the couch. It's all he does in the evenings. Lays in front of the TV and sleeps." Sam climbed into the back seat.

Jeff slid into the driver's seat, adjusting the mirror so he could see Sam. He redirected the conversation. "Your dad works hard. He probably needs a nap after work." He set the van in motion down the street.

As they drove, Sam looked out the window. "If he works hard, why are you trying to get rid of him?"

Jeff's head snapped toward the boy and then back to the road. "What?"

"Mom says you're trying to get rid of Dad. You've been trying to for a couple of years. But you can't find anyone to replace him, so you have to keep him. At least until you can find a way to keep the company going without him."

Why would Pam think that? *Tom.* What did he tell her?

Jeff searched for words in the world between "liar" and "respecting the father." Tough call. Tough call. "I'm not sure why your mom would feel that way. Your dad and I should have a talk about it this week. He's a valuable part of Trinity Builders. We aren't looking to replace him and want him to stay."

Sam shrugged. "I guess. I hear him talking to Mom sometimes. It never sounds like he's happy. I think he's sad and Mom's mad."

"I'll talk to him about it. I want everyone at the company to feel welcome and valued."

Sam continued to look out the window. "I wish he took me places like he does Brutus."

"Maybe when you're older."

"Maybe. Maybe when Brutus goes to college." Sam's face perked up, and then dropped again. "If he goes."

Again, Jeff risked a quick look at his passenger. "I thought he registered for the fall semester."

"He did, but Dad told him he'd have to wait until next year. Dad doesn't have enough money to pay for Brutus's tuition. Because Dad has to pay bills for me. He says I eat too much. Then he laughs at me." Sam interlocked his fingers in his lap, turning them inside and out.

Jeff swallowed his surprise. Tuition had always been a perk of working for Trinity Builders. Something Collin set up with her inheritance. Free to anyone who wanted to better themselves. Again, Jeff had to select his words. "I'm sorry to hear about it. Last I talked to Brutus, he seemed excited about starting college."

"Yeah, I know. He's really upset about it. And mad. He says it's not like Dad and Mom didn't know this was coming. He says they should have been ready for it. Now Wendy won't be able to go since she graduated, either."

Jeff pulled the van into the parking lot. "Okay, let's go have some fun. But no broken bones. Promise?"

Sam grinned. "Promise." They raced into the gaudily colored building.

* * *

The birthday party proved to be a success. All except the clowns. Whoever thought having six-foot clowns in oversized boots with gigantic mouths would be a good idea for a kid's party never worked with small children. Never. Collin could still hear the screaming. And right after the cake and ice cream, when they had full stomachs? Terror and gorged bellies did not go together. At least not for long. Clean-up had been a joy.

Her three were no exception. The trio rode in their seats in the back of the van, quiet, pale, and sleepy. Collin chuckled to herself. Ah, the joys of motherhood. She watched Caleb and Joshua nod off to sleep. Talitha watched out the window. Maybe now would be a good time to ask the questions. The ones she prayed she knew the answers to.

"Tee, what happened in the bedroom when you and Sam were alone?"

"Nothing, Mommy. Sam wanted to play doctor." Tee traced a circle on the window.

"Hands off the window, please. Did he tell you how to play?"

"He said I had to lay down and let him look at me like a doctor does."

Tension rose. Her hands gripped the steering wheel. *Relax. She's safe. Let go of the wheel.* "What did you do?"

"I told him I didn't want to play. If Caleb and Joshua weren't allowed to play, then I didn't want to play, either." Tee lay her head back against her car seat.

Tee's voice trailed off. Collin prompted, "What did he say then?" Keep your voice light. Surprised. "Oh! What did he say? Oh, my..." You know the drill. Light. Happy.

"He said they would play after we did, but I wanted all of us to play together."

Again, the sleepy voice. Tee's eyes were closing. Again, Collin asked, "What did he say then?"

Tee sat up straighter. "It made him mad. I told him I was sorry he got mad, but I still didn't want to play. Then you came in."

Collin breathed out. In. Out. In. Out. "You did the right thing, Tee. If your brothers weren't allowed in, then none of you should play. I'm proud of you." *And I want to strangle Sam.*

Tee nodded. Collin glanced repeatedly in the rearview mirror as her daughter's little eyes grew heavy, and she nodded off.

Lord...I want to skin him alive. I want to rip his heart out, and... And I want You to forgive me for my attitude. He's a child, too. A troubled child. He's not mine to discipline, not even for this. But how do we deal with it? How do we keep Tee and the boys safe? Am I being overprotective? Should I just let it go?

No! Nausea built in her gut. They're my children. My responsibility. I choose what lessons they learn and how.

She pulled up short. Within Your will, Father. Always within Your will. But I know this is covered under 'train up a child when he is young...' Show Jeff and me what to say to Sam and his parents. Give me truth in love, Lord. Please.

She prayed Psalms the remainder of the way home.

* * *

Jeff drove himself and an exhausted Sam home around four. If Sam had it right, Pam should come around four-thirty to pick the boy up. What should he say to her?

Sam grinned. "Thank you, Uncle Jeff. Today was the bomb. I've never had so much fun before." The boy bounced in his seat. Exhilaration overload.

Jeff chuckled. "Me neither, Sam." He leaned over to stage whisper in Sam's hearing, "Between you and me, not all of those flips were intentional. Don't tell Collin."

"Will she be mad?" Sam's eyes widened in joy.

"She'll be mad she didn't take you. She would have had a blast."

"Maybe the company could do this for an activity."

Jeff shook his head. "We've got too many people who wouldn't be able to enjoy it. And there are some people where it might not be safe for them. Then there's Erin and Walter down in drafting. They're both in wheelchairs."

"So? They could stay home." Sam waved off Jeff's objection.

"We want to make it so everyone can come and have fun. It wouldn't be fair to say, 'You can't bounce, so you can't come.' It's not what we do."

Sam shrugged. "Dad says they just spoil it for others. There's lots of things we could do. But because of the old people and the guys in the wheelchairs, we can't have fun." The boy looked out the window.

Lord, I'm getting tired of choosing my words carefully. Keep Your hand over my mouth. Please. "Having the lake days means we can all have fun as a group. There's something for everyone to do and some things we can all do together. You had fun when our two families went to the lake, didn't you?"

Sam's excitement returned. "Yeah. I love going up there. I get to climb rocks and trees. And I can go swimming and go out in the boats when someone takes me." He smiled at Jeff. "Like you do. When you pull all the floats. It's cool."

"See? It's not bad for a company to think of everyone. It's what Jesus would want us to do." *There. Maybe he'll chew on something positive.*

They rode in silence for several minutes. "You still go to church, don't you, Uncle Jeff?"

"Yeah, we go." Jeff glanced over to see what prompted the question.

"Why?" Sam continued to stare out the window.

"Jesus said if we loved Him, we would do the things He told us to do. One of those things is gathering together. We choose Sundays to honor Him. I love Him, so I do what He says to do." *Keep it simple. And honest.*

"I wondered." Sam drew on the glass. "I asked Dad why we don't go to church. He said he doesn't need someone telling him how to be a Christian. He can figure it out on his own."

Jeff pulled into the circular driveway in front of the house.

The garage door stood open, and Collin had small coolers sitting out. Jeff knew the food deliveries had already been made to the lake house. These ice chests were for the hour-and-a-half trip to the lake. Keep 'em happy. Makes life much easier.

The triplets sat on the front porch, waiting for Jeff to turn off the engine before mobbing him. As soon as he stepped out, it started. "Daddy! Daddy! They had a pony!" "There were animals." "I touched a snake. It felt yukky." "Well, I touched a spider. It felt yukkier."

Collin kissed Jeff. "Welcome home. How'd it go?" She slipped her arms around him.

Jeff pointed to Sam. "You tell her."

Sam glowed. "It was so cool. You could almost fly. I got so high up in the rafters." He raised his hands over his head and leaped in the air.

Collin grinned and tousled his hair. "I'm glad you had a good time. Nothing broken?"

Sam shook his head. Jeff chuckled. "Bruised, maybe. I'm sure I'll feel it tomorrow. But it's one fun park. When the littles get bigger, we'll definitely get a family pass." He stretched his arm around his back. And winced.

Collin crossed to the porch and held the front door open. "Okay. We're all going to go inside and read books for a while until Sam's mom comes to get him."

Joshua whined, "Can't we play in our room?"

"No." Collin's answer seemed a little short. Jeff could guess why. "You can bring the plastic blocks out and build a racetrack, though. Everything has to stay in the family room. And all in one spot. You hear me? I do not want to step on any blocks."

"Yes, Mommy." The foursome ran into the house. Collin jerked her head towards the house. "I don't want to leave them unattended."

Jeff drew in a deep breath and nodded. "Gotcha." Collin waved him through the door.

Collin and Jeff watched the racetrack be built, the blocks carefully corralled in one area. Jeff focused on his children but asked, "Did you hear from Pam?"

"No. Nor Tom. Do we talk to them tonight or at the lake?" Collin scooped up a wayward block and tossed it back with its mates.

"I'd rather do it sooner than later. Tonight might be pushing it, though. With Pam getting off work, I hate hitting her with it off the bat." Jeff slipped from the couch to the floor to watch the races.

Collin frowned. "I hate hitting her with it, period. This isn't something I ever thought I'd have to say to another parent."

Jeff eyed her. "When you were a social worker, did this ever come up?"

"Not with kids this young. We saw it with older teens, but never like this. This is…out of my experience."

Jeff took her hand. "Mine, too. But not the Lord's. We'll trust Him for the words."

It neared five when Pam stuck her head in the door and called, "Anyone home?"

Jeff and Collin got up, as did the children. Sam ran to his mom and hugged her. "Mom! I had the best time ever. Uncle Jeff took me to the Bounce Palace. It was fantastic."

The littles danced around Pam until she entered the door and sat on the couch. She grinned at their telling of the party antics. After five minutes, Collin said, "Okay, anyone under twenty, sit on the floor and play with blocks. The adults want to talk."

Jeff nodded. Where I can keep eyes on you all.

* * *

The focus shifted from play to people. Collin addressed the elephant in the room. "What happened with Tom picking up Sam?" *Let's get this out here right now.*

Pam hung her head. "I am so sorry. I am. Last night, he told me I needed to pick Sam up at noon. He didn't care what the attorneys said. They could fire me if they wanted."

She looked up, her eyes watering. "Then this morning, as I'm heading out the door, he says, 'Pick Sam up after you get off work. Jeff will understand. They're not going anywhere anyhow. It'll be fine.'"

Pam bit her lip. "I'm so sorry. I am. I don't know what to say when he pulls those stunts. I've told him I hate taking advantage of people, but he laughs and says you can take a joke."

Collin's eyes widened. "He thinks it's a joke what time he picks up Sam? Does he realize what it does to his son?" *Of course, he doesn't.* Collin sat back on the couch.

Pam lifted both hands, palms up. "He swears it doesn't matter. Sam will 'get over it.' I'm at my wit's end. I am. I don't know what to do."

"Do you know your phone is off?" Jeff leaned forward.

Pam shot a glance at Jeff. "What? No, it's not."

"It's off. It has been all day."

Pam reached into her purse and pulled it out. She showed it to him. "See? It's on. I would never leave any of my children—"

"Check the mode."

"What?"

"See if it's in airplane mode."

Pam shifted in her seat. "I promise you, it's not." She scrolled up the settings. Horror filled her face. Her eyes were hollow as she looked at Jeff and then Collin. "Oh, no. Oh, no. I am so sorry. Tom must have…" She trailed off and buried her face in her hands.

Jeff reached out and touched her arm. "It's okay, Pam. I'll talk to Tom about it." He leaned forward and lowered his voice. "Have you noticed any problems with Sam?"

Pam looked up sharply. "You mean like him trying to set the house on fire?"

Collin's face paled. Jeff's eyes narrowed. "Tell us about it."

"He burned the curtains in the kitchen. Not bad. But enough so you can't deny it happened. He swears he didn't do it. I think he did it to get Tom's attention."

"What did Tom do?"

Pam hung her head again. "Nothing. Like he always does. Passed it off. Since no one admitted who did it, he said let it go." Her face lost color. "Then I found the lighter in Sam's pocket. Tom still said it didn't prove anything."

Pam lifted her head and sat up straight. Anger burned in her eyes. "So I did something. I called a psychologist's office. I made an appointment to have Sam evaluated. Tom argued against it at first, but then he agreed to let it happen, but only to prove me wrong. He thinks I'm overreacting, and the evaluation would prove it."

"When is the appointment?" Collin moved closer to the edge of the cushions.

"Was. The psychologist had a cancellation on Friday, so we got in then."

Collin turned her neck. "You got in fast."

Jeff lifted his head. "That's what Tom meant about an appointment."

Pam's eyes narrowed. "He nearly bailed. Claimed he had a headache. I threatened him if he didn't come, he'd be looking for

36

somewhere else to live." She hung her head, the fire gone. "I'm ashamed to admit it. But how else could I get him to understand this is serious?"

Collin touched the woman's hand. "Do you want to tell us about it?"

She nodded. "The psychologist said Sam has an emotional IQ which bounces from a seven to seventeen-year-old. He needs to learn age-appropriate behaviors. And it's all about Tom." Pam studied her fingers, her palms, the nails on her hands.

Jeff cocked his head. "The psychologist said those exact words?"

"Exact words. It's all about wanting to be with his dad—wanting his dad's attention. The psychologist suggested a playgroup of Sam's peers and family counseling for all of us."

Collin kept her voice gentle. "What did Tom say?" *I know what he said. He said no. And you went right along with him. Pam…*

"He told the psychologist he'd think about it, check with his insurance, and get back to him." Pam gritted her teeth. "Which translates to no. On the way home, he told me Sam only needed Tom to spend more time with him. And Tom would…after his vacation. This retreat was all about work. Once it was done, he'd start doing things with Sam."

A cold chill climbed Collin's being. She narrowed her eyes. "What did the psychologist mean by 'age appropriate' behaviors?"

"He said Sam has interests in things inconsistent with his age group. Things he's picked up from movies Tom lets him watch."

You knew? You knew, and you still let Sam play with Tee? And didn't warn me? What…

Collin swallowed hard to bury her anger. "I have to tell you. And I hate doing it. Sam…he tried…"

Collin held Pam's gaze. She kept the bitterness out of her tone. "He tried to play doctor with Talitha alone in the bedroom. He also tried to get her to take her clothes off."

Pam's jaw sagged. Blood emptied from her face. *Good. I want you to feel bad.*

Forgive as you've been forgiven.

But this is my daughter.

Forgive as you've…

Oh, fine. "Nothing happened. Tee wouldn't go along with him.

She's fine." Collin held Pam's eyes. "I'm sorry I had to tell you. But it's something I think you need to know. He's acting out those behaviors he's seen on television."

Pam lifted her head, face to the ceiling, tears welling in her eyes. "How many times can I say I'm sorry?"

Jeff put his hand on her shoulder. "It's not your fault. Sam needs help. You're getting it for him. That's what matters."

Pam wiped her eyes and stood. She called, "Sam, we've got to go. Do you have your stuff ready?"

Sam got up. "Yeah, Mom. It's all in my bag." He picked up his pack and lifted it to his shoulder.

The bag fell open. Caleb's stuffed bear slipped out and fell onto the floor. Caleb grabbed the stuffie. "My bear! He sleeps with me."

Sam cocked his head. "How did that get in there?"

Collin offered, "Maybe you scooped him up by mistake when you picked up your clothes." *Maybe. Maybe the earth spins backward, too.*

Pam laughed, but it sounded forced. "Maybe I better see if you scooped up anything else." She took her son's bag and looked in it. She pulled out a stuffed lion.

Joshua yelled, "My lion!"

Grace. Give grace. Do it. Collin nodded. "They sit together on the bed. Sam's clothes were beside them." *Happy now?*

Peace, child.

Yes, Lord. I'm sorry. Forgive me.

Pam's eyes reflected shame and gratitude. "Yeah. That's probably what happened. Right, Sam?"

Sam looked from Caleb to Joshua. "I guess. Maybe."

"Tell the boys you're sorry."

Sam hung his head. "Sorry." He looked at his mom. "Can we go now?"

Pam directed, "Tell Collin and Jeff thank you."

Sam hugged Collin and then Jeff. "Thanks, Uncle Jeff. I had the best time ever."

Jeff smiled. "We'll do it again. After my muscles stop aching." He kissed the boy on top of his head. "See you at the lake, bud."

Pam passed out hugs. She and Sam exited the front door. Jeff waited until they were gone. He dropped his head and shook it. "Poor Pam. And poor Sam."

Collin directed, "Okay, trio, pick up the racetrack and all the blocks. Put them away, and then come help me fix dinner."

As the littles complied, Collin leaned into Jeff for a hug. Her whole body shook. Jeff kissed her head. "We'll get through this, milady. God's got us."

Collin nodded. Her voice came out small. "Right." She kissed him. "All of us."

SUNDAY MORNING

Sunday after church, standing in line for the ladies' room, Collin waited semi-patiently as two women in the separate stalls carried on a conversation.

"I just love seeing the young adults leading the service. It does my heart good to see so many ages and backgrounds represented on the stage."

"Yes, our pastor does love to mingle different worship styles."

Collin cocked her head. The words were supportive. But the tone carried shaded tones of sarcasm. *Maybe you should leave and come back in a little bit.*

The first speaker caught the undertone, too. "What do you mean, worship styles? We're all praising the Lord together."

"Some people like different music. I like traditional hymns. Some people like the new stuff. Some people like horrible rock music. I simply think those people would be more comfortable in their own church."

Now the sarcasm flipped speakers. "You mean in a church where more people looked like they do?"

"You know what I mean. The Bible says, 'God separated the nations.' I just think—"

Speaker one interrupted the woman. "Selma, you better change your thinking, or your first thousand years in Heaven will be miserable. Scripture says there will be people from every tongue, tribe, and nation. If you can't worship with people who don't look like you here and now, how will you do it in Heaven?"

Collin retreated out the door. Selma Fields. Married to Abbott Fields. Her brother Erin's coworker and friend. *Oh, dear.* She headed to the children's department. The facilities might be smaller, but they would definitely be friendlier. *Only You can change a heart with an attitude like that, Lord. She's all Yours.*

* * *

Life at the lake had been designed so attendees could relax. Trinity Builders added to the original family lake house, constructing cabins, a centralized cookhouse and dining area, and campsites for those who preferred tent or RV living. Meals were prepared and served at posted hours, or campers could fix their own. A central firepit created togetherness for s'mores and music, or there were individual BBQ set-ups for the introverts of the crowd.

The official "start" of the retreat fell on Monday. Collin, Jeff, and family arrived on Sunday after church to ensure everything was ready: food delivered, cabins cleaned and stocked, and the landscape raked and swept.

Jeff surveyed the grounds. Collin wrapped her arms around him. "Does your kingdom please you, milord?" She saw the pride in his eyes. *He loves this place. I love it for him.*

He nodded. "It does indeed, milady. All we need now are my loyal subjects to come adore me, and life will be complete." A theatrical bow followed.

Collin chuckled. "Ain't gonna happen." She kept her sarcasm light.

"A man can dream."

Collin waved at the triplets. "You've got three loyal subjects at your feet who adore you."

Jeff grinned at the trio pulling at his shorts. "They'll adore me more if I get the boat out."

"Truth. I'd probably adore you more as well."

He threw his hands in the air. "Fine. Fine. My subjects have spoken. I'll get the boat out. We can swing around the lake once before Tom gets here and wants to make it his private fishing spot."

The triplets jumped up and down. "We get to go in the boat. We get to go in the boat!"

Caleb asked, "Do we get to put on swimsuits?"

Collin shook her head. "Not tonight. Tomorrow you can." She looked at her daughter, and her heart jumped. *How do I protect her? How do I keep her safe?*

Jeff turned her to face him. "What is it, lady?"

"It's Tee. The whole bathing suit thing. She shouldn't have to cover up like she needs to hide because she's a girl. She's four years old. Her bathing suit is modest. She's not flashing anything to anyone. She can run, she can paddle around, she can splash, and nothing is going to show." Collin felt her resolve harden. "I will not start my daughter down this path of denying who God made her because there are people in the world who can't control their own base natures." She eyed Jeff. "Opinion?"

Jeff half-grinned. "Am I allowed one?" Collin sneered at him. He smiled. "Agreed. No burkas. She's four. We let her be four."

Collin ordered the trio, "Everyone down to the water, but stop there. No one sets foot on the dock until I say so. Right?"

"Right, Mommy." Three voices in harmony. Three bodies raced for the boat launch.

Jeff and Collin followed at a less frantic pace. Jeff asked, "Have you heard from Rob? Is he coming?"

Collin put on her best "dumb female" caricature. "Rob? You mean our son? The one we adopted together when he turned eighteen? Six years ago? That Rob?"

Jeff glared at her. "Yes, Rob."

Collin dropped the pretense. "He'll be up tonight. You two need to spend more time together."

Jeff humphed. "I will if he will."

"Oh, that's grown up."

"I thought so. Very."

The children and Collin sat in the back while Jeff piloted the boat onto the lake. Shouts of laughter, giggles, and cries of, "Faster, Daddy, faster" echoed on the water. Two hours of boating wore little people out enough Collin knew they would sleep through the night. And be ready to do it all again the next day. With friends next time.

As the boat pulled up to the dock, Collin saw Rob standing, ready to catch the line. He had a young woman with him. Collin recognized the cheery-looking blonde as a member of the young adult group at church. She also happened to be Abbott and Selma Fields's daughter. *This could be interesting. And a little complicated. Does Rob know how Selma feels about mixed-race dating relationships?* Her mind refused to think beyond a dating relationship. *Dating. Just dating. I'm not ready for anything more than that.*

Rob waved. "Ahoy, Cap'n. Bring her ashore."

Jeff instructed, "Mind the cargo. It's lively."

Collin ordered, "Do not jump. No jumping in the boat. You wait until you get your feets on the dirts before you jump. Everybody understand?"

"Yes, Mommy."

Rob lifted each child from the boat, supervised them as they made their way to shore, and then dropped down to their level to hug them. "Hi, buds. How you doing?"

The jumping began. The trio all started talking at once. "We saw fish jumping." "And bugs." "And fish eating the bugs." "And…"

Collin slipped beside her son and hugged him. She extended her hand to Gabby. "Welcome, Gabby. Very nice to have you here."

The woman smiled. "Thank you, Mrs. Farrell. Rob's been talking about this place for as long as I've known him. It's nice to finally get an invitation to come." She turned a full circle with her arms wide to indicate the panorama of trees. Green, lush, beautiful…

Rob dropped back aghast. "Get an invitation? I've been practically begging you to come up here on a family weekend, and you're always busy."

Gabby smiled and batted her eyes. "I wanted to keep you asking. I thought you might lose interest if I said yes too soon."

Rob's eyes flared. He glared at Collin. "You didn't teach me that trick."

Jeff came up behind Collin. "Your mom didn't play tricks. She'd look me in the eye and say, 'This is the way it is, you got it?' And I'd say, 'Yes, ma'am.' And that's how it went."

Collin rolled her eyes. "Gabby, ignore the men. We'll let them put away the boat, and I'll show you the house." She caught Rob's eye. "She is staying in the big house, right?"

"And I'm in the boat house. Yes, ma'am." Rob's mock sarcasm came through loud and clear.

Collin sneered. "I can always put you in a tent, you know." She threw her fists to her hips and glared him down.

Rob grinned. "I don't do tents. I set my cabin up yesterday."

"Good." I can't control the rest of the crowd, but my family sleeps married with their own partners or otherwise separate. So I

can say to the children, "I can't answer for what other people do. I only answer for us." And mean it.

The group made its way to the lodge, the littles racing ahead. Collin refrained from slipping her arm in Rob's, no matter how much she wanted to. She could feel the torch passing, and she didn't like the feeling. Not yet. *Will you ever?*

To that, she had no reply.

* * *

"Are you done packing the car yet? We're leaving in the morning. I don't want to drive back here because you forgot something."

"Almost done, Dad." The young man pushed the black trash bag full of cheerleading uniform pillows to one side, packing it down as much as possible.

"What are you doing with those? Throw those out of there."

"Mom wants to take them. She said she could work on them in the evenings."

"She's not going to touch those. Pitch 'em. And hurry up." The man stomped into the house.

The younger man ignored the command but called after his father, "Just making sure we've got everything." He shoved the fishing poles, tackle boxes, and beer cans away from the back of the hatch. Away from the auxiliary storage area—the one which held the worthless scissor jack. The one Dad couldn't bother to carry. Now the compartment sat empty. But just big enough for ammunition and a handgun. He covered the firearm with a towel so it didn't rattle.

He closed the lid. Latched it. Covered it with the carpet. Pulled the fishing rods back into position. Closed the hatch. "All done, Dad."

"Good. Took you long enough."

"Just making sure we had everything. We're going to have a great time at the lake. Best time ever."

"Long as they keep paying for everything, it will be. Turn out the light."

"Yes, sir. I will." He did.

* * *

Static. "Commander, we've got bogies on the lake."

"Unless they are wearing readily identifiable uniforms from our allies or our enemies, those are not bogies. Those are civilians. We will apply all diligence not to expose our presence. Anyone who does will find themselves in my office standing at attention for three hours before they are allowed to explain to me how they managed to screw up clear and detailed orders. Understood?"

"Yes, Commander."

"Spread the word. And Lieutenant?"

"Yes, ma'am?"

"You'll be standing with them explaining why they didn't get the orders or didn't comprehend said orders. Also understood?"

"Explicitly, Commander."

"Carry on."

MONDAY

Erin and Vy manned…personned…the welcome tent Monday morning. A small patio table and chairs were set in place, along with cold beverages in a cooler, snacks on trays, and the all-important clipboard with the list of who would stay where. Visitors steadily arrived for check-in. By one in the afternoon, Erin reached his limits. As another couple in line departed to their assigned cabin, Erin grumbled, "How hard is it to fill out the forms before you come up? And turn them in on Friday, so we know where to put everyone?"

Vy leaned down and kissed her husband's head. "Then you wouldn't have anything to grouse about this soon on the first day of the retreat." Her yellow sundress contrasted beautifully against her dark skin. A floppy hat covered her short black hair. Reflections sparkling off the lake gave her a heavenly glow.

Erin lifted his head. "Why do you put up with me?" He shifted in the wheelchair to ease pressure on a suddenly-protesting nerve and reached up to kiss his wife. "I'm glad you do, though."

Vy sat beside him. "How many more are coming?"

Erin looked at his list. "The Fergusons canceled this morning. Small child with a fever." He turned over the top page and looked deeper down the list. "The Wilsons thought it would be too hot, so they're not coming. Their teams run fine, thank you very much. They don't need this 'liberal team building' stuff."

Vy laughed. Lightly. To match her disposition. Everything about Vy was light and airy and filled with grace.

To Erin's mind, anyhow. Her job with the DEA required a second side which could be hard, cold, and professionally distant. Which she mostly left at the office. And when she couldn't, he was there for her.

They talked about her leaving the DEA. They talked about him leaving Trinity Builders. When the talking finished, they agreed they both liked their jobs and felt they were giving back to the community.

Erin pulled himself out of the rabbit hole and turned the page on his cabin assignment list. "Everyone's accounted for. Tom hasn't checked in yet."

"He'll be here. Be patient."

"Always." Vy gave him a jaundiced eye. "Sometimes." The look remained. "Okay, I'm a work in progress." Erin stretched his back. "If you can locate Jeff or Collin and tell them I'm done here, I'd appreciate it."

"Use the radio, dear. That's why we bought them."

"Oh, riiight. The radio." Erin smirked. "I know who has the brains in this family." He picked up the walkie-talkie and adjusted the signal. "Any Farrell who isn't otherwise occupied with official duties...I need a break here."

Jeff's voice floated back. "Working on a plumbing issue."

Collin responded, "Trio patrol until Harmon, Lacey, and Leesa get here." Harmon and Lacey, Jeff's parents. Leesa, Jeff's older sister. Born with Down Syndrome, but still quite capable of independent thinking.

Rob checked in. "I'll be there in five minutes."

Erin nodded. "Thanks, Rob."

"Is Vy with you?"

He looked over and smiled. "Usually."

Exasperation colored Rob's voice. "Is she there now?"

Vy nailed Erin with a stern look and took the radio. "I'm here, Rob. You need something?"

"Yeah. I'll tell you when I get there."

"Roger."

She handed the radio back to Erin. He tilted his head. "Who's Roger? I thought you were..."

The mock glare in her eyes stopped him. "Yes, ma'am. I'll quit."

"Wise man."

Rob walked up the paved path around the lake's edge, a young blonde woman at his side. She looked college-age, but the older Erin got, the younger people looked. Erin dropped the clipboard into his lap and waited for a proper introduction.

Rob put his hand on the woman's shoulder. "Erin, Vy, this is Gabby Fields. Gabby, meet Erin and Vy Winger, my uncle and aunt."

Gabby smiled and shook hands with Vy and then Erin. "Nice to meet you. Rob thinks the world of both of you."

Vy nodded. "It's mutual. How do you know Rob?"

Gabby looked at Rob. He nodded. She explained, "We're in the young adult group at church. And Abbott Fields is my father."

Erin smiled. "Of course he is. Good man. Good brother in Christ as well." *We've met you before. Before you were dating age.*

Rob pulled up two chairs. "Have you got a few minutes to talk? Or did you need to leave?"

Erin shrugged. "For you, I'll stay." He looked at Vy. "You're not needed elsewhere, are you?"

"Not when my favorite nephew needs me." Her eyes twinkled.

Rob and Gabby sat down, facing Erin and Vy. Revelers in the water shouted and splashed and generally made merry. A cool breeze wafted pine scents around the area. Rob hesitated a moment. "Okay, the question is, how do you work through the prejudice and kick-back about being a mixed-race couple? What do you do with people who disapprove?" He reached out and took Gabby's hand, squeezing it.

Erin raised his eyebrows at Vy. "You want to start?"

Vy's voice reflected her heart. "You love them. Live your commitment to Christ in front of them. And you pray a lot."

Gabby tapped her foot. "And when that's not enough?"

Vy looked from Rob to Gabby. "Enough for what? Their approval? Their blessing? Their permission? You may never get it. It's something you have to decide in advance." She leaned in. "Either the person you love is worth more than anyone else's approval, or they aren't. If they are, nothing and no one but the Lord matters."

Erin leaned back in his wheelchair. "It's not easy, I know." He took Vy's hand. "We know." He focused on Rob. "Collin told you how our biological mother reacted to Vy and me being a couple."

Rob snorted. "I was at the wedding. Geoff wanted to cast out her demons, as I remember."

Erin coughed. "Along with her." He frowned. "It didn't magically get better once we were married. We still catch flak. But we ignore it. We counter it with love."

Vy cleared her throat. "We?"

Erin cleared his. "I'm a work in progress. Vy counters criticism with love." Erin tipped his head to look closer at Rob and Gabby. "How committed are you two?"

Rob sat back. "I want to ask her parents' permission for steady dating. The 'find out if we're compatible' kind of commitment toward marriage."

Gabby looked at the ground. "My dad won't be the problem. Mom will. She's...let's say she's not a fan of people of color and 'white' people being together." The young woman looked up. "She talks a good game in public, but I know what she says at home."

Erin's eyes narrowed. "So you're going to ask Abbott first?"

Rob shook his head. "I thought of it. But it felt like a coward's move. I want to get everything out in the open right from the start." A thick body ran past them full steam into the lake, prompting cries of shock and awe and laughter. Lots of laughter.

Vy turned back to Rob and smiled. "I think that's very wise and very responsible." She touched Gabby's hand. "Have you thought about what you'll do if they say no?"

"Have I thought about it? Yes, I have. But I haven't decided what to do." She bumped Rob's shoulder. "We might not even be having this discussion except Rob felt it 'proper.' Especially since I'm still living at home. We're both legal age. We can do what we want." Erin detected a tone of defiance under her words. A little. Not much. But still...

Rob added, "We want to do this the Lord's way. Including being respectful of her parents."

Erin tapped his knee. "When are you going to talk to them?"

Rob grinned. "I thought about inviting them and Mom and Dad and you and Vy and having a 'cookout.'"

"Moral support, huh?" Erin grinned.

"More like safety in numbers. But I...we decided that wasn't fair to her folks. No one should have to hide their feelings about this. Tonight seems too soon. Thought about waiting until just before we all went home." He shrugged one shoulder. "Then if her folks say no, we'll at least have had the week to see each other with groups."

Vy stood and hugged Gabby and then Rob. "I think you're both doing a brave thing. I'll be praying it goes the Lord's way."

Erin added, "And I'll be praying He agrees with you about this." He turned his head sideways to look at Gabby. "Do you play basketball?"

She smiled wide. "Yes, sir. Lettered all four years."

Erin crowed. "Finally! Some competition for my sister!" He reached out and shook her hand, then looked at Rob. "Do not let this one get away, brother."

Rob grinned. "Not a chance. Not if the Lord agrees."

Jeff walked up carrying his toolbox. He set it on the ground beside the registration table. Vy asked, "Plumbing problem already? People haven't been here four hours."

Jeff shrugged. "Someone dropped their ring down the sink. I removed the trap and retrieved it. No big deal."

Vy shook her head. "So soon? Must be a newlywed. Someone not used to wearing rings on their ring finger."

Jeff grabbed a bottle of water from the cooler holding the beverages. He shook the condensation off the sides and took a long swallow. "Here comes Tom."

The SUV drove into the circle in front of the lake house, navigated the roundabout, and then exited to the boat ramp. Jeff snorted. "I know where his priorities lie."

Erin muttered, "Always have. Always will." Vy shoved him.

Rob and Gabby rose and walked off, probably to look for younger friends. Vy looked from her husband to her brother-in-law. "Excuse me, gentlemen, but are we gossiping behind someone's back?"

Jeff grinned. "Forgive us, Vy."

Erin held up his hand. "I'm not gossiping. Grumbling, but not gossiping."

"And that's better how?"

"It's not. It's just different."

Erin motioned to the latest—and last—arrival. "Registration is done now. Tell them number twelve. The keys are in the cabin on the counter."

Vy took hold of Erin's wheelchair handles. "Come on, dear. You've been in the shade too long." She wheeled him away from the table, into the sun.

"Where are we going?" Erin moved the clipboard from his lap to the table.

"Somewhere I can get out of this dress, into some shorts, and then maybe hit the lake." She pushed the chair toward the lodge.

"Can I come to?" *Rhetorical. I go where she goes.*

"Can you behave yourself?"

"Yes, ma'am. I'll behave just like myself."

Vy groaned. "Which is worse." She leaned in and kissed him. "I love you, Erin."

* * *

Jeff chuckled and watched them leave. If ever there had been a match for Erin, it was Vy. Sort of like Collin and him. Matches made in Heaven. And battled on earth. Jeff studied Tom as he directed Brutus in launching the boat. At nineteen, Brutus should be well-versed at attaching and detaching the requisite cables, ensuring the plug is in, and tying the boat to the dock. Wendy climbed out of the car, grabbed her backpack, and didn't look back as she headed directly lakeside. Sam watched the boat launch, standing off to the side. Observing but not getting in the way.

Jeff sighed. Pam swung her legs out of the car, stretched, and then began handing fishing gear to Tom. She waved at Jeff. He decided the wave should be invitation enough to warrant walking down and saying "hi." He smiled at the harried-looking woman. "Glad you all made it. I thought you were coming up this morning."

Pam shook her head. Her lips pursed, her eyes guarded. She handed a second tackle box to Brutus, who passed it to Tom. She shrugged. "Traffic got heavy. We had trouble getting out of town."

Tom grumbled. "That's what you get for starting this on a Monday."

"You think the weekend would be better?" Jeff waited for Tom's snide comeback.

"I think not having this event would be better. But no one wanted my opinion."

"We wanted it, Tom. We heard it. You got outvoted. Call this a mandatory family reunion. With people you might actually like." Jeff smiled to take the edge off.

Tom swung out of the boat. "That'll be the day." He stretched and bumped fists with Jeff. "I'm here. What happens next?"

"You relax, enjoy nature and the lake, and have a good time." *I can hope.* "You're in cabin twelve. Erin says the keys are there, on the counter in the kitchen."

Tom's eyes narrowed. "Did you tell everyone about the restricted boating hours?"

"We set it up so the lake is a no-wake zone from 8 p.m. until 9 a.m. Anyone who wants to go out on the lake to look at the stars can, and they won't bother your fishing."

"I'll take it. Took you long enough to think of it, though."

A cheerful answer deflects anger. And shuts down grumblers. "We'll see how it goes this time and adjust it as needed." He motioned over his shoulder. "You want the cabin, or are you gonna join us in the big house?"

"Did you get wi-fi in the house?"

"Nope."

"I'll stay at the cabin. At least I can watch shows I've downloaded."

Jeff saw Pam's eyes lower. He offered, "You know you're all welcome to come hang with us any time."

Tom laughed. "I'm around you clowns every day. Why would I want to spend an extra week when I don't have to?" Tom shifted items from the center of the hatch more to the back.

Jeff shrugged. "Team building. Morale boosting. Breaking down barriers. Building trust. To name a few reasons."

Tom held up his hands. "You go right ahead. I'll be out on the lake drowning worms."

Pam's eyes looked pained. Jeff suggested, "I think Collin is in the house with the littles. She's waiting for my folks to come up, so she's got back up with the trio. I'm sure she'd love to have an adult to talk to."

Tom cleared his throat. He directed his comments to Pam. "When you're done unloading the car. And since you let Wendy leave without helping, we'll be one hand short. I want to get everything put away and set up so I can go out tonight."

Pam lifted her eyes. "We'll have it done. You'll be able to get on the lake before sun-down."

"Good." Tom grabbed a bag of chips from the sack of groceries. "I'll take these." He sneered at his wife, his tongue part-way between his teeth. "See you." He walked away, tore into the bag, and began eating the chips.

Brutus stepped up. "I'll drive the car to the cabin, Mom. We can unload it there."

Relief filled the woman's eyes. "Thanks, Brutus."

Brutus shrugged. "Yeah." He motioned to Sam. "Get in the car, bud. We're going to the cabin to help Mom. You can go find someone to play with when we're done."

Sam kept his eyes on the ground. He nudged the dirt, and then climbed back into the car. Pam touched Jeff's arm. "Tell Collin I'll be up after we get settled."

Jeff hugged the woman. "We've been praying for you. We'll keep praying for the outcome."

"Thanks. We need it." She climbed back in the car, and the group left.

Jeff sighed. Lord, watch over the group. Pam is hurting, and I don't know how to help. Guard and guide my words. Please.

The walkie-talkie on his belt buzzed. Collin. "Jeff, can you come to the house for a few minutes? If you want to see your children live to start school, I need a break."

Jeff chuckled. "Be right there." He double-timed it to the house.

* * *

Static. "Status update?"

"Approximately fifty to seventy civilians."

"Quite a wide range, Lieutenant. Narrow it down."

"Commander, many of the persons are juveniles. They are circulating the area. It's difficult to keep track of them."

"How juvenile?"

"Under ten. Under five."

"Understood." Pause. "Maybe we can use this as an opportunity to practice night surveillance. I want three teams in position around the lake. Let's see what our people have learned."

"Yes, ma'am."

* * *

Early in the afternoon, Rob and Gabby found a gathering of young adults milling around on the east side of the shallows. Gabby pointed out two or three people she knew. "She's Mia. Gilbert. Peach. You know Brutus. I wondered if he'd make it."

As Gabby continued to name names, Rob realized how few of the crowd he recognized. It made him feel old. *Twenty-four, and it's like I'm a different generation.*

Gabby introduced him to as many of the group as would look up. Rob's eyes narrowed as he saw beverages in paper bags being consumed. Passed around and consumed. Should he say something? Report his suspicions? Or go along with the flow and turn a blind eye? At least until he had proof.

A man, maybe twenty, maybe under, asked Rob, "Are you related to the Farrells?"

Gabby laughed. "José, does he look like the Farrells?"

José shrugged. "No."

Gabby followed up quickly. "The Farrells' kids are four. Does Rob look like he's four? Collin's only what, thirty-four? Thirty-six? Does Rob look young enough to be her kid?"

José admitted, "No."

"Then answer your own question." She smiled and led Rob away.

He frowned at her. "Why'd you say I'm not a Farrell?"

"Jeff and Collin are cool, but everyone here knows they play by the rules. We want a break from all the parental stuff for a couple days."

Rob walked with Gabby as she continued to mingle among the young people. He objected, "But this is like Jeff and Collin's house. Shouldn't people respect the rules in someone's home?"

Gabby shrugged. "Jesus ate and drank with sinners. I think he'd be fine with someone having a beer."

"Even when the rules say no alcohol?" They meandered to another group of young adults seated on the stone benches.

"Those are the kind of artificial rules Jesus broke the most."

Rob stopped. He turned Gabby to face him. "Gabby, I think you're twisting what the scriptures say. Jesus didn't condemn people for their lifestyles, and neither do the Farrells. But that's a far cry from welcoming booze—"

Gabby waved at a dark-skinned woman as she passed. "Lilibeth! Hi!" She looked back at Rob. "We can finish this conversation later. I have to talk to Lili." She scooted off, leaving Rob alone.

He scowled after her, and then backtracked his steps. He found José sitting at a picnic table by himself. The younger man looked up as Rob approached.

Rob extended his fist. "I want to clear up what Gabby said. Yes, I'm related to Jeff and Collin. They adopted me when I turned eighteen. I'm their son."

José smiled. "I thought so." He tapped fists with Rob. "Jeff and Collin are good people. I've heard her testimony at church. Thought I saw you standing with her. I wondered if you would say something just now."

Rob shook his head. "I'm not sure what Gabby tried to prove there."

José grinned. "Who knows the mind of *una chica, eh?* Women."

Rob sat on the top of the picnic table. "Absolutely right."

José looked around at the milling group of people. "I'd love to meet your folks…" He stopped. "Do you call them your folks?"

"Of course. You want to meet them? My guess is they're in the big house with my 'bubbies.' Come on, and I'll introduce you."

"I don't want to interrupt anything. I meant sooner or later."

"This is sooner. Come on."

José laughed. "I'd love it, then."

"Let me tell Gabby I'm going." Rob looked over the heads of the crowd but didn't see her among them. After a moment or two longer, he shrugged. "I'll catch her later. Let's go."

The two men headed up to the house and opened the glass-paneled door. The lodge had been laid out with a central "courtyard," what Collin referred to as the "common" room. It served as the lobby, dining room, living/family room…sort of the "everything" room. Large skylights provided natural lighting.

The open floor plan contained an expandable dining table and chairs for more formal meals. Smaller tables and chairs for playing chess or other games dotted the room. An array of cozy furniture faced an impressive stone fireplace. It was a place where there were no prohibitions to eating on the couch, no "don't come inside with your wet swimsuit" rules. Kids and dogs (if there were any) welcome. An imposing polished wooden staircase led to the second floor. Multiple bedroom suites surrounded the upper level, open to the common room below.

A massive kitchen sat to the left of the entrance. A long butcher-block bar, seating five on a side, served as both the work surface and gathering place. Large windows ensured natural light and a view of the vast woods. Industrial refrigerators and freezers stood to the left of the deep farmhouse sinks. A multi-shelved walk-in pantry extended beyond the kitchen. Across from the fridges were the chef-top ovens and stoves. Rob had been in on the design. He made sure the kitchen would be family accessible.

A wall of windows ensured the cooking area would always have natural light. Beyond the kitchen were more paneled doorways—conference, billiard, game rooms, an office (seldom occupied) then more bedroom suites. The house felt large, warm, inviting. Made to be occupied and enjoyed. Which it usually was. The Farrells, extended family, and/or friends found time to visit often.

Jeff lay on the floor playing cars with the trio. All three Farrell children clamored to their feet and mobbed their big brother. "Rob! Rob. Rob!"

He swung each one up for a hug, and then set them down. "Hey, buds. This is a friend of mine. His name is José."

Suddenly the triplets got a case of the shys. Joshua stepped forward first. "Hi. I'm Joshua."

"Nice to meet you, Joshua." José tapped fists.

Caleb stepped forward, emboldened by his brother. "I'm Caleb."

"Pleasure, Caleb." Another tapped fist.

Talitha stepped out from behind Rob's back. She put her hands behind her back, her voice barely above a whisper. "I'm Talitha."

José kneeled down to be at her level. "*Hola, chica.*"

Tee's eyes lit up. "You speak Spanish? *Hola, José. Como estas?*" She spoke each word carefully and plainly.

José laughed. "How are you? You speak Spanish *muy bien.*"

Tee smiled. "My mommy teaches me."

Jeff reached out to shake José's hand. "Welcome, José." He hesitated. "Are you related to Buster Melendez?"

"His son."

"I thought I spotted a family resemblance. Nice to have you here."

José clasped Jeff's hand. "I want to thank you for the scholarship. I'm the first generation of our family to go to college. Made my mom over-the-moon proud."

Jeff smiled. "I'm glad we can make the perk available. I'm still trying to talk your dad into going. He keeps saying he's too old."

José laughed. "Yeah, we've talked about it, too. Don't give up on him. I think he's starting to believe it might be possible."

"Then we'll both work on him and see what happens."

Rob looked around. "Where's Mom?"

"Lying down. Fighting off a headache."

Caleb jumped up and down. "She said we gave it to her, and she wanted to pass it to her pillow to hold it for her."

Joshua matched his brother's energies. "Yeah. Daddy says we have to stay in the house until Grandma and Grandpa get here."

Caleb added, "And Aunt Leesa. Then we can go to the beach and play in the water."

Rob turned to José. "Have to have eyes on each one of them at all times. Especially at the water."

"Smart."

Jeff snorted. "Some say overprotective. I say just doing my daddy duties."

Rob laughed. "And there are a lot of them. Come on, José. I'll show you where the good food is."

"I don't want to impose."

"Hey, once you cross the threshold, you're family. Refrigerator privileges. Come and go up until eight p.m. After that, you wake one of the bubbies, they're all yours."

"I'll remember."

The younger men headed for the kitchen.

* * *

Collin rose from her nap. She, Jeff, Rob, and José walked with the trio down to the shallow part of the lake, to the artificial "beach" which had been dug out and cleared and cleaned. The bank ran out at four feet deep for a good ten yards. Enough to let children and non-swimming adults enjoy the water and still feel safe. But the trio wore floaties, and Tee wore her bathing suit happily.

Collin surveyed the area. Nothing but young children and their guardians. A few grandparents. Nothing to excite her Spidey sense. She turned her attention to her designated child: Joshua. The wild child. The "watch me do XYZ, Mommy" child. Jeff had Tee. Rob and José had Caleb. More equal distribution of labor. *Okay, I should have given Joshua to the boys. But...but I don't trust anyone to watch Joshua but me, right? Sigh. Yes, Lord. I know, Lord. I hear*

You, Lord. But…

Collin grappled with her fear for another few minutes, and then surrendered. "Rob, will you switch off with me and take Joshua? I'll watch Caleb."

Jeff dropped his jaw. Rob mirrored him. Both men, wide-eyed, stared at her. "What?" Jeff's tone sounded aghast. "You're asking Rob to—" He grabbed his chest.

Collin pointed to the water. "Watch your child. Just watch your child."

Jeff stepped over, kissed her, and then hugged her. "That's very mature of you."

She shoved him. "Go. Attend your duties."

Rob made as if to follow Jeff's lead. Collin's eyes narrowed, and she mock-threatened him. "Do not say it. Do not."

Rob grinned. "Love you, Mom."

"Yeah, yeah. I can be taught." Yes, Lord. See? I can be. Eventually.

Tom passed by on his way to the boat dock. He had Sam in tow, following behind him. Pam trod behind the two men. Collin couldn't read her friend's face. The lines on her brow were deep, the cheeks pulled taut. *Must have been a rough afternoon.*

Tom waved to Jeff. "Hope you got the lake stocked better than last time I fished up here."

Jeff shooed him by with a backhand. "All the ones you didn't catch then are that much bigger."

"I hear ya." He pointed to Pam. He scowled. "I want those pillows packed back in the car when I come back. I told you not to bring them. You know you won't touch them while you're here." He turned to Sam and clapped him on the shoulder. "Come on, Sam. Let's get started. Maybe we can get away from all these beached whales and find the cove I told you about."

"Yes, Dad." Sam increased his step.

Pam reached Collin's side and sat down on the sand. She pulled her knees up to her chest and sighed.

Collin sat beside her, keeping one eye on Caleb. He happily built castles with Tee. Collin looked at her weary friend. "Pillows?"

"I make pillows out of old cheerleader uniforms. I get paid to make them, a few bucks each. But it's something to do while Tom watches TV at night."

"You'll have to show them to me."

"They're nothing. Something to keep my hands busy."

"I'd still like to see them."

"Maybe later."

Why is she being so secretive? They're pillows. Collin let it drop. Minutes passed. Collin watched Caleb run into the water, run out, run in, then sit down and let the water lap over his legs. He looked into the murk he stirred up. "Mommy! There's little fish in the water." He made a grab for them. "I can't catch them."

He turned his cherub face to his father. "Daddy, can we go fishing here?"

Jeff smiled. "No, bubbies. These fish are too little. Like you three. You're too little to go fishing. You have to be very, very quiet for a very long time. Longer than you can."

Joshua crowed. "I can be quiet." He closed his mouth. Ten seconds passed. "That long, Daddy?"

"No, buddy. Longer."

Caleb tried. Eight seconds. "That long?"

"Longer. Much, much longer."

Tee sighed. "Fishing doesn't sound like fun." She went back to packing sand in her bucket.

Jeff laughed. "Not for little people. Not yet. Maybe later."

Tee sighed again. "I know. When we get bigger. How much bigger can we get, Daddy?"

"One day at a time, little one. Get bigger one day at a time. That's enough."

"Okay." Tee turned back to the water. "Watch me make it splash, Daddy!"

And he did.

* * *

Harmon, Lacey, and Leesa arrived and took over trio watching duties. Rob and José drifted back to the young adult gathering. A bonfire blazed in one of the many firepits. Hotdogs, marshmallows, and pretty much anything you could put on a stick and hold over a fire appeared. Rob scanned the area and saw Gabby sitting with three women and two men. Brutus was the only person Rob recognized in the group. José moseyed off to sit with some friends.

Rob walked over and stood beside Gabby. He smiled. "Is this seat taken?"

Gabby patted the sand. "Free for the asking." Rob sat. Gabby apologized. "I didn't mean to abandon you. Lili and I have been trying to catch up for ages." She lowered her voice. "She's having trouble at home. Her parents are pressuring her to break up with her boyfriend."

"Why?" Rob settled back for the long story.

"They think she's spending too much time with him alone. They're worried about what might happen."

Rob raised his eyebrows but remained silent. Gabby looked him in the eyes. "You agree with her parents?"

Rob shook his head. "I don't know the situation. Don't know Lili, don't know her parents. I can't offer an opinion one way or the other."

Gabby shrugged. "I guess." She motioned to Brutus. She lowered her voice. "He's in a bad way. And a bad mood. Wish I knew how to help him."

"What's going on?" Rob settled into the sand.

"Sam. Pam insisted he be evaluated by a psychiatrist, and Brutus doesn't like the results."

The other young adults all coupled off and left, leaving Gabby, Rob, and Brutus.

Rob waited to hear how the story would play out from Brutus's side. Did the younger man have any insights Pam didn't?

Brutus tossed a rock into the fire. He looked at Gabby. "Mom told us the psych thinks my little brother needs intensive counseling. Said he's a danger to himself. Maybe to others. And she said it's all Dad's fault." He pitched another rock hard, giving it some heat before it hit the fire. Sparks flew into the air, and wood chips scattered in the pit. "I could have told them without the evaluation. Dad never does anything with the kid unless he has to." Brutus snorted. "Took Sam out in the boat. Then he brought him back, dumped him off, and went fishing by himself. Sam gets in his way."

The younger man snorted. "Mom says he never really wanted Sam. He was happy with me and Wendy. Then Sam came along, and all Dad's careful plans about his future and retirement went out the window."

Rob wanted to support Tom, but how do you defend the

indefensible?

Brutus snarled. "All Dad cares about is himself. He's the one who needs to see the psych. But no. It's Sam who gets the short end of life. I worry about him. I really do. But what can I do?"

Rob offered carefully, "Can you spend time with him? When you're not in school?"

"School? What a joke." Brutus exploded. "Dad torpedoed me going to school. Said they couldn't afford it because of paying for Sam's upbringing. 'Takes a lot to raise a kid these days, you know.' Even before we knew about the evaluation. Dad doesn't want me leaving the nest. Mom says he wouldn't have anyone to run get his meds for him." Brutus nudged the firepit with his shoe.

"Meds? For what?"

"You name it. Depression. Anxiety. To help him get to sleep. To help him wake up. Pills for muscle aches. Pills for backaches. Headaches. He must take twenty meds every day. Washes them down with beer." Brutus's face darkened.

Rob's eyes widened. "With beer? Doesn't he know—"

"He doesn't care. It hasn't hurt him yet. And it's the only way he can unwind at night. So he says. Probably because Mom is always glaring at him. She thinks we don't notice. We do." Brutus looked at Rob. "I'm wrong, but I keep praying something will happen to Dad's boat, so he has to spend more time with Sam." Brutus leaned forward on his rear, moving closer to the ammunition pile of rocks.

Rob had to ask. "You really think it would make a difference?"

"Something has to." He tossed another rock. It landed gently in the center of the flames. "Dad turns on these R-rated shows, and then goes to sleep. Sam sits in there and watches garbage. It's no wonder he needs to learn 'age-appropriate behaviors.' Poor kid."

Which explains what happened with Tee. "I'm sorry, Brutus. What can I do to help?"

"Tell me how to sabotage a boat."

Gabby offered, "Put diesel in the fuel tank."

Rob turned sharply to look at Gabby. "What?"

"Yeah. Mom did it once to the car. Had to be towed and practically rebuilt. Cost Dad thousands. But she never did it again." Gabby laughed.

Rob didn't. "I'll bet."

Brutus perked up. "You couldn't fill the tank full, though." He rubbed his hands on his shorts. "You would have to leave some—"

Rob interrupted the flow of the conversation. "Can we not make the situation worse, please?" He caught Brutus's eyes. "Think about it. If the boat is out of commission, your dad will spend all his time trying to fix it. He still won't spend time with Sam."

"Unless Sam is helping him repair it. Dad could teach him how to use tools, how to fix things. Maybe."

"Maybe." *Breathe. Breathe. Stay under control. Walk in the Spirit…*

Wendy Quince joined the group, sitting beside her brother. José strolled over and took a place beside her. *Interesting.* Wendy looked as stressed as Brutus. Rob scrutinized the young woman. Something looked different. He hadn't seen her in a couple months, but…

Her weight. She's thin. Too thin. She looks pale. Lord, guide my words. Or shut my mouth. Don't let me say something hurtful. Or stupid. He smiled. "Hey, Wendy. Been a while since I've seen you. How are you doing?"

She shrugged. "Doing." She bumped her brother's shoulder. "Right? We're doing. You tell them about Sam?"

Gabby nodded. "Yeah, and I told him how to sabotage the boat." Gabby laughed. Brutus didn't. Neither did Wendy.

Rob tread lightly. "Wendy, what can I do to help?"

Wendy stared off to the lake. "Get me different parents. All they do is argue."

Rob leaned forward. "I'm serious, Wendy. What can I do to help? Both you and Brutus are hurting. I can see it."

Wendy gave Rob a sad smile. "Your mom taught you, didn't she?"

"To pay attention? Yeah, she did."

Gabby looked from Brutus to Wendy. "Pay attention to what? Hurting about what? That stuff with your brother? Were you serious?"

Rob deflected from Gabby's inattention. "I'm worried about you both." He touched Wendy's arm. "You've stopped eating, haven't you?" José reached over and took her hand.

Wendy shrugged. "What's it matter? I can just 'get over it' if I want to."

"Says who?" Rob had to swallow the heat in his voice. A little late, but…

"Dad. My school counselor sent home a note. She thought I was anorexic. That was the semester before I graduated." Wendy looked off at the lake again. "Imagine. What stress could there possibly be in my life?" She looked down and then looked Rob in the eyes. "Between Mom and Dad fighting all the time, Sam being ignored, and Brutus…"

Brutus's head jerked up. "I'm fine."

She lashed out. "So am I, right?"

José bumped her shoulder. "*Chica…*"

Rob tossed a rock in the fire. "Let me guess. Your teacher recommended counseling. Your dad said no."

"Bingo. Give that man a prize. According to Mom, he thinks all counselors are quacks. Actually, I really thought she agreed with him until she decided to take Sam to see someone."

Rob gazed from Wendy to Brutus and back. "What happens if you disobey him? Go for counseling anyway?"

"How?" Brutus snorted. "Takes money, you know? Yeah, we're both 'of age.' We could do it, but he'd kick us out of the house fast enough." Brutus shook his head. "Oh, I've got some friends I could stay with for a night or two. Maybe a week. But longer?" He shook his head.

Rob offered, "I could—"

Wendy cut him off. "You work with Dad. He'd tear the company apart if he knew you were helping us disobey him."

The heat returned. "I don't think he's as powerful as he thinks he is." Rob leaned in again. "Look, I know counselors. I know places you can stay. Not just stay but live. You have options. You gotta believe me. There are people who will help."

Gabby raised her hand. "Could you introduce me to some of them? Maybe they could get me away from Mom's constant nagging. 'What are you going to do with your life? When are you going to make something of yourself?' I graduated high school a year ago. I'm still trying to figure things out."

Rob smiled at her. "I'm sure your mom has your best interests at heart." He glanced back at Brutus and Wendy. "Think about it. Then do something about it. Call me."

José leaned over and kissed her cheek. "Listen to the man. He knows what he's talking about."

Rob swallowed a smile. "How long have you two

been…together?"

Wendy scowled. "We're not. Not officially. Not at all, as far as my dad knows. One more thing for him to go ballistic about. Mom says we should keep it hidden from him. Really think about things first, at least for a while. She keeps saying when the time is right, she'll talk to him about it."

Rob knew but asked anyhow. "And he would object why?"

José answered for her. "Because I'm the son of an immigrant. 'Undocumented' in Tom's opinion. Anyone not born here is undocumented until proven otherwise, he says."

Rob lowered his head. "Something else to bring to my Father."

Wendy's eyes narrowed. "Your dad? You mean he'd talk to my dad? That won't go over well."

"I meant my heavenly Father. God."

Wendy looked down. "Yeah, talk about a lost cause. If my 'heavenly father' is anything like my earthly father, I'm doomed."

"There's the beauty of it, Wendy. He's not."

She shook her head. "Every example I've ever heard says, 'Think of how your father loves you.' My father is not a shining example of someone who puts my interests first. How am I going to understand God?"

Rob gazed off over the lake. "I didn't have a father, either, Wendy. Never had a dad. Still don't know who he is." He looked back at the young woman. "Collin helped me. She didn't have a father who loved her." He snorted. "Hers tried to have her killed. When he wasn't trying to kill her himself."

Wendy sat forward. "I had no idea. That's horrid. So how did she get past seeing God as someone like her dad?"

"She told me to think not of my father and what he did, but think of myself as a father. How would I treat my child? Would I love them? Take care of them? Want the best for them? When she turned it around, I started to see how God might think about me."

He ducked his head to the side. "Of course, He's perfect, and I'm not. Jesus said something about it once. I'll paraphrase it. 'If you imperfect people know how to give good stuff—love, care, food, shelter—to your kids, don't you think your Father in Heaven will do the same, or even more?' Put yourself in the equation instead of your dad. It helps."

Wendy stared into the fire. Rob watched Brutus do the same.

Maybe he's getting it, too? Lord, help them. Both of them.

José nodded to Rob. "When you put yourself as the parent, God's sacrifice of His Son for us is far more impactful. Would I allow my child to die for someone else? Someone who didn't deserve it? Or even want it? But God did."

Wendy's voice sounded far away. "And all I have to do is say I believe?"

"Say it, and mean it. Can't just be something in your head. You have to bring it down to your gut, your soul."

Brutus shook his head. "Who gets to judge if it's real or not?"

"God. We can look at someone's life and say, 'Well, their actions don't reflect someone who is trying to follow Jesus.' But only the Lord can decide who is His and who isn't."

José chuckled. "Good thing. I'd have been written off a long time ago."

Rob extended his fist to tap knuckles. "Right there with you, *hermano.*"

Gabby yawned. "I think I've had enough for one night. Rob, would you walk me to the lodge? It doesn't count as a date, right?"

Rob shook his head. "No, it doesn't. I think we're safe."

José's head came up. "You two are a couple?"

Gabby gave an exaggerated sigh. "Not until we get the okay from my parents. Rob thinks the proper thing to do is ask first. We're going to talk to my folks later in the week."

José raised his eyebrows. "Interesting. Let me know how it goes."

Wendy stood as well and addressed José. "Since Brutus is here, will you walk us to the cabin? It won't look like you and I are alone, either."

José eyed Brutus. "You okay with the idea?"

"Yeah. I'm down with it."

Everyone stood, dusted off their jeans, shorts, capris, or whatever they wore, and went their separate ways.

Rob and Gabby went on into the lodge together. Gabby stopped at the staircase. "Thanks for the conversation tonight. Kind of heavy, though. Maybe tomorrow the five of us have some fun? Go out in the boat and have a good time? Brutus and Wendy look like they could use it."

Rob nodded. "We'll try. Night, Gabby."

She smiled, turned, and disappeared up the steps. Rob watched her go. He sighed. Only a little. *Lord, direct me. Amen.* He headed out the door and to his cabin.

* * *

Late in the night, Jeff woke suddenly. He looked around. What woke him?

A gunshot rang out in the distance. Jeff cocked his head. The clock said two-thirty. Who went out shooting at two-thirty? *No one good, for sure.*

Two more shots echoed. Jeff guessed the shooter had to be across the lake. Maybe up on the ridge. Well away from the lodge. Nothing to worry about tonight. He'd notify the sheriff tomorrow. In the morning. After breakfast. Yeah. Then.

* * *

Static. "Lieutenant, tell me that was *not* one of our people shooting at shadows."

"No, Commander. Squad leaders have checked in. Not us."

"Get eyes on who it is. I want to know what they're firing, what they're wearing, and what they had for dinner. You copy?"

"Copy. I'll get a squad on it."

"Good. I don't want to answer questions about a firefight on a training mission."

"Yes, ma'am. On it."

Silence returned to the ridge.

TUESDAY

Tuesday morning, Jeff filed a report with the sheriff's office about the shots being fired. Erin and Vy sat at the table with him as he spoke to the deputy, taking the information over the phone. "Yes, a handgun. I heard five shots. I think one more woke me up, but I'm not certain. What kind of handgun?" He looked around the room in confusion, one palm lifted in the air.

Vy offered, "Glock 19."

Erin declared, "Glock 17."

Vy glared at him. "I'm the firearms expert. Nineteen."

"I've got the better ear. Seventeen."

Jeff called it a tie. "My experts say Glock but can't agree on the caliber. I have no clue."

Erin muttered, "Neither does she." He turned his back to Vy.

Vy tapped him on the shoulder, and then gave him the stink-eye. "What did you say?"

"Nothing, dear. Absolutely nothing." Erin leaned back and kissed her.

Jeff swallowed his chuckle. "Thank you, Officer. We'll let you know if we hear anything more."

He hung up. "Report filed. Let's go get the boat set up."

Erin nodded. "I think you have an excellent idea. Do you want to come, my love?"

Vy sneered at him. "No. When the work is done, I'll come out and ski. You two don't need me for all the mechanical parts."

Erin rolled out in his wheelchair beside Jeff. He muttered, "She wouldn't understand it anyhow."

"I heard you." Vy's voice rose over their departing shoulders.

"No, you didn't." Erin ducked.

The men scooted out the door.

Jeff and Erin prepped the boat for a day to be spent hauling tubers, maybe a skier, and definitely a raft or two. Jeff wanted to be sure the new set-up would accommodate Erin getting in and out of the boat with his wheelchair. Leave no man behind.

Tom idled his craft into the dock as he returned from fishing the night before. He called out, "You gonna go stir up the lake?"

"Yep. You're done fishing for the morning. How'd it go?"

"Eh. I've caught bigger. Not here, but better lakes."

Jeff let the jibe go. He debated only a moment. "Sam was upset you left without him."

Again, Tom passed it off. "When he's old enough to sit still and not tangle our lines, he can come."

"Is that how your dad taught you?"

"Yes. He made me learn to take responsibility for myself. I know how to raise my son, Jeff."

Jeff fell silent. Not the time to push it. Tom motioned behind him. "Thought I heard a gunshot up there. Saw a flash. You might have hunters up in the woods."

"Where?"

"Below the ridge."

"Can you show me? Take me there?"

Tom tossed his tackle box out of the boat. "Only if we take your boat. Don't want to use all my gas running your errands."

Erin interjected, "I'll stay here."

Jeff jerked his head sideways to Tom. "Get in. Let's go."

Tom climbed in, and they took off. Jeff pushed the "no wake zone" to its max. He wanted to race it out to the hills but reminded himself, *God has this. Hurrying won't make it any different. You're either for me on this, or You're not.*

Tom nudged him. "This as fast as this thing goes? Open the throttle, man."

"I'm being considerate of the fishing crowd, remember? Someone complained."

Tom frowned and took a seat up front. "Far side. About halfway round the lake."

Jeff increased his speed when they hit the middle of the lake. He knew there weren't any people out but him and Tom. They could risk a few waves on the shore.

As they neared where Tom pointed, Tom pulled out his cell phone. Jeff's eyes narrowed. "Thought we all agreed no phones for the duration. The lodge has a phone for emergency contacts. It's part of the contract, man."

Tom sneered. "Your contract, not mine. And since I have the GPS coordinates, you're going to forgive me, right?"

Jeff burned inside. How many times? When will I speak up? Or out?

After we clear up this shooter issue.

"We'll talk about it after."

"Yeah, yeah. I'm not worried." Tom stuck his tongue partway out at Jeff, and then laughed. Jeff didn't. Tom scowled. "What? Can't you take a joke?"

Jeff stayed silent on the matter. "Where'd you see the flash?"

Tom consulted his phone. "Right up there." He pointed to a small area, just large enough to beach the boat.

There were no rocks, fallen trees, or other dangers to the hull of the boat. Jeff idled in. Tom watched for obstacles. Jeff monitored the sonar. The lake bottom proved clean. Tom jumped out of the boat with the rope. Jeff gunned the boat up the shore. Tom tied it off, and Jeff jumped out to follow him.

Tom pointed. "That way."

The two men climbed the hill and began searching for any sign of someone in the woods. After several minutes, Jeff spotted something. He called out, "Tom. Over here."

Tom walked over. "What is it?"

Jeff pointed to a makeshift target hanging from a tree.

Tom drawled, "Well, I guess we found our shooter. Someone in the woods trying to scare us off."

"Why? We're families with kids. And this is our land. It doesn't make sense."

"Criminals never do. Come on, let's head back, take this thing to the police. I want to get a shower and go to bed."

Jeff stared at the target again. He moved around the area, examining nearby trees, bushes, and anything growing. Did they have an illegal pot farm here? Was someone—

A shot rang. A chunk of tree over Jeff's head flew off. Jeff ducked behind it. Tom mirrored Jeff, flattening out on the ground. "Where'd the shot come from?"

Jeff pointed. "There." He counted to three, tossed a stick left, and then dashed right behind another tree.

Nothing. No more shots. Tom picked up a dirt clod and pitched it as hard as he could in the direction Jeff pointed. Still nothing.

They waited another moment. Then another. Another. Still nothing.

Tom rose with extreme caution. "You think they're gone?"

Jeff listened hard but heard nothing. No bushes rustling, no twigs snapping. Nothing to indicate anyone moved. "I don't know." He inched his head out from behind the tree.

Another chunk of tree flew out. Jeff ducked back down. Tom followed. Jeff yelled, "What do you want?" *Or should it be, "Who are you?"*

No answer. A third shot blasted a tree branch above Jeff's head. He ducked as it fell beside him. Then he heard feet running away through the brush.

Jeff waited, counted, breathed… Finally, he inched around the tree again. Nothing happened. He stood up straight and stepped out in full view.

Nothing. No one fired. Trees stayed intact. The shooter had gone.

Tom stepped out from behind his hiding place. "What do you think that was all about?"

"If I had an idea, I'd tell you. I don't understand any of this. Let's get back to camp and call the sheriff. Maybe he has some explanation."

"Yeah, well, have him come out here. I don't want to waste my time in some podunk law officer's digs while they try and figure out how to turn on a cellphone."

Jeff stared at him. "You are…why are you so against everything?"

"I'm not against anything. I just don't like interruptions to my time."

The two men walked back to the boat. "Your time? When did it become all about your time? Other people have time, too."

"Fine. Let them have their time. But not on mine."

"You know the world isn't all about you, right? There are other people with needs and wants and hurts."

"I know there are."

Jeff snorted. "You just want what you want when you want it, right?" He climbed into the boat.

"You got it." Tom shoved the boat off the bank and jumped on board. "I look out for my family. I provide what they need. You can't say I don't."

Jeff hesitated. "We kept Sam for two days. He needs time with you. He's desperate for time with you."

Tom nodded. "And I'm going to spend time with him. When we get back home. This is a work week, right? When I'm done working, I'll start spending time with him."

This was going nowhere. Jeff pointed the boat to the opposite shore and the dock. He wanted nothing more than to go hug his wife and children. Maybe even Rob. Definitely Rob. They did need to spend more time together. Starting when Jeff got back to shore.

* * *

Static. "Not us. Commander. Not our people."

"I don't like this, Lieutenant. Your team better have answers for me and fast. Or the platoon will run laps with Smokey the Bear up and down the hills."

"Understood. We're on it."

"Consider this urgent, Lieutenant. You've got ten minutes to gather your recon and tell me who is threatening civilians. I don't need local mounties up here chasing us around."

"Got it, Commander. I'll get you the information. Right away."

"Don't disappoint me."

"No, ma'am."

* * *

Jeff spotted Collin sitting at the top of the ramp when he and Tom pulled up. Collin caught the rope Tom threw her. She wore a cautious smile. "Where have you two been out so early?" She looked at Jeff, her eyes questioning. "I heard shots."

Jeff killed the engine. "Yeah. We did too." He disembarked, wrapped his arms around Collin, and hugged her hard.

She pulled back from him slightly. "You're shaking."

"Post-trauma. It's sinking in. We got shot at."

Tom corrected him. "You got shot at. They weren't aiming at

me, remember?" The man grabbed his pack from his boat. "I'm going to the cabin. If you need me, I'll be there. But don't need me until at least two. I'm going to rest up for tonight's battle with the fish." He saluted Collin and walked away.

Collin hugged Jeff again. "What's going on?"

As they walked back to the lodge, Jeff explained. "I don't think they were singling me out. I think it was a 'you're not welcome here' statement. Which we heeded. I need to call the sheriff's office. We need to get his advice."

"Should we send everyone home?"

"It's a possibility. I think we'll wait until we talk to the authorities. Maybe they can give us some advice. I hate to cut and run, but…"

"…but we have families and children here. I agree." Collin hesitated. "Did you talk to Tom?"

Jeff felt the anger build inside him. "Yes, I did. And we'll discuss it later. You and me. And maybe Vy and Erin. And Rob."

"All of executive management? It's that serious?"

"Possibly. I thought more like his brothers and sisters in the Lord."

"Ah, I see. Okay, then. One problem at a time."

"The only way to do it."

Jeff called the sheriff's office and filed a report. The operator assured him someone would get back to him. No time frame. *As soon as we can, sir.*

He hung up, and then proceeded to hunt down every member of his family and hug them. Including Rob. And Gabby being with Rob, Jeff hugged her as well.

Rob's eyes twinkled with amusement. "What's this all about?"

"Maybe I don't show it enough. But I love you." Jeff sank into a chair.

Now Rob's eyes narrowed. "What happened?" He stood beside his father.

"Tom. Then we got shot at. But mostly Tom."

Rob nodded. "I see. I think."

Jeff turned to Gabby. "Are you coming out on the water this morning? We're going to haul rafts and anything else we can float."

Gabby eyed Rob. He nodded. She smiled. "Sounds like fun. I'll stay in the boat, however."

Rob laughed. "Aw, come on. Live dangerously. Jeff drives like an old lady anyhow."

Jeff grinned. "But I'm letting Erin drive."

Rob raised his eyebrows. "Ooo. Different story." He turned to Gabby. "Maybe I'll stay in the boat with you. Erin drives like a maniac."

* * *

Erin rolled into the common room. "I do not. I've never once gotten a ticket for my driving."

"I meant on the water."

"Ah, different story. But still never got a ticket for it."

Jeff tapped the table. "Are we going to do this or not? And when?"

Rob snickered. "I thought about having breakfast, but if Erin's driving, I'll pass. Less to come up."

Erin sneered at Rob. "Coward."

Collin waved her hands. "Um, we will have small children in the boat."

Jeff shook his head. "Maybe not the first trip. We can take them and my folks after we drown the younger crowd."

"Sounds like a plan. I'll see if Mom and Pop will watch them this morning. If not, I'll stay on shore and watch the carnage."

Vy entered the room and the conversation. "Carnage? What'd I miss?"

Erin jumped in before anyone else could comment. "They have wounded me, my love. They are casting aspersions about my ability to pilot a boat. Safely." He laid his hand on his chest.

Vy bent down and kissed her husband. "Oh, you poor thing. I'm sure they have your best interests at heart."

Collin chuckled. "I'm not. We were thinking more of the people he's going to be towing."

Vy lifted her head. "Ah, those kinds of aspersions." She patted Erin on the shoulder. "Then I have to agree with them, dearest. You think your purpose is to dump them as soon as possible."

Erin gave Vy a wide-eyed, innocent look. "Isn't it?"

Jeff shook his head. His brother-in-law lost the levity in his smile. "I'm considering an intervention with Tom." Silence filled the room. "I don't want to butt into his personal life, but he's going to lose his kids if he doesn't change course."

Collin's voice softened. "Scripture says if you see your brother messing up, someone should help him." She smiled. "Very loose translation."

Jeff grinned. "Close enough. But yeah. If you saw me headed for a train wreck, I'd want any of you to stop me."

Vy asked, "Except we know how Tom will react."

"Then we need to pray the Lord opens his eyes."

"And his heart." Collin lost her smile.

Jeff kissed her. He pointed to Erin. "Go check the board and see who and how many signed up to go. We can make plans from there."

Erin saluted, and then moved outside to the sign-up board on the dock. Life. Family. Family lived with the Lord. Yeah. He wouldn't trade it for anything.

Ten people had signed up to go rafting. Ten more wanted to watch. It would be a busy day on the water. Maybe they could scare all the bass to the shallows, and Tom could enjoy catching more fish. Priorities.

He saw Brutus at the dock. The young man poured gas into his father's boat's gas tank. He smiled as Erin passed. "Hey, Erin. How goes it?"

"Going well. Keeping the tank full?"

"Yeah, Dad told me he needed a refill before he went out tonight."

"You going with him?"

"Not tonight. You gonna have some room for Wendy and me on the boat this morning?"

"I'll make sure you two get out. You tubing or skiing?'

"Tubing. I'm not good on the skis yet."

"Good place to learn. No other boats to run over you."

Brutus laughed. "You got a point. I'll think about it."

"First load is leaving at nine. Second goes out at eleven. Anyone left over can go in the afternoon."

"I'll talk to Wendy and see what she wants to do." Brutus finished pouring the gas into the tank. "There. Now he'll be happy. When he wakes up."

Erin hesitated. "How's Sam?"

"He and Mom are hanging out with some kids more his age.

Mom figures even if he doesn't get to go where the psychologist says, he can still find kids his own age to play with. Whatever works."

Erin hesitated again, and then decided to go for it. "Jeff is talking about doing an intervention with your dad. Christian brother to brother. What do you think?"

"Honest opinion? You're wasting your time. He doesn't want to hear it." Brutus shrugged. "Mom's tried. Wendy and I've tried. Nothing. Oh, he may say he'll change, and he does for a few days. Maybe a week. But then it's right back to the 'me first' thing." Brutus shrugged again. "I wrote him off last year when he said I couldn't go to college. As long as I live under his roof, I have to obey his rules." He looked at Jeff. "I'm saving my money for deposits on a place of my own."

Erin prayed. *Do I interfere? Is passing on information interference? Lord?* "You know the company offers full-ride scholarships to employees and their families, don't you?"

Brutus's jaw dropped. His eyes widened, and then narrowed. His expression went from wonder to anger to disgust. "No, I didn't know. Dad never mentioned it." He lowered his head but lifted his eyes. "What would I have to do?"

"Sign up. We have the forms online."

"Any college?"

"If you can get in it, the company will pay for it."

"Full ride means?"

"Tuition, fees, books, housing, meals. A small stipend for extraneous stuff."

"What if Dad quits the company?"

"Once you're enrolled, the company pays until you graduate. They don't cut you off in the middle."

Brutus tapped the side of the boat with his foot. "Does it matter what the major is?"

"If you can show it will benefit the company somehow—and the benefit can be pretty tenuous—then it's fine. You do have to maintain a 'C' average. But that's about the only requirement."

Brutus lay his hand on the boat. "If I wanted to study Marine Biology?"

"Show how the company would benefit from looking into floating houses. Tiny homes on stilts in the bay. Be creative."

The corner of Brutus's mouth turned up. "I can be creative."

Erin grinned. "I'm sure you can."

Brutus scowled. "Dad's not gonna like it."

Erin shrugged. "The world doesn't revolve around what your dad likes or dislikes. I care about your dad. He's a good worker and can be a good friend. But even so, you have a life to live. Live it." He stopped. "I'd like to tell you to pray about it, but I don't know where your heart is with Him."

Brutus nodded. "Yeah. I will pray about it, though."

Erin clapped him on the shoulder. "You're a good man, Brutus." He paused. "And yes, you can tell your dad we talked, and I told you about the scholarships. I'll take the heat."

Brutus hugged Erin around the shoulders hard. "Thanks, man. I owe you."

"Nah. Just have fun today. Whenever you want to go, let me know."

"I will. I better get this can back to the shed." Brutus walked off with the gas can in hand. The younger man whistled as he walked.

One good deed. Thanks, Lord, we can provide for others. I hope it helps him.

Erin went back to organizing the whos and whens.

* * *

The day on the water proved a rousing success. No one drowned, no bones were broken, and no one got seriously hurt. There were some bruised egos and a whole lot of laughs. Jeff actually made four runs. The final boatload came in about five, well before the 'no wake' restrictions. The churned water would have plenty of time to calm down before Tom went fishing.

The man emerged from his cabin in time to watch Brutus getting up on skis for the first time. He stood beside Collin and Pam as they watched the younger man stand, and then circle the lake victoriously. Pam turned to Tom. "Be proud of him. He worked hard to get up."

"I'll be proud when he can get up on one ski. Two is nothing."

Collin corrected, "Two is harder. You've got both legs wanting to go in different directions. He's done good."

Tom shrugged. "Whatever." He turned to Pam. "Did he get the

gas in the boat before he went out to play?"

"Yes, dear. He said he filled the tank."

"Did you check it?"

"No. I trust our son."

"Eh. He's screwed up before. I wouldn't put it past him to lie about it."

Pam wilted. "If he said he filled the tank, he filled the tank."

"We'll see. If I get stranded in the middle of the lake, he'll be the one swimming out to get me."

"You won't get stranded." Pam motioned to where Sam played volleyball with a group of youths. "Do you see him? He's enjoying himself."

"Good. Maybe it'll keep him out of my hair for the night."

Pam shook her head. "But you told him he could go with you."

"We'll see if he's ready when it's time to leave." He looked around. "Brutus left a note saying he wanted to talk to me. Tell him he's got half an hour, so he better make it quick." Tom headed back to the cabin.

Collin waited for Jeff to toss the rope as he idled the water taxi in for the last time of the evening. She tied it to the dock. The skiers, tubers, and rafters all unloaded. Harmon climbed out, followed by Caleb and Joshua. Then Lacey stepped out, followed by Talitha and Leesa. Collin let out a small sigh. Everyone home safe again. Perfect.

She directed the trio to the house. "Baths."

Lacey smiled. "They've been in the water all day, Collin. I think they could go an evening without." She nudged Collin's shoulder. "And as worn out as they are, they're liable to fall asleep in the tub."

"Good thinking." She raised her voice. "Forget the baths. Pajamas." Her offspring jumped and hopped and made their way to the house.

Collin waited for Jeff. "What did the sheriff's office finally say? I know they called just before you went on this last run."

Jeff frowned. "They think as long as we stay out of the woods, we're fine. The bad guys were warning us away from anything up in the hills. They'll scour the area after we send everyone home. Then, if they find anything, there's less chance of wild shots or hostages being used."

"Yeah, let's not have any more problems. Been there, done that.

Don't want to ever do it again."

"Me either, milady." He slid his arm around her shoulders. "What say we stay up late and watch the stars? We could paddle the kayaks out to the middle of the lake, float, and admire what God created."

"Sounds like a winning idea. After the kids are asleep. If Mom and Pop don't mind."

"I doubt it will be a problem."

"You're still gonna ask, right?"

"Absolutely. Why wouldn't I?"

Collin sighed. "Guess I listened to too much of Tom's attitude. I don't want it to rub off on us."

"No chance. Not as long as we stay centered on the Rock."

"Right." Collin hesitated. "You want to invite Erin and Vy?"

Jeff half-closed his eyes. "Yeah, we can. If they want to come. Erin got beat up by the boat today. He may not be up for it."

"We can ask. Vy said they wanted to talk to us. Maybe this is a good time."

Jeff laughed. "Out in the middle of the lake is as secluded a place as any. Any idea what this is about?"

"I think she's pregnant. They may want to tell us but not make it public knowledge." After the last two miscarriages, Collin understood why.

Jeff chewed his lip. "Yeah, I can see why they'd keep it secret. Okay, you ask them, I'll ask the folks, and we'll meet in the kitchen at after sundown."

Collin kissed him. "Sounds good."

* * *

Erin prepped the kayaks for the midnight tour. Tom's boat sat at the dock. Strange, the man hadn't left yet. It had to be close to seven. Maybe he'd found something to do other than fishing.

Tom stalked up the path to the dock. Erin saw fire in the man's face. *Must have talked to Brutus. Here we go.*

Erin sat in his chair, waiting. Tom's eyes were narrowed to slits. He stomped up the dock. He stared Erin in the face, and then, in one motion, grabbed the armrests, and dumped him from his wheelchair.

Erin rolled to face the raging man. He pulled himself to his feet, leaning against the dock rail. Tom lashed out and pummeled Erin, knocking him to the deck, kicking him in the face. He seethed, "Don't you ever mess with my family, you hear me? Ever. I tell them what's best. Not you, not anyone. You got it?" He emphasized his point with a final kick to Erin's middle. Then he climbed in his boat and circled away from the dock.

Erin dragged himself into his wheelchair. He breathed hard, getting himself under control. Blood trickled from his eye. Dribbled down his cheek. Oozed down his chin. Erin drew on reserves and training from his past, settled himself, and maneuvered his way into the lodge.

Collin sat at the table. She looked up as he came in. She jerked to her feet and yelled, "Jeff!"

Erin didn't try to stop her ministrations to his wounds. Jeff walked into the room, took one look at him, and went into paramedic mode. He grabbed a towel, soaked it in water, moved Collin out of the way, and began dabbing at the wounds on Erin's face. "What happened?"

Erin waited until Jeff removed the towel, wrung it out, and applied it again to Erin's eye. He gritted his teeth at the discomfort of Jeff pushing on the laceration above his brow. "I poked a bear. He didn't like it."

Vy entered the kitchen. Her eyes widened, and she strode to his side. She didn't get in the way of Jeff's doctoring but asked through clenched teeth, "What bear?"

Erin tried to smile, forcing the bruised muscles to obey his will. "An angry bear."

Jeff stepped back. "Those are the wounds I see. What else happened I can't see?"

"Blows to the shoulder. Kick to the midriff. I'll live."

Jeff pulled up Erin's shirt and pressed on his middle. Erin swallowed any reaction to pain and repeated his mantra, "I'm fine. It's nothing."

Jeff's eyes narrowed, and his jaw clenched. "And you'd tell me if it wasn't?"

Erin reached out and clasped Jeff's arm. "Yeah, bro. I would. I'm sore. But I'll live. Other than the face, he didn't hurt me."

Jeff sat down. Collin and Vy joined him. All three waited for an explanation. Erin stared at the wall. "I told Brutus about the college scholarships. Tom objected." He looked toward Jeff. "Said I messed with his family."

Silence ruled. Erin watched Vy closest. Her reaction mattered most.

She leaned back in her chair. Her eyebrows rose. "Are you going to press charges?"

Collin's head swiveled from Vy to Erin to Jeff. Erin knew his sister's thinking. Her brother had been attacked. But this company belonged to Jeff and Collin. And Vy and Erin, but mostly Jeff and Collin. Did he want to press charges? *Lord? What do I do? Hold him accountable? Or give grace? He won't ever admit guilt for this. I know he won't. He feels justified...*

A thought interrupted his prayers. *What about Brutus? And Pam? Are they okay? Did he hurt them?* He motioned to his sister. "Go check on Pam and the family. Make sure they're not hurt."

Collin nodded. She walked purposefully out the door. Erin prayed, Help her work it off, Lord. Calm her down before she gets there. And let them be okay. I never intended to set Tom off. I didn't think he'd...okay, I didn't think, period. But protect his family. And Tom.

Erin looked to Jeff. "It's your call, man."

Jeff lowered his eyes. He looked up. "He attacked you. We can't let his assaulting you go. We can't. But pressing charges...how does an arrest help him?"

Vy nearly exploded. "Him? Him? He attacked my husband! What about Erin?"

Erin reached out and took Vy's hand. "I'm fine, Vy. I am. No permanent damage done. I want to do this the Lord's way."

Vy wasn't having it. "Fine. Call him back and let him kick you on the other side. Would you feel any better?"

Jeff shook his head. "My first inclination is we call him in privately. Tell him we're forgiving him. But any further offenses on his part, we contact the police." He raised his eyebrows at Erin. "Thoughts?"

Erin ran a million different scenarios in his head on how Jeff's plan would play out. All in a matter of moments. "If Vy agrees, then, yes."

Vy sighed. "Agreed." Her eyes narrowed again. "But any repeats, and you'll have to call the police on me."

Erin leaned in and kissed her. "I love you, Vy."

She chuckled. "I love you, Erin. God knows why, but I do."

Collin slipped back into the lodge. She rejoined the group, sitting down next to Jeff. "Tom slapped Brutus. He didn't touch Pam. Sam got hysterical, and Tom walked out. They all had calmed down when I got there. I told them they could sleep here, but Pam said she'd rather stay and 'work it out.' I told her about Tom attacking Erin."

Vy's tone came out frigid. "What did she say?"

"She apologized, said she never wanted anything like that to happen, and what could she do to make it right?"

"And you told her?"

"Tom needs to make it right, not her. I told her we'd let her know what we decide about pressing charges."

Erin snorted. "Which went over well, I'm sure."

"Like you'd expect."

Jeff looked around at the group. "I think we call off the kayak circle tonight. The stars will be there tomorrow. I suggested the solution but didn't give us time to pray about it. Or listen for the answer. Can we table this for tonight? Come back together in the morning and see if it still flies?"

Erin glanced to Vy. "My love?"

She nodded. "Yeah. I need time to work on my attitude as well."

Erin turned to Jeff. "Yes on our part."

Collin chewed her lip. "Can we meet back here at six? Before the trio gets moving."

Erin groaned. "Kick a wounded man when he's down. Six? Can we do six-fifteen?"

Vy swatted at him, her smile finally returning. "Hush, husband. Six is good." She eyed Jeff. "As long as someone has coffee ready."

"For you, Vy, I'll have coffee."

Erin sighed silently. We're good. Finally. Okay, Lord. Speak to us. And make it a consensus so we know it's You. Any pain You want to take away would be great, You know? He snorted mentally. Of course, You do. Thanks, Dad.

As the group headed for their rooms, gunshots rang out. Erin counted. *1...2...3...4...5.* Silence. Nothing more. Erin pursed his lips. "Guess they're done for the night."

Jeff scowled. "I'll call the sheriff in the morning. They can add this to the file."

"Right. Night, all."
"Night."

* * *

Static. "Two civilians wearing hoodies. Difficult to distinguish features. One is a dead shot. Same one who did the shooting this morning. The other figure can't hit the tree, much less the target, from ten feet."

"That's fear. Or lack of desire. I want eyes on their location in the campground. I want eyes on who they talk to, who they fight with, and who they eat with. I want the topflight on this, not the rookies."

"Yes, ma'am."

"If there's a threat, I want to know about it before it happens. Understood?"

"Understood, ma'am."

"You have your orders. Carry on."

WEDNESDAY

Collin got up at five to put the coffee on. She'd slept well but woke up twice. Each time she prayed for God's solution to the Tom problem. And each time, she received the same answer. *Peace, child.*

The triplets slept with Grandma and Grandpa and Aunt Leesa. The boys stayed with their grandparents. Leesa and Talitha slept together. Collin guessed the whole group would sleep in later than the usual eight a.m. "get up" time. Which meant she could have time to kayak the lake. She needed time with the Lord. Him and her. Him speaking, her listening.

The six a.m. meet-up brought no further wisdom through the night. Jeff's idea to approach Tom privately still seemed the best decision. Jeff would meet him at the dock when Tom came in from fishing.

Collin slipped out to the dock and climbed in her kayak. The weather promised to be clear and warm as the sun rose over the trees. But now, a slight breeze cooled the lake. Collin shivered. Rowing would warm her.

She paddled halfway round the lake, and then let her craft drift. She lifted her face to the sky. "You are God. Creator. Maker of Heaven and Earth. My Father. My Savior. My Lord and King." Collin let the words sink into her soul. He was all she could describe and more.

"So much more. Why would You choose me for anything? Why do You even know me? Who am I?"

She knew the answer to the *who*. "I am loved. I am Your child. I am a daughter of the King. I am forgiven and accepted. I know who I am in You. But I don't know why."

Except God reserved the *why* answers to Himself. Collin drifted, letting the silence fill her. She bowed her head. "Speak, Lord, for Your servant hears you." She smiled. "Or at least I'm listening. Make me hear You. Only You."

Warmth and quiet and peace filled her. Not just her soul but her whole being. She breathed in deeply. Tension, worry, concern, confusion...all dropped away. The "gotta go gotta go gotta go" compulsion stilled. Peace. Life. Light. Joy.

Collin sat for half an hour before she resumed her circuit of the lake. Further up the lake, Tom's boat drifted along the shoreline. The man paced the length of the vessel, disappeared under the gunwales, and reappeared. Even from this distance, she heard him cursing. *Ooo...he's not happy. Wonder what happened?*

Do not gloat when your enemy falls...

I'm not gloating. I'm wondering.

Collin paddled closer. "Tom! What's wrong?"

Tom glared at her. "Someone sabotaged my boat. There's kerosene in my fuel tank."

Collin cocked her head. She chose her tone carefully. "I'm sorry. You need some help?"

His voice dripped sarcasm. "Sure. You gonna tow me back to shore?"

Collin shrugged. "I probably could. Once we're both floating, your boat won't weigh anything. There's no current to fight, so I could do it."

Tom eyed her. "Yeah. But I'll do the towing."

"Do you know how to handle a kayak?"

"What's to know? You get in, and you paddle. How hard can it be?"

Collin let it go. "Up to you." She pulled her kayak up to the side of his boat, handed him the paddle, and then carefully climbed aboard.

Tom stepped off into the smaller craft, weebled, wobbled, and fell in the lake. Collin swallowed every hint of a smile. "It happens." The soaked man climbed over to the bobbing craft, grabbed it by the side, and pulled it to climb in.

And flipped the kayak over his head and him under it. Collin had to cover her face. *Oh, Father. Thank You. But help him.* Collin envisioned the Lord on His throne, intoning, "I am. I'm teaching him humility."

Tom came up for the second time, spluttering and coughing. He shoved the kayak away. Collin watched it float past the boat, dove in the water, and retrieved it. She towed it back and shimmied out of the water into the boat. She eyed Tom. "Do you want some help?"

Tom muttered a curse word Collin ignored. He jerked his head toward the kayak. "You're so 'women can do anything men can do.' You pull it."

Collin stared around the coast of the lake. It had been designed with gently sloping shores. Some rocks, yes. Some trees, of course. But all in all…

Collin shoved her kayak up on Tom's boat. She unfastened the tow rope, took Tom's tow rope, and tied them together. She gave him a straight-lipped smile. "Come on. *We* are going to tow this thing around the shore."

"Do what?"

"We're going to walk it around shore back to the dock. Pretty sure it will be faster this way." *At least, I hope so.*

Keeping the fishing boat in deep water, with Tom leading, they pulled, pushed, floated, and maneuvered the watercraft around the shore. It took another hour, but they finally walked their "puppy" home on its leash.

Collin saw the welcoming committee on the dock waiting for them. Jeff, Erin, and Vy stood at the edge, watching Tom and Collin. Jeff jumped in the water to help with the final yards. "What happened?"

Tom growled. "Stupid son of mine put kerosene in the gas tank."

Jeff eyed Tom. "Brutus knows better than to do something like—"

Tom snarled, "Don't tell me what my son does or doesn't know."

Jeff jumped up on the dock to tie the boat to the mooring. Erin deflected, "Why didn't you shoot off a flare? We would have come and got you." The bruises on her brother's face were a deep purple. One eye had swollen nearly shut. He moved stiffly. Vy stood protectively beside him, her hand resting on his shoulder. Her gaze was ice as she glared at Tom. *Guess there needs to be some more work on the attitude. But I know how she feels. I absolutely do.*

Tom glared at the ground. "Shot them off for the fourth of July.

Never got around to replacing them."

Erin drawled, "Well, there's your problem."

Tom's eyes narrowed, and he scowled at Collin's brother. Erin held Tom's eyes. No accusation. No animosity. Simply held the man's gaze.

Finally, Tom dropped his head. "Yeah, wasn't the smartest thing I could've done."

Erin took the lead on the confrontation. Meeting. Intervention. Whatever they wanted to call it. He continued talking in quiet, even, helpful tones. "I'm sure we have a siphon pump somewhere. We can empty your fuel system, run gas through it, and it should be fine."

Tom nodded. "Good idea. Glad I thought of it." He sneered in his customary way, tongue halfway between his lips. He laughed. "No hard feelings about last night. You were messing with my family. Telling Brutus about scholarships? Pretty low, man."

Vy's eyebrows lifted. Her voice held an edge. "Lower than knocking a man out of his wheelchair and beating him?"

Tom pretended to think her question over. "Yeah. I'd say. Who would do such a thing?" He laughed.

Erin didn't. "You're facing assault and battery charges, Tom."

"You wouldn't. Think of the company's reputation."

Her brother held his head a bit higher. "I'm thinking of our company's values. What would Jesus do? How would the Lord want us to handle this?"

Tom chuckled. "He'd want me to hit you again on the other cheek."

Erin didn't smile. "He'd want us to forgive. But forgiveness isn't license to excuse bad behavior."

Tom's eyes narrowed. "Bad? You want to talk about bad behavior? What about interfering in a man's family? Tearing it apart? Turning my kids against me? What about your behavior?"

I know this game. It's never his fault. It's always someone else. Fourteen years of hearing everything bad happening was my fault, not my father's. Anything good, well, he got all the credit. Erin lived it longer than I did. He knows.

Collin watched her brother's eyes. His face. His hands. Her brother remained calm. Composed. Controlled. The only tell, the twitch in his good eye. And only Collin saw it. Erin moved his wheelchair around to get closer to Tom. "We can talk about my behavior toward your family if you want. After we agree, there will never be a repeat of you striking me or anyone else."

Tom stared at Erin. He nodded. "As long as you stay out of my family's business, I promise never to hit you again." He turned and walked away from the dock back toward the maintenance shack.

The group at the dock stood silent for several breaths and heartbeats. Finally, Erin quipped, "Well, that went better than I expected."

Vy glared at her husband. "Did we accomplish anything?"

Jeff nodded. "Yeah. We warned him. He knows he can't get away with anything like this again. His getting the last word salvaged his ego. But he knows."

Collin pulled her kayak off Tom's boat. "I'm going to get cleaned up and in dry clothes." She chuckled. "So I can follow the trio into the water and get wet again."

Vy smiled. "Which is what mamas do."

Erin nodded. "I'll hang around here and help Tom repair his boat." He grinned. "Which is what Christ-followers do."

"Amen."

* * *

Families at the retreat spent Wednesday much like they had Monday and Tuesday—playing in the water, riding in boats, fishing along the shore, hanging out in the sunshine. Eating. Decompressing. Unwinding.

There were a few questions about Erin's injuries. He joked in response, gave them some unbelievable story of cowboys and aliens, smiled, and let it go. Twice they heard gunshots in the hills away from the lake. The echoes sounded more distant. Maybe the shooter had moved off? It could be hoped.

Collin enjoyed a day of rest while Harmon and Lacey, with Leesa, supervised the trio. She even allowed the children to play in the water under strict observation. Just not hers. The day proved almost as restful as her morning on the lake had been. The part before she encountered Tom.

Until the afternoon. Pam emerged from the cabin with Sam. The boy found children his age and got involved in a game of volleyball. Pam dropped down in a lounge chair next to Collin and let out a long sigh.

Collin raised an eyebrow. "How's it going?"

"I think we've got it settled down. Tom apologized for slapping Brutus. Told him he didn't mean to strike out like he did. It was the shock. Hearing about it took him by surprise. Of course, he wants Brutus to go to college. And Wendy, too. But he feels they're not ready yet. Tom wants them to go when they both have the best chance of succeeding. But as their father, he can tell now is not the time. Another year, they'll both be older and more mature. Then they can think about college. But not yet."

"How did Brutus take it?"

Pam shrugged. "It's his dad. What's he going to say?"

Collin shooed a fly off her shorts. "Oh, I don't know. How about, 'No, Dad, I think I should go now.'"

Pam shook her head and smiled. "You don't understand the family dynamics, Collin. Tom has the children's best interests at heart. He's very successful in what he does. Brutus and Wendy can learn a lot from their dad if they swallow their pride and listen to him."

Never his fault, right? Pam, you know better. Defend your children.

Maybe it's safer not to.

"What are Brutus and Wendy up to today?"

"I'm not sure. They left early this morning. I think they're going hiking. They really do love each other."

"Good." Someone needs to love in this family.

Collin switched topics. "Sam seems happy." She motioned to the boy on the volleyball "court," if a patch of earth could be called a court. Diehards played in the sand. The less able-bodied played on dirt.

The younger crowd finished their game and ran off the court, looking for drinks and snacks. Collin grinned as Jeff and Erin made their way to the battlefield. Erin used his wheelchair. Collin knew her brother still hurt from the beating he'd taken. But it wouldn't slow him down. Erin called out, "Players assemble! Come on, people. Let's get a game going."

Cat calls, boos, and some more emphatic "nos" answered. Erin sighed. "Aw, come on. Doesn't anyone want to get some exercise?"

More boos. Jeff shrugged. "Guess they told us."

Sam ran forward. "I'll play. Can I play?"

Right on time, Tom strolled up to the volleyball court. He looked from Jeff to Erin, and then put his hand on Sam's shoulder. "We'll play. Two against two." He laughed. "Well, one and a half against one and a half. We're still even."

Pam lowered her head. "I'm sorry. He's—"

"*—Joking. I know." Collin breathed in slowly. Don't say it. Don't say it. Don't think it.*

Sam danced around his dad. "Where do you want me to be, Dad?"

"You play the back. If anything gets by me, you make sure you keep it off the ground." He leered at Jeff. "No counting strokes, right? However long it takes to get it over. Aren't those the rules you play with?"

Jeff nodded. "Usually. We can change it if you want." He tapped Erin on the shoulder. "My partner and I can play any rules you want to make. As long as they apply to both sides."

Tom laughed. "So I can't make a rule saying, 'I win'?"

"No."

"Well, if you're going take the fun out of it, we'll let the two liabilities have three touches. You and I'll get two."

Erin eyed Jeff. Jeff nodded. Erin called, "I'll stick to two. Sam can have three. He's the rookie out here."

Tom's smile said it all. "We'll serve."

Pam covered her eyes. "I'm so sorry, Collin. He thinks he's still got something to prove."

"I hope he's ready, then."

Tom served. Into the net. He grinned. "I get two touches, right?"

Jeff waved at him. "Whatever it takes."

Tom served again. Into the net. His eyes darkened as he threw the ball under the barrier to Jeff. "Your turn."

Jeff tossed the ball to Erin. Erin lobbed the ball over the top. Tom went for the slam. Jeff met him at the net, blocking the shot. Tom caught the ball, passed it to Sam. The youngster tapped it up in the air. Tom slapped it over to Jeff. Jeff set Erin up. Erin tapped it back, Jeff spiked it. Tom missed it.

Sam rolled the ball back. "One for your side."

Tom laughed without humor. "Don't keep score for them. Let them do it themselves if they can."

Jeff exchanged glances with Erin. Together they called "One." Erin served again.

Collin deciphered Tom's strategy in short order. He targeted Erin with all his spikes and slams. He intended to humiliate her brother. If he couldn't hurt him outright.

Except Erin rose up to the challenge. Shots which went over his head he left to Jeff, who managed to hit them over Tom's defense. Tom tried to hit everything coming over the net, leaving Sam useless. Jeff made sure to sail balls beyond Tom, so the boy got to return some of the shots. The players even got a string of ten volleys back and forth before Erin missed a comeback. Jeff and Sam clapped and laughed. Erin grinned as he sailed the ball under the net. "Great exchange. Good job, Sam."

The boy beamed. "Thanks, Uncle Erin."

Tom barked, "He's not your uncle. Serve the ball."

Sam stood holding the ball. His face fell. His head followed. Tom yelled again. "Serve the ball!"

Sam gave a half-hearted swat at the ball and missed it. Jeff called, "Come on, Sam. You can do this. Serve it hard. We're ready, aren't we, Erin?"

Erin nodded. "I'm ready. Hit it, Sam."

Sam smiled. He tossed the ball up and slammed his fist into it. Erin dug it out, Jeff tapped it back. Erin set up the spike. Tom leapt to block it. Jeff barely tipped the ball over the net. The ruse worked. Tom missed the gentle tap. And score another point for the good guys.

Pam shook her head. "He's going to be impossible this afternoon." She glanced over at Collin. "He'll take it out on Sam. I know he will."

"Can you stand up for your son?"

Pam seethed. "Don't you think I do? I'm the only one defending our children. I'm the one who has to take care of them and make sure they have what they need. I have to take them to their appointments, to games, to school activities. I'm the one who has to leave work for them. I sacrificed my career for them. I'm the only one who loves them. Don't tell me I'm not standing up for them."

Collin held up her hand. "It's not what I meant, Pam. I'm not criticizing, and it wasn't an accusation."

Pam settled down. The darkness on her face said she could jump again if provoked by the wrong words. Collin tread lightly. "I don't know what your life is like. I don't. All I can do is pray for you, Tom, and the children." *And pray and pray and pray…*

The game broke up. Collin smiled at her husband and brother. "Well? What's the score?"

Erin called to Sam. "Hey, what's the score?"

Tom growled, "You guys are ahead by five points. We suspended the game, so I can get ready to go fishing."

Sam beamed. "And I'm going with him."

Wendy and Brutus drifted over to the group. Pam asked, "How did the hike go?"

Brutus nodded. "Good. There's some great trails up there."

"I worried. I heard gunshots."

Wendy shrugged. "Yeah, we heard them, but they were a long way off."

José passed by on his way to wherever. He smiled in the general direction of the group. "Hey, people. *Como estan?"*

Tom muttered, "Can't even speak English. Neither can his father. Useless illeg—"

Jeff cut him off. "Stop, right there. Hector is as American as you are. I've seen his certificate. And he speaks four languages. His English is better than mine some days."

Erin quipped, "Most days."

Jeff took a quick look at Erin, and then back to Tom. "Most days. Because Hector speaks so many languages, including Spanish, we can do business with multiple partners in multiple places. He's invaluable to our company. And I'm happy to call him my friend and brother in the Lord. José is helping me and my children learn Spanish. Don't insult him."

Tom held up his hands. "Hey, I was only joking. Guess I'm being politically incorrect or something. I'll have to learn better." He put an arm around Sam. "Come on, buddy. Let's go get ready for our fishing trip tonight."

Wendy waited until her dad had disappeared to the cabin before she sighed. She took José's hand. "I'm sorry."

José smiled. "I'm immune to people like him. Water off a duck's back."

Collin gave him a thumbs up. "There's the attitude."

Erin grumbled, "I know what I'd like to do with that duck some days." He numbered, "Peking Duck. *Duck a L'Orange. Canard aux cerises.* Tandoori Duck. Duck Risotto. Duck—"

Pam laughed. Jeff tossed the ball at Erin. "We get the idea."

Pam stood. "I should go help the men. Make sure Tom packs everything he needs. Wendy, are you coming?"

Wendy shook her head. "Nah, I'm going to hang out with this crowd for a while."

Pam lost her smile. "Don't let your dad see you." She smiled at José. "Not yet. Not until I've had time to talk to him."

José nodded. "I understand. I understand very well."

Pam lowered her head. "One of these days, maybe I won't have to apologize for your dad's behaviors. I keep praying." She walked away.

Vy, Rob, and Gabby ambled over to the group. Vy kissed Erin. "How did the game go?"

"It went. Two on two with Tom and Sam." He scowled. "One and a half versus one and a half."

Jeff clapped a hand on Erin's shoulder. "Let it go, man. Quack."

Collin stretched. "I should go check on Pop Harmon and Mom Lacey. See if they need a break from the trio."

Vy smiled. "Harmon and Lacey are doing fine. They have the littles racing laps around the sandcastles they built. Chasing dragons which are trying to nest. Wearing the bubbies out thoroughly."

Collin grinned. "Nothing like experience. I'll go join them, anyhow." She turned to Rob. "Have you talked with Abbott and Selma yet?"

"Tonight."

Gabby let out a wounded sigh. "I think this whole permission thing is overblown. We're adults. We can do what we want. You know, easier to ask forgiveness than permission?"

Rob shook his head. "I respect your dad too much. And I'd like to get off on the right foot with your mom."

Gabby snorted. "There is no right foot with her. I ignore her advice as much as possible."

Rob cocked his head. "That's not what you said in the young adult group. You were talking to Amy about her parents and told her to listen to them. They've been there. They know things she doesn't."

"Yeah, well, those are her parents, not mine. Or not my mom, anyhow. She's so far off I can't listen to her."

Collin stood. "I'm outta here. I'll see you at dinner?"

Rob nodded. Gabby shook her head. "Some of the college group are planning a bonfire on the beach. I'm going to sit with them." She smiled at Rob. "You don't mind, do you?"

"I'll come get you when we're done, I guess." Only Collin heard the disappointment in Rob's voice.

Gabby grinned. "Thanks, Rob." She raised her eyebrows to Wendy. "You coming?"

"We'll see."

"We can cover for you and José to have some alone time. Without supervision." She smiled, and then walked off.

Rob sighed slightly. Very slightly. Collin wanted to reach out and hug him. *He's a grown man. If he wants a hug, he knows where I am.*

Vy didn't wait for the invitation. She hugged Rob. "Keep praying, my brother."

Rob nodded. "I am. Hard."

The group broke up and headed their separate ways.

* * *

Late in the afternoon, Collin and Mom Lacey sat with the trio at the beach. No swimming, just sand-castle building. And building. And building. "We're gonna make it so high it reaches the sky, Mommy." Colorful buckets and plastic shovels dug and filled and dug and filled and dumped…

"You go right ahead, bubbies. Grandma and I will watch." The warmth of the shore felt delightful on Collin's legs. She stretched and tossed a handful of sand over her knees. "Sunscreen."

Lacey chuckled. "Uh-huh." She rearranged a loose white shirt over her shoulders. "The bubbies are so tan. My little brown berries."

"They'd live outside if we let them." Collin swallowed a grin. "There are days…"

Lacey patted Collin on the shoulder. "Oh, believe me, I do remember those. I wanted Harmon to build a shed in the back where I could corral Jeff and his brothers for a few hours. I would have loved a chance to sit and read a book. Drink a glass of tea. Paint my nails."

"Yeah, I hear you. I think I know exactly where Jeff should put it, too." Collin squeezed her mother-in-law's hand.

Tom and Sam passed by. Pam followed behind with a six-pack carrier of glass bottles. Collin couldn't see the logo, but she had a reasonable suspicion they weren't soft drinks. *Leave it. No sense in escalating anything.*

So he gets away with even more?

Leave it.

Fine.

Collin growled to Mom Lacey, "I so want to nail him."

"Let the Lord do it. He'll do a much better job."

"Yeah, but sometimes He takes too long."

Lacey bumped shoulders with Collin and laughed. "I heard that."

Tom and Sam stopped at the dock. The boat floated, ready for its occupants. Tom took the bottles from Pam. He smiled at Collin. "Gotta stay hydrated out there."

He knows I know. And he's daring me to say something.

Don't.

Collin waved him off. "Don't get too hydrated. It might cloud your navigating."

Tom sneered. "Never." He turned to Sam. "Did you bring the worms?"

Sam kneeled on the dock, opened his tackle box, and looked. His eyes opened wide. "They're not here! I put them in, I swear I did. I had them. I really did. Mom, you saw them in my box, didn't you?"

Pam nodded. "They were there when I looked."

Tom growled. "Well, they're not there now. Go back and get them. Now. Hustle."

Sam left the box and took off at a frantic run.

Collin caught a smirk in Pam's eye she didn't understand. What was going on? Did Pam know something? Tom untied the boat, climbed in the craft, and started the motor. He backed the boat away from the dock.

Collin continued to watch Pam out of the corner of her eye. The woman had a satisfied look, almost a smile of...what? Victory? Why would...

You're imagining things. You're losing your skills of

observation. Why would a mother be happy her son missed going fishing with his father?

Pam noticed Collin looking at her. She lost the smile and yelled, "Tom, wait! He'll be back in a minute. You can't leave without him!"

Tom yelled in return, "He'll learn not to forget things next time. That's how my dad taught me." He swung the boat around and roared across the lake, away from the shore.

Pam bowed her head. "Not again. Not again." Tears poured down her cheeks.

Collin seethed. "How can he be so…so…" She choked on all the words she wanted to say at once. Too many thoughts, and none of them came out.

Lacey shared a few. "How hateful can a father be? And justify it because his father did it? Why? How?" Her face hardened, and her eyes narrowed. Lacey Farrell angry wasn't someone Collin saw often. With good reason. Lacey radiated fury, climbing to her feet and glaring after Tom's shrinking boat. She picked up a stone and flung it as far as she could.

Sam passed by at a dead run, the worm container in his hand. He kicked up puffs of dirt as he raced to the dock. He panted and screamed. "Dad! Dad!" The boy reached the end of the pier and sank to his bottom as his father disappeared from view. He stared in silence.

After a moment, Sam picked up his tackle box. He walked down to his mother. "He left without me." His voice sounded broken. His shoulders hung down. His hands shook.

Pam stood to hug him. "I'm so sorry, Sam. I…"

Tears streamed down the boy's face. "I had the worms, Mom. I had them. They were in my box." He looked at her, pleading. "You saw them, didn't you?"

Pam consoled her son. "Yes, Sam. I saw them in your box."

Sam repeated, "You saw I had them. Someone put them back in the refrigerator. Someone didn't want me to go!" Sam hurled the tackle box in rage. It struck Caleb in the shoulder.

Caleb shrieked in pain. Collin flew to her feet. Sam hacked at the castle, pounding it with his fists. He pummeled and kicked anything and anyone within his reach. Including Talitha and Joshua.

Pam tried to grab him, but he slammed his head into hers,

knocking her back, stunned. Collin caught the boy. She wrapped her arms around him, pinning his arms to his side. He continued to butt her with his head and kick at her legs. She didn't release him, she didn't try to calm him. Collin let him exhaust all his anger until he had no fight left in him. He leaned into Collin and cried. "He left me. He left me."

Collin shoved Sam to his mother and turned her attention to the triplets. Lacey sat on her knees, hugging and soothing them. Caleb had the start of a nasty bruise and scrape on his shoulder. Talitha suffered a cut to her chin. Jacob had sand in his mouth and eyes. All three were wailing. Collin picked up Talitha and Jacob. Lacey lifted Caleb.

Pam moaned, "I'm sorry. I'm sorry." Whether she apologized to Sam or the triplets, Collin didn't know. And didn't care. She and Lacey dashed the children to the lodge for help and first aid.

They carried the sobbing babies to the kitchen. Fury seeped through Collin's soul. She grabbed two bags of frozen peas, tossed one to Lacey for Caleb, and put the second on Tee's chin. She soaked a tea towel in water, passed it to Joshua, and ordered, "Hold this over your eyes."

Lacey and Collin cooed and comforted and hugged and held all three wailing children. Every cry drove a knife into Collin's being. Every sob hurled an accusation: *you're a bad Mommy. Good Mommys don't let their babies get hurt. You failed...*

Jeff raced in from the common room. "What happened? What can I do?"

Mama Bear whirled and ripped into him. "You can tell me how many more members of this family Tom is allowed to hurt!" She drew a breath. "And wash the sand out of Joshua's eyes."

Jeff took Joshua, held him over the sink, and began sloshing water in and over the boy's eyes. Collin pulled the peas from Tee's chin and examined the cut. Collin hugged and kissed the sup-supping girl. "No stitches. It'll be all better. Keep the peas on it."

Lacey repeated Collin's instructions to Caleb. But it set off another round of crying. "I don't like peas!"

Rather than argue, Collin grabbed the offending bag and replaced it with frozen corn. "There. Now you have corn."

Tee pulled the bag away. "But I want corn, too."

Collin shook her head. "You'll live. You're not eating them. It's to make your chin feel better."

Caleb settled down, as did Joshua. Everyone was treated and deemed "okay" by their father. Collin sent them to their rooms to nap for half an hour. She assured them they would feel better when they got up.

Only after the trio had been settled in their beds did the adults sit at the kitchen counter. Collin bowed her head. Her hands wouldn't stop shaking. Her voice kept time with her hands. "I'm sorry I attacked you. I was wrong. I won't justify it with excuses."

Jeff pulled her to himself. "I understand. I do."

Lacey slipped out of the room. Collin watched her go. *I love her. She never interferes when it's me against Jeff or vice versa. We're on our own.* Collin lifted her head. "Tom promised Sam he could go with him but left without him. Sam lost it and attacked anything he could find. The bubbies. I restrained him until he ran out of steam, then gave him to Pam."

She took in a deep breath and felt her ribs catch. For the first time, she realized she'd been battered as well as the children. She lifted her shirt and looked down. Circular bruises pockmarked her chest.

Jeff kneeled beside her and pressed carefully on the sore spots. Collin breathed slowly. "Yes, it's tender."

"Here?"

"No."

"Here?"

"Bingo. Yep, that one hurts."

Jeff ran his hand along her ribcage, and then sat back. "You probably cracked one."

"It'll heal. No treatment for cracked ribs. I'll take it easy for a while."

Jeff cradled her in his arms. "I am so sorry, milady. I should have done something more after Tom assaulted Erin. Then this wouldn't have happened."

Collin leaned into him. "Apology accepted. Promise me you'll do something tomorrow."

"I will. As soon as he pulls into the dock in the morning. I promise."

"What will you do?"

She felt his muscles tense. He sighed. "I don't know. But the

Lord and I are going to talk about it."

Collin settled her shoulders. Tom Quince would steal no more of her life. "Don't forget we're going to go kayaking tonight to look at the stars."

Jeff sat back. "You think that's wise?"

"If I don't use the muscles, they will tighten up on me, and I'll hurt worse than I do now. It'll be fine. Erin and Vy still want to talk to us."

Jeff climbed to his feet. "I'll make sure Mom and Dad are okay with another night of sleeping with the kids." He grinned. "I don't think it's going to be a problem."

"I agree."

* * *

Rob caught up with Gabby at the beach. She sat surrounded by friends, talking and laughing. He caught her eyes and smiled. *Why am I so nervous about this? Lord? You with me? If You're not, then break my ankle before I get too far.*

Gabby did a mock groan. "There goes the party." She stood and brushed off her shorts. "You know how to take the fun out of an evening, don't you?" She grinned at him and offered him her hand.

Rob took it. "It can't be that bad. Your mom seems to like me when we talk at church."

"When she's at church, yeah. But this will be here." Gabby swung her hand with Rob's. "How can I put this delicately?" She paused. "I can't. Mom's a bigot. There, I said it. My mom disapproves of men of color dating 'white women.' She disapproves of people of color in general."

"But your dad—"

Gabby huffed. "Daddy is as accepting as it comes. You'd think being married to him would have altered some of Mom's prejudices, but it hasn't."

Rob processed the information. Or tried to. *You're sending me into a lion's den? With no warning?*

A thought crossed his mind. Several thoughts. Or have You given me warnings, and I've ignored them? Lead me, Lord. Guard my words. Put a clamp over my mouth. Don't let me say something to dishonor You.

Abbott and Selma, Gabby's parents, had eaten dinner with Collin, Jeff, Erin, Vy, Harmon, Lacey, and Leesa. *No, I won't do this in front of the whole group. We'll talk privately.* There were lots of rooms available. And suitable. He drew in a deep breath and opened the door for Gabby.

They walked into the main dining room. When fully occupied, it sat twenty with no problem. If the doors on the sides were opened, you could fit another twenty. The Farrells liked to be inclusive.

The diners were done and the dishes had been carried to the kitchen—no wait staff, just old-fashioned "carry your plate to the counter" civility. Rob and Gabby stopped at the table. Rob waved to Jeff's dad, now Rob's grandfather. "Pop Harmon. Good to see you here." He smiled at his grandmother Lacey. "Mom Lacey. You're looking beautiful."

"Why, thank you. You lie so well." She grinned at him.

Rob turned to Abbott. "Sir." He nodded to Selma. "Ma'am. Can Gabby and I have a word with you?"

Abbott and Selma exchanged glances. Abbott's eyes twinkled. "Certainly, young man."

Rob caught Jeff's eye. "Anyone in the billiard room?"

"Nope. All yours."

"Thanks." Rob motioned toward the side of the room. "We can go in there and talk."

Selma's eyes were guarded. They flicked from Rob to Gabby, back to Rob, and then settled on Abbott. But Mr. and Mrs. Fields rose to follow Rob and Gabby.

Only after the group settled in the leather-bound wing-backed chairs did Rob clear his throat. "Gabby and I have been talking. We see each other weekly at church, and I've grown fond of her." *Why did this sound so much better on paper?* He breathed. "I…we…would like permission to see each other off campus, so to speak." He looked at Abbott. "In short, I want to date your daughter."

Abbott raised his eyebrows. "To what end, young man?"

Gabby reached over and caught Rob's hand. "To see if we are compatible in the Lord's eyes."

Abbott nodded. "I see." His eyes continued to twinkle. Selma's did not. But Abbott had the floor, so Rob focused on Gabby's father.

"May I ask what you do for a living, young man?" Abbott

stopped. "Oh, of course. You work with me. Which is certainly in your favor."

Rob wondered at the formality in the tone, but it fit the mood. He was, after all, asking permission to date. An old-time tradition. The old-time language worked.

Abbott continued his questioning. "And you go to church?" He interrupted himself. "Of course you do. I see you every weekend." He smiled. "And I know your heart for the Lord. I'd be pleased if you were to date my daughter. But there are conditions."

Selma interrupted. "Wait a minute. No. I'm not pleased about this one bit." She glared at Gabby. "You know better than this, young lady." She smiled at Rob. Or tried to. "Rob, you're a fine man. And like my husband said, we know you have a heart for serving the Lord. But dating Gabby is out of the question. It won't work. It isn't...natural."

Abbott held up his hand. "Stop." His eyes held Selma's. "This is where it ends, Selma. All the whispers and looks and nudges. It stops here and now."

Gabby jumped into the fray. She leaned forward and caught her mother's eyes. "Rob is everything you've taught me to want in a man. He loves the Lord. He treats me with the utmost respect. He's responsible. He works hard, and he loves children. I can't ask for anything more except the Lord's blessing." She scowled hard at her mother. "I'm willing to fight you on this. That should tell you how serious I am."

Selma's eyes narrowed, and her voice hardened. "If you're willing to disobey your mother, then it proves how wrong you are. 'Children, obey your parents.' Remember the scripture?"

Abbott leaned forward. "Unless the parent is wrong. And in this, you're wrong. The color of a man's skin means nothing compared to the character of his heart."

Selma sat back. "I still say no. If my vote means anything, it's no."

She glared at Abbott, Gabby, and Rob. Rob especially.

She wants me to say, 'Fine, I'll leave.' Not gonna happen. Erin, Vy, thanks for the advice. I'm standing my ground.

Abbott looked from Gabby to Rob. "I said there were conditions. Hear them out, and then decide. You know what the scriptures say about being unequally yoked. There are more yokes than simply believer-unbeliever. There's maturity. If both are striving together, fine. But if one is committed and the other isn't, you're unequal. And there's a problem. If one is frugal and values hard work, and the other spends what they don't even have, you're unequal.

"These things can be overcome, but they must be recognized. So, here are the conditions. Gabby, you have to enroll in college or begin a career. Until then, you need to start pulling your weight at home. You need to prove you're responsible enough to date."

Gabby's eyes flared. "Responsible enough?"

"Yes. Able to manage on your own. Pay bills. Buy groceries. Create a budget and stick to it." Abbott's face crinkled. "Put gas in your own car. I appreciate Rob too much to let him date someone so unprepared for the future, even if she is my daughter. Especially my daughter."

Rob swallowed his smile. And any other facial tell which would expose his feelings. Neutral. He would be neutral.

Gabby motioned to Rob. "And what does he need to do?" Rob couldn't tell whether she meant the smirk on her face to be serious or in jest.

Abbott nodded. "Rob needs to be willing to attend counseling with your mother and me."

Selma jumped to her feet. "I'm not going to any liberal counselor who'll tell me what I have to believe. I know the truth." She glowered at Abbott.

Abbott held Selma's glare. "I'm talking about spiritual counseling with the pastor. There's a cancer of intolerance and bigotry in our church, and we need to weed it out. And we're starting with this family."

"If I refuse to go?"

Abbott's face softened. "You want me to quote scripture at you? 'Wives, submit to your husbands in all things.' You want to have a battle of who knows more Bible verses?"

If glares could ignite rooms, Selma would have charred the lodge to cinders. Abbott kept his voice even. "But I don't believe in beating someone over the head with cherry-picked verses to shore up my position. We"—he made a round-the-room motion with his index finger—"are going to dig into what the Savior said. And we're going to obey Him. Because that's what we do. It's who we are." Love poured through Abbott's eyes. "Isn't it, Selma? When we married, wasn't it what we said?"

Selma's eyes watered. She sucked in her lower lip, turned her head to the side, and then nodded once.

Rob realized he held his breath. He breathed out. And recognized he had to say something. He touched Selma's hand. "If all this works out, Gabby and I will be family. You will always be part of us. As much or as little as you decide. It will be up to you. But you will be loved and welcomed. I need you to be clear about it. I care about your daughter. I maybe love your daughter. We want to find it out."

He turned to Abbott. "Thank you, sir."

Abbott smiled. "Thank me after you date her awhile."

Gabby held up her hand. "So we can start dating now?"

"No, it means after you enroll in college and start your first semester, or you begin training in a career other than food service at the corner fast food joint. Then you can date."

Gabby looked at Rob. "Will you help me fill out the application for OSU online? Then line up the scholarships?"

Abbott gave Gabby a stern look. "He can help. He can't do it for you."

Gabby nodded. "I hear you, Daddy. Pull my own weight. Yes, sir. I will. I'll show you."

She stood and hugged him. She hugged her mother. Selma remained unmoving. Rob stood as well and shook hands with Abbott. "Thank you, sir." He took a step toward Selma. Her eyes warned him off. Rob raised a hand. "Thanks, Mrs. Fields." He took Gabby's hand and murmured, "I think we should leave."

Abbott stage-whispered, "I think you should."

The two young people headed out through the main dining room. It was empty save Collin. Rob bumped her shoulder. "Hey."

"Should I ask how it went?"

Gabby smiled. "As expected. Daddy said yes. Mom said no. We'll start dating after I start school in the fall."

Collin nodded. "Great. What will you study?"

"I haven't decided yet." She grinned at Rob. "Maybe race relations."

Rob chuckled. "That would be amazing."

Gabby's eyes matched her grin. "Wouldn't it, though?"

Rob looked at the clock. Just past eight. "Missed saying

goodnight to the bubbies. I'll make it up in the morning."

Gabby pulled on Rob's arm. "Come on. We can still make the bonfire. Maybe there's some marshmallows left."

"Good idea. You coming, Mom?"

Collin shook her head. "No, I'm going to take a nap. We adults"—she smiled at Gabby and Rob—"are going to kayak to watch the stars. Then I want to kayak the lake early for my quiet time."

Rob hugged her. "Then night, Mom."

"Night, Rob. Night, Gabby."

* * *

Static. "Anything more?"

"Three people entered the area. No one saw them come."

"Description?"

"Um…you'll hate me, but they're dressed like ninjas."

"Ninjas."

"I know, I know. Everything is black. They're wearing black headgear and gloves. The clothes they're wearing seems reflective because they're not showing up on the thermals. We pick them up on the infrared but not the thermals."

"We have ninjas. Greaaaaat."

"Sorry, Commander."

"Not as sorry as I am. Keep eyes on them. Infrared. I want to know everything they do."

"Yes, ma'am."

* * *

Near midnight, Erin and Vy met up with Collin and Jeff in the kitchen. When Harmon, Lacey, and Leesa had gone to bed, the boys happily climbed in with Gramma and Grampa. They were asleep, snuggled on either side and between them. Tee, of course, slept with Leesa. "Another girl. Not always boys."

Erin looked around. "Is this a 'bring your own snacks' trip?"

Collin waved him off. "No food. You're worse than the trio. You don't have to be eating all the time."

"But I'm hungry."

Vy waved a finger at him. "Down, boy. No food."

He sighed. "Yes, my love."

Jeff motioned to the door. "Are we going or not?"

The four adults padded out the door of the lodge and down to the dock. Solar lights created a path to the water's edge, where the kayaks were tied. They loaded into four of them and slipped silently to the center of the lake.

The surrounding forest kept the lake in pitch darkness. It also shadowed any dusk-to-dawn lights which provided comfort for city dwellers not accustomed to total darkness. But the middle of the lake offered an unobstructed panorama of the universe. They tied the kayaks together, and then stretched out. Lying back in the kayaks, the four had a light-free view of the galaxy.

Awe and wonder. A million billion stars sang above them, all reflecting the glory of the Creator's Hand. Collin's soul feasted on the spectacle. Worries, concerns, thoughts, and plans were reduced to nothing compared to the heavens above. The constant voices in her brain fell silent. Who was she, what was she compared to the stars above? How could she matter at all?

Erin whispered, "The earth spins on its axis at over one thousand miles per hour. It circles the sun at sixty-seven thousand miles per hour. The solar system circles the galaxy at four-hundred eighty-three thousand miles per hour. The celestial dance is perfect. The stars know their places."

Vy murmured, "When I consider the heavens, the work of Your fingers, and the moon and the stars which You have created, what are we that You take any thought of us?"

Jeff added, "Lift your eyes to the heavens He created. He calls each star out by name."

Collin finished, "But You knit me in my mother's womb. Your eyes saw my unformed body. All Your thoughts towards me are like the sand of the sea. The stars in the heavens. Unfathomable. Great is Your glory, Lord."

Four voices whispered, "Amen." The silence returned.

Erin broke the serenity after about ten minutes. "Vy and I are pregnant."

Collin asked, "How far along?"

Vy answered, "About twenty weeks. I want to make it to twenty-four before I say anything to anyone other than my family and you."

Jeff assured her, "We'll honor your wish."

Collin sat up in her kayak. "Should you have been water skiing?"

Vy's gentle laugh peeled. "You can't shake a baby loose skiing. My doctor says I can do anything I want except skydive."

Jeff asked, "Why skydiving?"

"Because he hates it."

"Fair enough." The kayaks bumped gently on the wave created by Collin's motions. A gentle, rocking motion, as if the lake swayed in time to the celestial music.

Erin cleared his throat. "Um, her folks don't know, but the ultrasound showed two heartbeats."

Collin grinned. "Twins?"

Vy chuckled, "If you're any example, it could be more."

Collin coughed. "Sorry."

Erin cleared his throat. "For boys' names, we're thinking about Geoffrey-with-a-G."

Jeff remained silent for a moment. "I'm honored."

Vy's voice drifted across the darkness. "We've talked about Caitlin for a girl."

Collin felt her face burn. "You don't have to."

Erin snipped, "Don't get too proud. Her folks have yet to weigh in. There could be some naming tradition Vy doesn't know about yet."

Collin smiled. "That works. Shouldn't you be able to tell boy or girl by now?"

"If we asked. We haven't." Vy sounded definite on the issue.

Erin added, as Erin would, "What are we going to do, send it back if we don't like it? People were surprised and pleased long before ultrasounds."

Jeff sat up in his kayak. "Okay, before this devolves into colors for the nursery and curtains and stuff, we should head back in."

Collin splashed water at him. "You're no fun."

Jeff splashed back at her. Vy called, "Children, children. Let's not get—"

Erin hit her with a paddle full of water. Vy grabbed his kayak and threatened to overturn him. Erin yelled, "Wait! I'm sorry! I wanted to hit Jeff."

Vy let go. "Sure you did."

"Honest. I wouldn't splash you. Not where I couldn't get away from you."

"Exactly what I thought."

Jeff laughed. "Okay, come on, people. Let's go."

A shot echoed in the hills. Four heads whirled around to look for the flash.

Jeff said it for all of them. "Nothing. I don't see anything."

The group paddled as quietly as they could back to shore. Collin whispered, "Kind of late for target practice."

Erin suggested, "Unless they're trying to sight in a nightscope. Those are cool."

Vy cleared her throat. "You don't put a nightscope on a handgun, husband."

"Hmm. Good point. Maybe they're wearing night-vision goggles, and trying to figure out how to make them work."

"You'd need night-vision goggles to get into the woods without lights. You should know how to make them work by then."

Jeff asked, "Can we go back to the nursery colors?"

The group docked, tied the kayaks up, and climbed out. Collin made sure her craft sat on the outside, easiest to access. Jeff looked at her. She shrugged. "I'm coming out early and paddling the lake. Gives me my quiet time."

"You want some company in the morning?"

"No. I love you, but no. As bad as my attitude has been, I need this alone time. I've got a lot of listening to do."

Jeff hugged her. "I need more of listening time. And I need to make time."

The group parted in the common room. Good-night hugs and kisses, whispered "Congratulations," and both couples headed to bed. Collin watched Erin swing Vy past the refrigerator for one last stop, and then they disappeared to their room. *Which one has the cravings, I wonder? Thank You, Lord. Watch over them. And if it's Your will, please, can these babies be born strong and healthy? I know Erin and Vy will take whatever You give. But if there's room, let them be healthy. I love You.*

* * *

Static. "And?"

"Four persons. One shooter."

"Why one shot, I wonder?"

"Accidental discharge."

"You know we're under obligation to report a threat, right? And if we do, we compromise our operation here. Not to mention our existence as a unit in this area. I'm reviewing the transcripts."

"All they are is chatter, ma'am. Wanting to be free of someone doesn't constitute a genuine threat."

"What does 'He'll drink the beer. The beer will take care of it,' mean?"

"We're not sure. We'll have a device in place in the next hour." Pause. "You know the local authorities were contacted by the campers. Doesn't that clear us?"

"Legally, maybe. I have to answer to my conscience. Don't let this slip past us."

"No, ma'am."

"Very good."

THURSDAY

Collin set her internal alarm for five a.m. so she could be up and on the lake before the sun. She dressed without waking Jeff, grabbed a cup of coffee on the way out the door, and hiked down to the lake. The trees were silent. No wind, no rustling of branches or pines. Even the birds were asleep. Collin touched the water. Yep, ice cold. At this hour, what else did she expect? She straightened her kayak out, climbed in, and then pushed away from the dock.

Clockwise or counterclockwise around the lake? Did it matter? No. Not really. She decided to go clockwise. She'd stay in the shade first, and then warm up with the sun on the return side. Collin hummed praise choruses as she paddled, trying to match the rhythm and beat to the dip of the oar. She didn't really have enough coordination, but hey, she could try.

Halfway round the lake, she stopped and allowed herself to drift. She whispered, "Good morning, Lord. Thanks for this time. 'Speak, for your servant hears.' And I need to hear You. I'm sorry, Father. I've been running unchecked the past couple of days. I didn't want to forgive Tom the other day. I wanted to do to him what he did to Erin." She lowered her head. "May as well admit it. You already know it." She looked up at the trees and the disappearing stars. "Then when Sam freaked out on the triplets… I know I should be praying for Tom. Praying You move in his heart. Praying he can recognize he needed to ask for forgiveness."

She dragged her paddle through the water, making small circles in the quarter-light. "But I don't want You to forgive him. I want You to blast him. To tear him up the way my babies were torn up."

Tears drained down Collin's face. She let them fall, let her nose run. Gross, but it matched how she felt. "I am wrong, Lord. I know it. I fooled myself into thinking I'm better than him. So holy. So mature. And it only took the attack on my family to show me how far I am from anything resembling 'good.' I don't know why You tolerate me. Much less why You love me."

She floated on the ripples. Condemnation flooded her. Guilt, shame, disgrace…they were all there. Them and a thousand other accusations. *Useless. Worthless. Contemptible. Vile. Loathsome. Unloved. Unlovable.*

Collin bowed her head. Consider the sparrows. They do nothing profitable. But I know every feather. I love you with everlasting love. Not because of what you do. Never because of what you do. You can't do enough to earn My Love because it's free. It cost me everything. But I gave it to you for free.

Collin let the grace, the mercy, the forgiveness sweep through her. Clean. He washed her clean. Again. And He would wash her as often as she needed to be reminded of her identity in Him. His child. His beloved. His chosen.

Collin bathed her face in the water, washing away the tears and snot. "I love You, Lord. Thank You."

She let the kayak float unguided for ten, fifteen, twenty minutes, breathing in the freshness of the morning. At last, she sighed. Collin smiled again and whispered, "Thanks, Dad. I'm ready. Let's do this. Whatever this is. I love you."

She resumed paddling around the perimeter of the lake. As she came out of the shadows, she saw Tom's boat drifting along the shoreline. It bumped the rocks with every movement of the lake. Not anchored. Drifting.

Collin shook her head. "Again?" She stopped. "Okay, Father. If this is my test, help me pass it. This time."

Tom sat slumped over the steering wheel. Collin pulled up beside the boat. "Tom?" She climbed in, stepped behind him, and shook his shoulder.

"Tom?" She checked his breathing. Slow. Shallow. Not good. Collin shook him harder. "Tom! Talk to me. What's wrong?"

Empty beer bottles clinked under the man's feet. Three…no, four. Could he simply be drunk? Collin slapped him. "Tom. Wake up."

A pill bottle rattled in his pocket. Collin pulled it out. Lorazepam. Anti-anxiety meds. The prescription had been filled on

Friday but looked half-empty. "Tom! Wake up. Don't do this, man."

The breathing stopped. Collin shook him, yelled, slapped him. Anything. "Do not do this! You've got a family who needs you."

Collin dragged Tom to the floor and checked for a pulse. Nothing. She began CPR. Over and over. Pumping. Pumping.

The heart began beating. Collin twisted to start the engine. She had to get him to Jeff. *He's a paramedic. He knows what to do.*

It didn't start.

On the floor, Tom again stopped breathing. Collin pounced on him. "Oh, no, you don't. Not while I'm here." She checked the heartbeat. Again, nothing.

CPR. Over and over. Over and over. Over and over.

She gritted her teeth. "I'm supposed to do this until a paramedic comes. But no one is coming. No one knows we're here. Lord, I need Your help. Tell me what to do." She searched for the flare gun. Found it. No flares.

"Tom!"

Pump. Pump. Pump.

Gunfire broke out. Collin ducked, but not fast enough. A bullet slashed across her back, knocking her sideways off the boat. She felt the burn of a whip lashing her skin. Collin dived for deeper water, ducking under the waves

Silence. Collin risked swimming up. A shot skipped across the water. She dived again. Saw the blood trail in the water. Collin kicked to the side of the boat, took a lungful of air, and then forced herself to float out into deeper water. She floated face down, her arms out to her side, bobbing lifelessly. Hopefully. *Lord, help me.* She slipped beneath the waves, disappearing to the bottom.

Moments before her lungs wanted to burst for lack of air, she resurfaced. Grabbed a breath. Waited for the next rifle shot.

Nothing. Are they gone? Is it safe? Father?

Collin kicked to the kayak, her arms dragging beside her. She couldn't paddle back across the lake. No way. She tread water in the shallows, too weak to climb out.

Jeff would come. He'd search for her. She would wait here. Trust someone else to rescue her. *For once.*

Maybe five minutes passed before Collin heard the sound of a boat slicing through the water full throttle. She watched Jeff race by on the far shore, and then cut across the lake to reach her. He killed the motor, jumped off the bow, and yanked the boat onto the shoals. He splashed through the shallows to Collin's side.

"What happened?" He pulled her to his chest, letting the water buoy her up.

She drew in a breath and swallowed the cry wanting to escape her lips. She motioned with her head. "I think Tom's dead. I tried..."

Jeff carried her to their boat. He lifted her over the side, placed her gently on the floor. She lay on her side to watch Jeff climb into Tom's boat. He felt for a pulse from the stricken man.

Jeff bowed his head only a moment before returning to Collin's side. He grabbed the first aid kit and began swabbing at the wound on her back.

Collin gritted her teeth. "Beer. Medicine bottle."

Jeff's face darkened as he scowled. "Don't talk. Lay there and be still." He tossed bloody bandages into a pile, trying to staunch the bleeding.

Collin forced herself to focus on anything but the pain. "How do we tell Pam?"

"This is going to burn." Jeff poured antiseptic on the wound. Collin jerked straight but made no sound. Jeff's tone softened. "We tell her the truth. But we need to get the sheriff out here. He needs to see this as soon as possible."

Collin closed her eyes. "We need to send the people home."

"Yeah. As soon as I call the sheriff." Jeff finished up his work. "That'll have to do until you can see a real doctor." He left Collin lying on the floor, climbed in the pilot's seat, and raced the boat back to the dock.

* * *

Static. A string of curses. Lasting several moments.

"Commander, we were under orders to be invisible. How were we supposed to intervene and not be detected?"

"I understand the issue." More curses. "Law enforcement will be all over this area. Pull our people back over the ridge. Keep eyes on the shooter. I want to know everything they do. And pull those audio files. Make sure they're clean and clear. If we have to submit them as evidence, I do not want anyone to say, 'I can't understand what they said.' You got it?"

"Yes, ma'am. We'll make sure the files are perfectly audible."

"Get a mark on where the weapon landed. Launch point. Trajectory of the throw. Velocity. If the locals don't find it, we'll need to show it to them."

"Yes, ma'am. We'll mark the coordinates."

"Very good." Long pause. "Thank you for doing what you could. We couldn't stop it, but we will avenge it."

Slight chuckle. "Understood. Nice reference, by the way."

"Carry on."

* * *

Erin, in his wheelchair, Vy, and a small crowd of people waited as Jeff idled in. Erin's eyes narrowed to slits as Jeff slid Collin over the side. Collin stood. The world pitched and whirled. She sank down on one knee.

Erin came beside her, pulling her into his lap. "Come on, Cane. I've got you."

"So weak."

Jeff's anger cut through her. "You lost a lot of blood, Collin. I'm calling the squad."

Vy suggested, "We could drive her to town faster than they could get here."

She muttered her mantra. "I'm not going to the hospital."

Erin jostled her. "Shut up and breathe. We're taking care of you, like it or not."

Collin closed her eyes. "Fine." She lay her head on Erin's chest. Her eyes closed. Collin pulled internal, focusing on nothing. The nothing closed around her. Darkness took hold. She passed out.

* * *

Jeff ordered, "Take her to the hospital. I've got to call the sheriff and get him out here." People grabbed at him. "What happened?" "What's going on?" "Did someone get shot?" "Where are they taking Collin?"

Jeff ignored them all and dashed to the house. As much as he wanted to follow Erin to town with Collin, he had a hundred or so other people to be concerned about. Living people. People he wanted to keep alive.

And one dead one. He grabbed the landline and hit 911.

"What is your emergency?"

"A man has died, and a woman has been shot out at Farrell Acres. We need the sheriff, a coroner, and a forensic team."

"Your name?"

"Jeff Farrell."

"Is this the best number to reach you?"

"Yes."

"We'll have someone there in twenty minutes."

"Thank you." Jeff hung up and looked for any responsible adult he could find. Gabby stuck her head out the door of her room upstairs. Her face paled as she stared at Jeff. He realized he had blood on his clothes. Gabby whispered, "I heard gunshots."

"Gabby, I need you to monitor this phone."

Her face drew down into fear. "What's going on? Did someone get shot? Who?"

"Collin. But I've got to…" He stopped. How exactly did he evacuate one hundred people in an orderly fashion? *Runners. I need runners.* He turned to Gabby. "Where's Rob?"

"Still in his cabin, I think."

He spun to leave. Gabby called out, "Jeff!" He turned. Fear filled her voice. "What's going on? You look terrible."

He took a deep breath and settled down. "Tom Quince was…is…dead. Collin got shot in the back and is on the way to the hospital. I need to send everyone home…"

He stopped. What if they're suspects? What if the police want to talk to everyone? What about the crowd at the dock? They want to know what happened. I ran in here and didn't say a word. And I have to tell Pam…

He sank down on a stool. Gabby slid down the stairs and took his arm. "Tell me what's going on? Tom is dead? Someone shot Collin? Is there a crazed killer out there?"

Rob ran in through the front door Jeff left open. He looked as panicked as Jeff felt. He saw Jeff's face, the blood, and demanded, "What happened? They're saying Mom got shot. She's dead?"

Jeff held up his hand. "No, no. Yes, she got shot. She's on the way to the hospital." He struggled to his feet. "I need your help, Rob."

Harmon walked in from the grandparent suite, his voice louder than it needed to be. "What's the shouting about?"

Jeff yelled, "Both of you. Calm down."

Harmon raised his eyebrows. "I will if you will."

Jeff swallowed and nodded. He motioned to the kitchen bar. He sat, and the others followed suit. "Collin found Tom Quince unconscious this morning. While she was giving him CPR, someone shot her across the back. Erin and Vy are taking her to the hospital right now. Tom didn't make it. I've got the sheriff and his men on their way."

He circled the room with his eyes. "I've got a crowd of people outside who want answers to what just happened. Then there's the rest of the crew. Do I send them home? What if they're suspects? Will the authorities want to speak to everyone? But what if the shooter picks another target?" He paused, dropped his head. "And I have to tell Pam Quince her husband's dead."

Rob pointed at Harmon. "Pop Harmon?"

Harmon put his hand on Jeff's shoulder. "Breathe. Everyone." The senior Farrell waited until everyone inhaled and exhaled a few times. "One, we calm the crowd outside before it gets any worse. Two, tell everyone to stay out of the woods and off the lake. Three, you talk to Pam before she hears anything from anyone else. Four, you wait for the authorities to determine about sending people home." He raised his eyebrows. "Sound right?"

Jeff let out a small breath. "Yeah." He stood. "I'll go talk to the people—"

Harmon interrupted. "Rob, will you go calm the crowd and tell them to stay put, preferably inside'?"

Rob nodded. "Do I tell them about Tom?"

"Not until Jeff leaves to tell Pam. Jeffrey, I'll get your phone out of the lockbox. You go speak to Pam. Priorities, son. Go."

Jeff nodded like a ten-year-old. "Right." He got up and headed to Tom's cabin.

Brutus and Sam stood in the crowd at the dock, trying to find out what had happened. Jeff took them by their arms. "Come with me."

Brutus pulled back, looked at the blood on Jeff's shirt, and then followed. "What's wrong?"

"Come with me. I need to speak to all of you."

Brutus's eyes flared. His tone sounded hollow. "Dad didn't come back last night. Did something happen?"

"I want to find your mom."

Brutus wrenched away from Jeff and broke into a run for the cabin. He dragged Sam with him. "Mom! Mom! Something happened to Dad."

Jeff lifted his eyes to Heaven. *Lord, guide my words. Tell me what to say. And how to say it. Speak Your peace, Lord.* He doubled his speed and reached the cabin door as it opened.

Pam and Wendy stepped out. Wendy, still in her pajamas, Pam fully dressed. She closed the door behind her. "Jeff? What is it? What happened?"

Jeff motioned to the table and chairs on the patio. "Sit. Please."

Pam's face drained of color. "What happened?"

Lord, I've done this before. Help me. "Collin found Tom in his boat this morning. He wasn't breathing. She did CPR, but he didn't respond."

Wendy's voice trembled. "Is Daddy alive?"

Jeff swallowed hard. "No."

Wendy shrieked and dropped to the ground, flailing and crying. Pam slipped out of her seat and caught her daughter in a hug.

Sam shouted, "No! No!" Brutus grabbed him and forcibly held him. Sam pounded on Brutus's chest. "No! No! No!" Tears coursed down Brutus's face, baptizing his little brother in their fountain.

Jeff didn't know who to comfort first. *Maybe there is no comfort. Maybe there is only sitting in silence and being present.* Jeff remained still and waited.

Campers came over to see what they could do to help. Jeff rose and moved to Brutus's side. Sam gave up pounding his brother's chest and sobbed. Inconsolable. Jeff laid his hand on Brutus's shoulder. "I'm here."

Brutus lowered his head onto Sam's. He nodded. "Help Mom."

Jeff turned to Pam and Wendy. He helped them both into chairs. They clung to one another. Jeff kneeled and touched Pam's hand. She looked at him. "I'm here, Pam. We'll do everything we can. And we'll take care of everything."

Pam looked around. "Where is Collin?" Her face became a mask of fear. "Did she get shot? Oh, Jeff, is she—"

"She's alive. She got grazed by a bullet. Erin took her to the hospital."

Sam ran into the cabin, slamming the door. Brutus went in after him. Sam screamed and screamed. Jeff closed his eyes. *Lord, help him. Please.*

Five minutes. The screaming stopped. Brutus and Sam walked outside without closing the door. Brutus kept a tight hold on his little brother.

Pam stroked her daughter's hair. "I love you, Wendy. I love you."

Jeff noted she didn't say, "It's okay." Because it wasn't, and it wouldn't be for a long time. Anger filled his gut. His fists clenched. This family didn't deserve this.

Does any?

The out-of-the-blue question snapped Jeff's mind and heart back to center. Of course not. No one deserved it. People made choices. Good ones. Bad ones. Tom made bad choices. Did he deserve to die?

No, but there were—are—consequences to choices made. Tom made his. Now his family would suffer the loss. Oh, Jeff could see they suffered no financial loss. Brutus and Wendy, and yes, Sam, when they were ready, would all go to college. There would be retirement and pensions for Pam. He could fill any financial gap.

But no one would fill the gap left by Tom's passing. I know You're there, Lord. I know You fill the emptiness. But even You can't replace the hole Tom leaves. You mend the heart. But the hole remains. At least this side of eternity. Do what only You can do, Father. In Jesus' Name, amen.

* * *

It took the family a good forty-five minutes to pull themselves together enough to face Jeff with the "Where is he?" and "What do we do now?" questions.

He motioned to the lodge, where he saw blue and red lights flashing. "The sheriff's people are here, now. They will want to talk to you."

Pam walked with one arm around Wendy and the other around Sam. Brutus fell in step with Jeff behind his mother. "Someone murdered him, didn't they?"

Jeff breathed slowly. "I don't know, Brutus."

"People at the dock said Collin got shot. Did she say anything?"

"She said your dad was barely breathing when she found him. The boat wouldn't start." Jeff envisioned the scene in his mind. "She tried to do CPR. Then someone shot her. She fell into the water. The shooting stopped. I took off on the lake when I heard the shots and found Collin with your dad. He was gone. I brought her back, and that's all I know."

Brutus did not respond. His eyes pitched back and forth, but he said nothing.

A sheriff's patrol corralled the group at the boat landing. A few of the people pointed at Jeff and Pam. Rob stepped out of the mass and walked to meet up with Jeff. A uniformed officer accompanied him.

Rob made the introductions. "Dad, this is Sheriff Manning. Sheriff, my dad, Jeff Farrell."

Manning did a quick head turn from Jeff to Rob but and then focused on Jeff. "You're the one who saw what happened?"

"Not exactly. You would want my wife. I got there after the shooting stopped. But I can take you where the…" Jeff stopped, and corrected his speech. "…the boat is." Before the sheriff could say anything hurtful, Jeff motioned to Pam. "This is Tom's wife and children."

Manning doffed his hat. "I'm sorry for your loss, ma'am. Son. Young woman. Son." He pointed to a female officer setting up at the table outside. "Deputy Lane will have some questions to ask while we retrieve your husband."

Thank You, Father. He's got a heart.

Pam nodded and led the group up to the table where they all sat.

Manning put his hat back on. "Now. Tell me everything you know."

Jeff motioned to his boat. "I can take you out there."

Manning whistled shrilly. Three men popped their heads up and turned his direction. Manning lifted his hand, circled it in the air. The men grabbed their gear and joined Jeff and the sheriff. Five men loaded into the boat. Jeff took off, roaring across the lake, but slowed as he neared the shoreline by the silent vessel. He idled into the shore. One deputy jumped overboard, grabbed the rope, and tied it to a rock.

Everyone disembarked except Jeff. *Stay out of the way. Speak when spoken to. Be invisible.*

Manning examined the crime scene. "How long has he been here?" Two of the deputies climbed in Tom's boat. One began searching the surrounding area.

Jeff answered, "He went out about six last night. I don't know how long he sat grounded on the shore."

Manning turned to Jeff. "Tell me again what your wife saw and did."

"Tom was slumped forward in his seat. She climbed in, felt for a pulse. Tom was breathing but stopped while she checked him over. She tried to revive him, did CPR. She got a heartbeat and tried to start the engine, but it wouldn't fire. Someone fired a weapon. She got hit, fell overboard, and stayed low. They fired a second shot, and then stopped. She waited in the water until I showed up." His hands shook. Post trauma. *How is she? Is she even alive?*

Stop. The bullet grazed her.

But she lost so much blood...she could be dead.

She's not dead.

Sheriff Manning eyed Jeff. "How did you know where she'd be?"

"I didn't. I knew she'd gone out in the kayak. With the gunfire, I came out looking. Saw the boat, raced across here, and found her."

"Did you touch anything in the boat?"

"I checked to see if Tom had a pulse. He didn't. Then I worried about my wife. She bled heavily, and all I cared about was taking care of her." He lowered his eyes. "Sounds bad, I know." *I didn't care. I don't care.* Jeff straightened.

Manning huffed. "Sounds human. I'd have done the same."

One of the men looked up. "The victim died before the shooting. No bleeding."

Jeff cleared his throat. "Tom Quince. His name's Tom Quince."

"You knew him well?"

"We, uh...we worked together. Five years. Our families got together." Jeff had to swallow the crag in his throat. "He'll be missed." He shifted his weight in the seat.

A deputy held up the prescription bottle. "Found these. And empty beer bottles."

"Bag 'em and tag 'em." Manning turned back to Jeff. "You filed complaints about gunfire up in the hills?"

"Yeah. There would be a few shots. Then nothing for hours.

More shots, and then nothing. Sometimes in the morning. Sometimes in the middle of the night. Tom and I searched the woods and found a target, but nothing more. Then we got shot at." Jeff hesitated. "I'm certain the shooter only wanted to scare us off."

"So you said in your report. Why?" Manning's eyes narrowed. He leaned forward.

Jeff explained, "We were both standing in the open when whoever fired the first shot. It went five feet over our heads. Second shot did the same." He held up his hand. "No, they weren't just a bad shot. They brought down a four-inch branch over my head with no problem. They were trying to scare us out of the forest."

He scowled. "It worked, too. I made sure everyone at the retreat knew not to go into the woods." Jeff gripped the steering wheel. It gave him something solid to hold on to.

Manning nodded. He called to a deputy. "Lancer. You think we can tow this thing across the water?"

Lancer's eyes narrowed. He jumped in the water, walked around the craft, tipped it over, and looked under the hull. "I think we can." He sniffed. "I smell kerosene."

Manning walked over and joined Lancer. He drew in a long breath through his nose. "I do, too." He turned to Jeff. "Your wife said the engine wouldn't fire?"

"Yeah. The starter turned over, but no fire." *At least, that's what I think she said.*

"If someone put kerosene in the tank instead of gas, it would explain it."

Jeff shook his head. "Tom's son messed up the day before yesterday and put kerosene in it. But Tom drained it and cleaned out the fuel system. He had the boat running fine last evening."

"Anyone have it out for Mr. Quince?"

Jeff had to stop. He would not indict Pam and the kids. "No one I know of."

Manning snorted. "No one ever does. All perfect people."

Jeff raised his hand. "I'm not saying he's perfect. Yes, Tom would rub people the wrong way. But no one I know of would deliberately sabotage his boat." He stopped. *Tell the truth. The whole truth.* "His sons were upset with him. But I can't see either of them trying to hurt their dad."

"We'll look at everything and everyone. It's what we do."

Jeff nodded. "And you do it well. Thank you for coming out so soon and being considerate of Pam. She's going through a lot." He refused to say more. Let Pam tell about Sam's problems.

Manning scanned the lake. "You have another dock where we could pull this up without people gawking?"

"There's a boat launch area off the highway. It's not paved, but it's smooth. You could get a flatbed trailer down there." Jeff pointed south of the lodge. "Maybe halfway round the shoreline."

"Should be what we need." Manning called for his additional resources. "And transport for the body. Right away. Right."

It took another hour to get everything in place—the boat loaded on a flatbed trailer, the body wrapped and placed in the coroner's wagon. Manning shook Jeff's hand. "Sorry for your loss, Mr. Farrell. We'll be in touch. We'll need to interview your wife to get her statement."

"I'll let her know as soon as I see her." He chewed the inside of his mouth. "Should I send everyone home? We planned to run until Friday morning."

"It will have to be your decision. We'll want a list of everyone who came and how to get in touch with them. I'll have my men and the rangers comb these woods for whatever is hidden up here. Once law enforcement moves in, the bad guys usually take off. I think your people will be safe. But I won't give a guarantee."

Jeff nodded. "Thanks. I can give them the options." He gripped the wheel tighter. *How long has she been gone?*

"Up to you. We'll be in touch." Manning climbed in a cruiser and left.

Jeff ground his teeth. He pointed his boat back to the dock and the crowd waiting there. He searched the shore for Erin or Vy but didn't see them.

Rob caught the rope and tied the vessel to the mooring. Jeff jumped out and hugged Rob. Hard. Long.

Rob didn't pull away. He waited until Jeff gathered himself. "You gonna be okay, Dad?"

Jeff nodded. "Yeah. I used to do this all the time."

"But not with people you knew."

"Right." He squared his shoulders. "Any word about Collin?" *Tell me she's safe.*

Rob grinned. "She's fighting with the medical staff. They want to admit her, and she's protesting."

Jeff snickered. "I'll bet. I'll call and tell her to settle down." *My girl.*

Rob's face grew solemn. "What do they think happened?"

Jeff looked over the patio and saw Pam and the kids were gone. He eyed Rob. "Pam?"

"The sheriff's people took her and the kids into town."

"Okay." Jeff put his arm around Rob's shoulder. He walked to the patio and raised his voice. "Listen up." Faces turned. "Tom Quince died this morning. The sheriff's office is investigating the shooting." He stopped. "It appears the shooting happened after Tom passed."

Murmurs increased. Someone asked, "How'd he die, then?"

Various heads nodded. Jeff held up his hand. "The sheriff's office will have to determine that. All I can say is it appears Tom died of natural causes." *If a mix of booze and pills can be called natural.* "Most of you know Tom and Pam. I'm sure you want to support her in any way you can. But giving the family some space is what they need most right now."

He paused. "I talked with Sheriff Manning. It's up to you whether you feel safe staying until Friday or want to leave today. The Sheriff feels the shooter is probably gone. We should stay close to shore, maybe not go kayaking to the far side of the lake. Stay out of the woods. We can still enjoy the beach and the company. But no hard feelings and no pushback if you go home. And yes, you can still take the rest of the week off. Each family should decide for themselves. Talk it over and let me know."

Someone asked, "What are you going to do?"

"I'll have to talk to my people, too. After they get back from the clinic. With my wife."

A chuckle took a tiny edge off the devastated mood. Jeff held up his hand. "Anyone who wasn't here, please pass the message on. Tell them to talk to me. Last speech. We don't help anyone, especially Pam and her children, by gossiping or circulating 'I heard' rumors. What you heard from me is what we told the sheriff's office. Let's keep the chatter to ourselves. Got it?"

There were nods, and people milled away from the patio. Rob bumped Jeff's shoulder. "What are you going to do, Dad?"

Jeff sighed. "Stay. It's our place. Our property. I'm not running away because someone decided to poach our hills." He eyed Rob. "Which doesn't mean you have to stay."

Rob ignored the comment. "Are you going to send the triplets back with Pop Harmon and Mom Lacey?" They walked side-by-side back to the lodge.

Jeff scowled. "I'll have to talk it out with Collin. She's not big on letting them out of her sight."

Rob snorted. "What gave you that idea?"

"Intuition. Observation. Self-preservation."

"Especially the last." The two men walked into the house.

And were mobbed. "Daddy!" "Daddy!" "Rob!" "Rob!"

Talitha pointed to his shirt. "Daddy, what's on your shirt?"

Jeff realized he was still covered in Collin's blood. A shiver passed through him. He patted his daughter's head. "Yeah, Daddy's dirty. I'll go get cleaned up and be right back."

He walked to his room, went into the bathroom, and scrubbed at the blood on his arms. Legs. Hands. Brow. Another shiver jolted him. Jeff leaned against the wall. "Oh, Lord. Oh, Lord God. Father, please. Please. Make sense of this. Help me. Help me."

He bowed his head and waited for... He didn't know what he waited for. Peace. Comfort. Answers? The "still, small Voice?"

He received quiet. A chance to breathe. And to remember Who held the world. Including Jeff's small part of it. He nodded. "Thank You." Jeff stripped out of his clothes, tossed the garments in the trash, and put on something clean. He let out another calming breath, and then walked back into the common room.

Harmon and Lacey entertained the trio. Harmon lifted his head as Jeff entered. "Have you heard from Collin?"

"Not yet. I should drive to town and see how she's doing."

Lacey suggested, "Or wait. You might miss them on the road. You could call the hospital and see if she's been admitted or sent home."

Rob sneered, "Or if she's torn the place down trying to get out."

Harmon smiled. "A definite possibility."

The door opened, and Vy walked in. Collin followed stiffly, and to Jeff's eye, defiantly. She wore a hospital gown draped over her shoulders. Erin brought up the rear in his chair.

Jeff caught hold of Collin. He bent to look her in the eyes. "How are you?"

"A dozen new stitches, and I'm fine." Defiance burned in her eyes. But weariness draped her body.

Erin added, "And a pint of blood and an IV. But yeah, she's fine. Totally fine. Not a pain in the world. "

Collin glared at her brother. "Enough. You're one to talk."

The triplets, not understanding the exchange, tried to mob Collin. "Mommy!" "Mommy!" Four adults ran blocker. Jeff dropped down to their level. "Look, Mommy has a hurt back, so she needs to rest for a while, okay? She'll lay down for a few minutes, and then get up and play with you."

Talitha's face became still and solemn. "Mommy, you have a hurt back? What did you do?"

Joshua touched the gown. "This is funny. Where is your shirt?"

Collin addressed Talitha's concern first. "Yes, honey. I hurt my back out on the water. But I'm okay, and I'll be better than okay when I get up from a little nap." She tapped her daughter's nose. "Got it?"

Talitha nodded. "Yes, Mommy."

Collin turned to Joshua. "I left my shirt at the hospital."

Caleb noted, "You have dirt on you like Daddy did."

Talitha pointed to Erin. "So does Uncle Erin."

Jeff jumped into the conversation. "It's the same dirt. Mommy will get washed up after her nap. Uncle Erin will wash, and then we'll all be clean and shiny."

Joshua laughed. Collin kissed her children, including Rob, on the cheek. Lacey and Harmon patted her shoulder as she went by. Jeff led her to the bedroom and got her situated. Lots of pillows for support. She lay on her side. After she stopped moving, she asked, "How'd it go here?"

Jeff filled her in on the investigation as he saw it. And what the officers said and did. Collin listened, and then hung her head. "Maybe I could have saved him. If I'd pulled him in the water instead of leaving him there—"

"—you'd both been killed. And Tom didn't die from the gunshots." Jeff held her hand. "You couldn't do anything to save him, Collin. You have to know that."

Collin bit her lip. "It doesn't make it any better. It won't make it any easier next time I see Pam." She looked up into his eyes. "How is she?"

"Like you'd expect. Wendy had a meltdown. So did Sam. I worry most about him." Jeff replayed the scene in his mind. He stopped. *She asked me about Collin. How did she know? No one told Pam about Collin getting shot.*

Maybe he remembered it wrong.

"Yeah." Collin's voice quivered. "He's going to have a tough time of it. I hope Pam gets him therapy. Maybe they all should go."

"We'll suggest it after all the arrangements are made and done." He patted the pillows. "Rest. Sleep if you can. You need anything for pain?"

Collin shook her head. "I'm good. I'll sleep and get up for dinner."

Jeff kissed her. "Then we'll decide what to do about staying the rest of the week."

Collin sank back into the cloud Jeff built for her. "Yeah. We need to talk about it. Later." She closed her eyes.

Jeff stroked her hair until he heard her breathing even out. Then he got up and walked back to the common room.

Gabby and the rest of the Fields family sat beside Rob, murmuring. Harmon and Lacey read to the trio. Erin and Vy were in the kitchen fixing lunch. Erin had changed clothes so there would be no more "dirt" for the trio to wonder about. Jeff cleared his throat. "Can I have everyone's attention?"

Erin, being Erin, replied. "No."

Vy bopped him on the head. "Yes." The Wingers joined the rest of the crew. Vy sat beside her husband.

Jeff straddled a kitchen stool. "I told the others it's up to them whether they stay until Friday. I'm staying. What are your thoughts?"

Erin exchanged glances with Vy. She nodded. He turned to Jeff. "We're staying."

Rob spoke. "I'm staying. Like you said, this is our place, and I'm not gonna be run off."

Abbott lay a hand on his wife's arm. "We'll be leaving." He held Jeff's eyes. "It's not—"

Jeff held up his hand. "No one needs to give a reason. I understand people wanting to leave. Doesn't hurt my feelings. I will send food home with you. We've still got enough for fifty-plus people for another day. You'll have to take your share with you."

Abbott smiled. "We'll work it out."

Gabby eyed her father. "So do I have to go with you?"

Selma cleared her throat. "I think you ought to come home."

Abbott overruled his wife. "You're an adult. You can make your own decision."

Harmon's eyes twinkled. "Rob and Gabby will be properly chaperoned at all times, I assure you."

Rob snorted. "Got that right."

Selma burst out. "You're making jokes, and a man died! A man you worked with. His family is suffering, and all you're worried about is too much food? How cold are you?"

She turned away from the group and sobbed. Abbott caught her and pulled her to his chest. "Selma, Selma." He stroked her head. "We're not cold. When there's something we can do, we will." He glanced over at Jeff. "Maybe a prayer would be good?"

Jeff nodded. Heads bowed. He closed his eyes. "Lord...You're the Only One Who can make sense of what happened. We know You love Tom. You loved him more than we ever could. You died for him. Please, shower Pam and the kids with Your Presence. With Your Peace. Wrap Your arms around them in ways they can feel and know. Help them turn to You for comfort. Hold them."

Erin's voice. "God, You know Tom. You know us. Show us what You want us to do now. How do we help? How do we honor Tom and his family in ways meaningful to them and You?"

Harmon. "Father God, Lord of All, keep us leaning on You. Always."

No one else spoke. Jeff intoned, "Amen."

Selma bit her lip. "Thank you."

Abbott stood. "Come on, Selma. We have packing to do."

Selma faced Gabby. "I still say you should come home with us."

"Daddy said it's my decision. I'm staying." Gabby remained defiant. Selma's eyes burned. But she stood and followed her husband up the stairs.

Erin quipped, "That is not a happy couple."

Gabby snickered. "No, it is not. I have no doubt Mom is going to give him an earful when the door is shut. And all the way home."

Rob squeezed her hand. "Gabby, maybe you should go back with them." Her eyes widened. Rob continued. "It would create some peace with your mom. Show her your 'responsible side.' And maybe she'll think better about us."

Gabby glared at him for several moments, and then nodded. Her face remained angry. "I hate it when you're right." She hugged him. "Okay. This time she wins."

Rob hugged her in return. "It's a win for all of us, maybe."

Gabby huffed but went up the stairs to the bedroom suite. "Mom, I'm coming home with you."

Jeff faced his dad. "What about you?"

Harmon lifted his head, turned his eyes to his wife. "We'll go home."

"Leesa?"

"I think she'll come with us."

"Where is she?"

"At the beach. She's loving the water."

Lacey chuckled. "And the freedom to do nothing. It's going to be tough to get her back in a routine when we get home."

Jeff smiled. "This is her vacation, too. I need to spend time with her." *I need to spend time with everyone. I need to stop trying to "find" time and "make" time. Now.* He sat on the floor with the triplets. "Come here, bubbies. Daddy needs a hug. Dogpile."

Immediately all three children jumped on top of him. Jeff rolled to the floor and let the crew wrestle and wiggle and bounce on him. He let the play go on for about five minutes, caught his breath, and then called a halt. "Okay, let's get our bathing suits on and go to the water."

Cheers of "Yea!" "We're going swimming!" filled the room. Jeff crawled to his feet and eyed Rob. "Chess game after swimming."

He pointed at Erin. "You and me on the hoops court after Rob beats me at chess."

"So I can beat you at roundball?" Erin's eyes narrowed with glee.

Jeff grinned. "If you can."

"How many losses can your ego take in one afternoon?"

"As many as necessary." His throat choked.

Vy ducked her head. Her voice reflected her understanding. "You don't have to make it all up in one day, Jeff."

Sadness welled in Jeff's soul. He closed his eyes. "I can try."

Vy crossed the room and hugged him. "I know. God knows."

Jeff held her longer than maybe he should have. But he needed the hug. And Erin didn't object. He pulled away finally. "Thanks, Vy. Love you, sister." He kissed her cheek.

The boys came back into the room in their swim trunks. Talitha had on her suit, looking more like a ballerina in a tutu than a swimmer. But hey, she was covered. And that's all that mattered.

Jeff smiled at his children. "Okay, let's go."

Caleb asked, "What about you, Daddy? Aren't you going to put on your swim trunks?"

"Nope, I'm going to swim in my clothes. This time."

He held his hands out. The trio grasped his fingers, and they headed out the door. A train of grandparents, aunt, uncle, and one older sibling followed. He closed the door gently behind them.

* * *

Static. "All personnel clear of the area. We have eyes on the law enforcement searchers."

"Make sure they don't lay eyes on you."

"Copy."

"You still monitoring the ninjas?"

"Yes, ma'am. They're laying low. Waiting."

"Maybe we can disrupt their plans."

"Ma'am?"

"Who's your best operative?"

"G-5."

"Have him hit the cabin. Bring everything to camp."

"Yes, ma'am."

"No mistakes. No slip-ups."

"Yes, Commander. He'll get in and out."

"Good. Time we did something besides watch."

THURSDAY AFTERNOON

Collin woke and looked at the clock. Nearly three p.m. She'd slept long enough. Time to get up and face the world. Such as it was. The stitches pulled as she rolled out of bed and put her feet on the floor. She grabbed a button-up shirt and pulled it on. Much easier than a pull-over. Which she might not manage to put on. Clean shorts, ones not stained with blood, completed the outfit.

Collin steadied herself at the door. Her knees were weak. Wobbly. In need of something. She looked down. "Behave. Get it together. We are walking to the common room, and we will appear whole and well. You got it?"

Strength enough to walk steeled her legs. She could do this. Collin opened the door and walked out. Rob and Jeff sat locked in combat over the chess set. Harmon lay on the floor playing cars with the boys. Tee and Leesa drew pictures. Vy and Mom Lacey were in the kitchen doing something creative with knives and spoons.

Collin walked over to the chess players. She slipped her hand on Jeff's shoulder. "How goes it, my love?"

"Great." Jeff didn't look up from the board. "He's about to beat me for the third straight time."

Collin swallowed a smile. "I'm sure you'll redeem yourself."

Rob quipped, "I'm not."

Jeff warned, "One of these days. One of these days." He searched Collin's face. "Should you be up?"

"Are we going to start a fight?" She held his eyes.

"No." He kissed her hand. Collin drew her hand across his back, and then drifted to the kitchen. She watched Vy and Lacey working. "Where's Erin?"

Vy chuckled. "Sulking in his room. Jeff beat him at hoops."

131

"Poor man."

"He's blaming it on the chair. Says it had a flat tire."

Collin scowled. "He has hard rubber tires."

Vy grinned. "I know. Any excuse. How are you feeling?"

"Tight. Sore. But I'll make it." She looked outside. "How many left? Meaning how many didn't stay?" *Breathe. Breathe. Focus. Smile.*

"I think most of the families pulled out. A few stayed. Maybe two or three."

Mom Lacey shook her head. "We've still got all this food to get rid of."

"We'll split it up." Collin sat down on one of the stools. "Has anyone seen Pam?"

"The family is staying in town. It might help if we gather some things for them. We can take them later after dinner."

"Makes sense. Do you need a hand here?"

"Nope. We've got this covered."

"I'll walk down to Pam's cabin and see what I can pack up."

"No, you won't." Vy set her ladle down. "You're not walking all that distance after getting an IV and blood. You'll stay right here. Pull up a stool and help Mom Lacey."

Collin tried to argue. "I'm—"

Vy picked up the ladle and pointed it at her. "Don't make me use this thing. Stay. Now."

Collin rolled her eyes. "Yes, ma'am. Of course, ma'am. I'll sit right here and be a good girl."

Vy nodded sharply. "Good. You have children to think of. Your superhero days are over."

Collin waved her off. "Go. Do whatever. Be free."

Vy laughed. She started out the door, and then stopped. "Do we have permission to enter these cabins?"

Jeff looked up from the chessboard. "I would assume so. We own the property. We're not charging anyone rent. I can walk into any room in my home."

"What about privacy issues?"

Pop Harmon rolled over on the floor. "I believe we're trying to assist a friend. I don't think it should be an issue."

Vy chuckled. "Law enforcement. It sticks in your head."

* * *

Vy walked to the cabin. Her mind continued the debate. *Ownership or privacy? Which would take precedence?*

The cabin door stood open. *Solved one question. Thank You, Lord.* Vy passed the SUV parked on the grass. *Tom never did think rules applied to him.* She poked her head into the room and called, "Anyone home?" Yes, she knew no one was there. But it felt better. Less intrusive.

Vy saw evidence of lives interrupted. Pam's purse stood open on the dresser. Pill bottles lay beside it. Her brain registered the name of the drug. Nothing more. The small table had leftover food on the plates. Vy stepped closer and ran her hand over the table. The last meal as a family.

Her fingers picked up a foreign substance. White powder smeared the surface. Someone tried to wipe it away but failed. Vy looked closer at the residue. She kneeled down and sighted across the surface.

Particles of what might have been crushed pills sat on the table. Her DEA training went into full alert. She backed away immediately. *I need to leave and call the sheriff's office. Now.*

Vy stepped outside, locking the door behind her. As she passed the SUV, she noted the back hatch had been left partially open. The light still burned. *Someone's going to have a dead battery.* Vy reached out to close the hatch with her hip but stopped.

A spent shell casing lay half-buried in the soft ground beside the back tire. Vy closed her eyes. *Lord, what is going on here? What is all this about?*

Her mind battled. *It's a set-up. Whoever killed Tom—*

You don't even know if he was murdered.

Don't I?

You know Pam. You know Tom and the kids.

And I know people have a breaking point.

Not yours to decide. Call the sheriff.

Close the hatch and walk away from all of it. Leave it. They've suffered enough.

Which justifies murder?

You don't know that.

The sheriff will.

The sheriff will suspect. He'll build a case, so he has one to close. Walk away.

Vy walked back to the lodge.

Erin had come into the room. He glanced at her. "I'm done pout— What's wrong? It's all over your face."

"The door was open. I found...some...things... Maybe evidence..." Vy pulled herself together. This wasn't some perp off the street. These were friends, a co-worker. Almost family. She met Erin's eyes. "There's a shell casing by the car. And crushed pills in the cabin. Empty Lorazepam bottles on the dresser. I need to call the sheriff. This could have been murder."

Jeff shook his head. "No. No. Not Pam. She wouldn't. Tom mixed his meds. She told us before."

Erin lay his hand on Vy's arm. "I agree. The sheriff needs to know about this."

Jeff threw his hands in the air. "She's been through enough. Being with Tom and all he's put her through. You know how he could be. If anyone deserves a break, it's Pam. You don't know if any of it matters. Do you really want to accuse her of murder on top of everything?"

Vy continued to maintain her level demeanor. "Jeff, I'm not accusing her of anything. It's evidence. The sheriff needs to know about it." She held his gaze. "If this were a stranger, would you ignore it?"

"It's not a stranger. It's our friend. And her children." Jeff sounded desperate.

Vy snapped, "Don't you think I know? You think I want to call the authorities? But I have to. It's my duty. My job."

Jeff eyed her. "Is it what Jesus would do?"

Vy's jaw dropped. She stared at him. After several seconds she nodded. Her tone came out flat. "Yes. It is."

Jeff jerked the phone from his pocket and all but threw it to Vy. "Here. You do it. I'm not going to be the one who accuses her."

Erin caught the phone. "I'll place the call." He glared at Jeff. "Because my wife isn't accusing anyone of anything. She's reporting facts. Remember those? Remember truth?"

He dialed, and then waited. "Yes, this is Erin Winger. I'm out at Farrell Acres. I have some information which might have a bearing on Tom Quince's death. Empty prescription bottles and what could be crushed tablets were found in the cabin where they were staying. Yes, sir. Lorazepam. Right. And a shell casing by the car. No, I don't know what make or model."

Erin listened. "Right. The scene has been secured to prevent tampering. No, no unlawful entry. The door was open."

Vy's gut settled. Peace, child. Peace.

Erin turned his head. "Really? Oh, I see. I'm sorry. I am. Yes, we'll be here at the lodge. Thank you, sir. I appreciate your help."

He disconnected the call and handed the phone to Jeff. Then he held Jeff's gaze. "Pam refused the autopsy. Said her religion forbids it." He moved across the room to the kitchen bar.

Jeff's head snapped up. "What?" There were tears on her brother-in-law's face.

Erin nodded. "Yes. But with this new evidence, the coroner will override her request. Unless she can prove she and Tom both adhered to a religion which forbids autopsies."

Collin's voice remained calm and quiet. "She won't be able to. She'll have to have witnesses."

Jeff's was bitter. "And we certainly won't cover for her, will we?"

Harmon laid his hand on Jeff's shoulder. "I think you need to take a walk, son. A long walk. You're not thinking straight."

Jeff glared at Harmon. For a moment, Vy thought Jeff would snap back at his father. But her brother-in-law pulled himself up, nodded curtly, and stalked out the door.

Vy squeezed hands with Erin. He pulled her head down and kissed her.

Collin sagged. "I don't understand. What's gotten into him?"

Harmon shook his head. "I don't know. Give him some time. I suspect…" Harmon stopped. "Give him time." He resumed pushing a racecar on the floor with the boys.

Half an hour later, Mom Lacey called, "Dinner is ready."

* * *

Collin let the other adults seat her children. She stepped out the front door. Jeff sat in a rocker, tears streaming down his cheeks. Collin kept her voice soft. "Mom says dinner is ready."

Jeff nodded but made no move to get up. Collin stepped behind him and put her arms around his shoulders. The motion pulled on her stitches, and she closed her eyes against the pain. But she asked, "Talk to me about it?"

Jeff sucked in his lips. He wiped his face with his shirt. "Dinner's waiting. Later." He rose and walked into the house. Collin followed.

Jeff sat between Caleb and Tee. Collin sat between Tee and Joshua. The rest of the adults picked a spot, and everyone sat. Jeff's voice cracked. "Dad, will you say the blessing?"

Harmon prayed for Pam and the family, those who left, and those who stayed. He prayed for the shooters in the hills, and the family gathered around the table. He kept it short, direct, and to the point. Collin appreciated it. Especially when the littles were at the table. The children might go long in their prayers, but no one else could.

After dinner, Collin got shooed from the kitchen to "rest." She eyed Jeff. He shrugged, and then motioned to the front. Collin followed him out.

He sat in the rocker again, looking out over the lake. Collin sat beside him on the floor of the porch and waited. He would speak, or he wouldn't.

"I'm sorry. I was out of line." His voice sounded stiff. Controlled.

"I know. Can you tell me why?" *Will you?*

Tears filled his eyes. "I worked with him. I know what he's like." He held Collin's eyes. "Day after day after day. No break. Yes, I loved him like a brother. But the constant pick pick pick…I got to hate it. And he wouldn't stop. We had to write him up one time. A woman in billing had a run-in with him. He loved to come up behind her and scare her. She laughed the first time he did it. The second time, she asked him not to do it again. But he kept doing it. She finally complained to Human Resources. Abbott had to call him down to tell him to either stop or she would file a harassment charge against him. He never did get why she became upset. It was just a joke."

Jeff looked at the sky. Tears drained into his mouth. He tossed his head. "Just a joke. His excuse for everything." Jeff lowered his head again. "I got to where I wished he would quit. Then I wouldn't have to put up with him anymore."

Jeff went silent. Collin waited, and then Jeff picked up the story.

"Now he is."

"Wishing it didn't make it so, my love."

"Could I have saved him? Or did I leave him there on purpose?"

Collin touched his knee. "What did you tell me? It wasn't my fault. I couldn't have saved him. Neither could you."

Jeff stared at the lake. "If I'd have looked for you earlier."

"If I'd have reached him earlier. Jeff, ifs won't change what happened. Tom died. If the pills and beer didn't kill him, the shooter would have."

Jeff lowered his head. "You think he knew the Lord?"

Collin put her arms around his legs. "I know Tom made a commitment to Jesus. We were there when he surrendered his life five years ago. We saw him baptized, telling the world he'd decided to follow Jesus."

She softened her tone. "I know he walked away from all of it. I know his life didn't reflect his words the last year or so." She leaned her head against his knees. "I'm not God. Neither are you. God is God. He's the only One Who determines who is or isn't His. I know He is good. I know He is Love. I have to trust Him for the rest."

Jeff swallowed and closed his eyes. He rocked back and forth slowly. She rocked with his motion.

They stayed locked together for several minutes. Ten. Fifteen. Twenty. Jeff drew in a deep breath. "Okay, then. There's a good reason I'm not God. And I trust His judgment. Like you said, He is good, He is God, and He is Love. And Love wins in the end."

He stood, pulled Collin to her feet, and then hugged her. He smiled sadly and kissed her. "I love you, milady. Thank you for hanging with me."

"I love you. And there's no one I'd rather hang with." She kissed him back.

A sheriff's car pulled into the driveway. Collin hung her head. "I'll go talk to them."

Jeff pulled her close. "We'll go together."

They walked to the car and waited as the officers exited the vehicle. The law officers put their hats on before greeting them. "Sir. Ma'am. Deputy Norton." He pointed to his partner. "Deputy Barnes. Were you the one who reported possible evidence regarding Mr. Quince?"

Collin shook her head. "They're inside. I'll get them for you."

She motioned to the house. "I've got the keys to the cabin inside."

Barnes held up his hand. "Do you have permission to access the cabin? Does it belong to you or to Mrs. Quince? Did she rent it from you?"

Jeff answered for her. "We own the property. This is a company event. We allow people to use the cabins for the week. There is no fee."

"So she's not renting it for the retreat? Nothing charged for lodging?"

"There are no fees or charges for the entire week on anything."

The deputies raised an eyebrow. Norton chuckled. "Can I join your company?"

Jeff waved at the house. "Law enforcement is always free to join us. Food's on us."

Norton grinned. "After I get off duty." He grew sober again. "May we search the cabin?"

Collin ducked inside, grabbed the keyring, and handed it to the deputy. "Cabin twelve." She hesitated. "The keys to the car are on the keyring. I don't have permission to search it. As a friend, I have permission to put things in and take things out, but only if I'm directed. I don't think it constitutes legal permission."

"We have a warrant just in case. We appreciate your help."

The deputies walked the pathway to the cabins. Collin leaned into Jeff. "Pam won't appreciate the help, I know." She looked off into the distance. "I think I just lost a friend."

Jeff hugged her. "It's justice, milady." He looked at the ground. "Obey the authorities over you. Don't turn a blind eye to injustice."

Collin turned to him. "Which injustice? What Tom did to Pam and the family all the years? Or what happened to Tom? If anything."

Jeff stared at the lake. "We're about to find out."

The deputies worked for a good hour before returning to their vehicle. They had several items in plastic bags, including a gun and ammunition. Norton tipped his head to Collin and Jeff as he passed them. "Thank you again. I think this will help the coroner."

Jeff repeated his offer. "You're welcome to stop by any time. Pass the word along."

"We appreciate that. We do." The men climbed into their car and drove away.

Collin and Jeff walked back to the house. Inside, Jeff cleared his throat. "Apologies all around for my behavior."

Count on Erin. "Accepted. Remembered, but accepted."

Jeff shook his head. "Thanks, bro. I appreciate the vote of confidence."

Jeff's phone rang. He looked at the number and then answered. "Hello? Pam. I didn't expect...okay. Yeah, Collin, Erin, Vy, my folks, and my sister are here." He looked up. "She wants me to put it on speaker."

He complied. "What is it, Pam?"

"They want to cut Tom open. They want to do an autopsy. I don't want them to. They say the only way to prevent it is to say my religion forbids it. I need you to back me up. Tell them we belong to a sect which prohibits desecration of the body. Somehow it will keep him from going to Heaven. I don't want him all chopped up. Please. Help me."

Collin turned her eyes to the floor. Jeff coughed. "Pam, I don't think we can't lie for you."

"Why not? Tom never wanted to be cut open. He swore he'd haunt me if I had it done."

"You're not the one choosing this, Pam. And he can't exactly haunt you. He's with Jesus. You don't come back from there."

"You don't know. I'm asking you as my friend, as Tom's friend. Please tell the coroner our church prohibits autopsies. For Tom's sake. For my sake. For Sam's sake."

Jeff choked. Collin took the phone. "Pam. What is this?"

The woman on the line snapped. "Don't talk to me. You left him to die. You could have saved him, but you saved your own precious life instead."

Collin closed her eyes. She lifted her head but said nothing.

Pam continued her diatribe. "I'm right, aren't I? The great Collin Farrell. So strong. So smart. So invincible. But when it came down to it, you jumped like a scared rabbit. You could have saved him. If you'd kept doing CPR, he might have made it. But no. Someone starts shooting, and you bail on him to save your own life. Like you're the only one who mattered."

Collin let the words roll over her. Her one defense... *Lord?*

Be still, My child. I love you. There is no condemnation for those who are in Me. You did nothing wrong.

Pam snarled, "Give me to Jeff."

Jeff took the phone back. "I'm right here, Pam. I have to agree with Collin. There's nothing in our statement of faith forbidding an autopsy."

Statement of faith? What about defending me? What about saying, "No, she couldn't have saved him?" What about my defense?

Pam continued arguing. "Yes, there is. There's my wish for it not to happen. And you should love me enough to support me. You're turning your back on Tom and me. Are you feeling guilty, too? You should. You were his friend. You should have—"

"Pam, you're not thinking straight. Come back to the camp, get some rest, and let yourself heal. Or at least see things more clearly. We love you."

"Really? Really? They think one of the boys did the shooting. One of them murdered Tom. Now are you happy? It takes the guilt off you, doesn't it? They did it, not you. Well, you can pretend all you want, but it doesn't change a thing. You two let him die. It's your fault. It always will be. Live with it."

She hung up. Jeff put the phone in his pocket. He looked around the room. "I'm sorry you had to hear her."

Harmon stood, crossed the room, and put his hands on both Collin and Jeff's shoulders. He lowered his head. "Father. You heard the accusations. You know they're lies meant to destroy and kill. Turn the weapons back on the enemy. Surround Pam with Your love, mercy, and healing grace. Help her and her children to see clearly, to think clearly, and to trust You for all their needs. I can ask nothing more in Jesus' Name, amen."

* * *

Those who stayed behind at the lake held a memorial for Tom on Thursday evening. The triplets went home with Harmon, Lacey, and Leesa. They were as excited as Collin was apprehensive. But Jeff agreed it would be best for everyone if they left. Safest. Collin couldn't argue. Wanted to but didn't. At least not out loud. The internal discussion would continue until the bubbies were all safely home in their own place. With Mommy and Daddy. *Sigh.*

The bonfire for Tom gave it a Celtic or Viking feel. *We should sacrifice some fish. We could each say something, and then throw the fish in the fire. And eat them at the end.*

Collin shook off the inappropriate—but fitting—thought. Not helpful. She looked around the circle at the twenty-some participants. Most knew Tom only from work. They spoke of his hard work, his cheery attitude, his helpfulness.

Erin stood. "Tom Quince could be a complex man." He paused. "He loved a joke." Pause again. "Even when others might not. He cared for his family. Provided them with food and shelter and laid up for their futures."

Erin stopped. "Tom's good points will be missed. His shortcomings forgiven. May justice be done in finding his killer."

He sat. It fell to Jeff to close the session. Collin watched her husband draw a deep breath, stand, and then lower his head. "Lord, You gave us Tom as our co-worker and friend. You brought him into our lives to teach us lessons of Your choosing. Help us learn them, grow from them, and be better persons because of them. Be with his family. Draw them close to You. Draw us all close to You. In Jesus' Name, amen."

Collin felt like there should be a closing hymn. But nothing felt appropriate. Silence would close the session.

Someone got up and moved away. Others followed. Eventually, only the Farrells and Wingers remained. It felt fitting. Right. A chance for private closure.

Erin squeezed Vy's hand. "He really was a hard man to know. He could be the best worker we had, and then make bad decisions which cost us."

Jeff nodded. "Complex. You hit it right. I loved him, but he could get under my skin. And he knew it."

Collin decided to change the trajectory. "What can we do for Pam and the family?"

Jeff shrugged. "She'll get his salary and eventually his pension. The kids will have the college scholarships if they choose to take them." He tossed a chip into the fire. "Brutus seemed excited about being able to go. Before Tom passed, of course. It'll remain to be seen what he does now."

Vy added, "And what Pam lets him do." She slid her arm around Erin's shoulders. "She may want to honor Tom's wishes. Or say she needs him at home. It may be hard for him to leave."

Erin nodded. "With Sam needing extra support, Brutus may decide to stick around on his own. They need time to work it all out."

Collin's voice caught. "Do you think she'll blame us forever?"

Jeff squeezed her hand. "God will heal her heart. He's the only One Who can. Give it time, milady."

Rob pitched a stick into the firepit. "What are we going to do tomorrow?"

"Enjoy our last day. Be grateful for life and breath and God's provision in our lives."

Rob pitched another stick. "You think Brutus will feel grateful?"

Jeff stared into the fire. "I don't know. We can pray. It's all I know to do."

Collin lifted her face to the stars. It's all we've got, isn't it? Wrap Your arms around them. All of them. And thank You for keeping this family together. Watch over the littles. I love You, Lord.

FRIDAY MORNING

Jeff took the boat out Friday morning. Erin and Vy joined him. He wanted—needed— to make a statement. The lake should be fun. Those who stayed behind could feel safe. Vy took advantage of Jeff's driving and skied again. Erin went on a tube and managed to hang on the whole time.

Collin watched from the shore, under orders not to get her stitches wet. She sat with Rob and watched the boaters having fun. Collin frowned. Rob noted. "No pouting, Mom."

"I'm not pouting. I'm expressing disappointment. I can't have fun."

Rob laughed. "It's good for you to learn there are limits."

Collin narrowed her eyes. "Listen, Mister. Don't you talk to me about limits, or I'll limit your refrigerator privileges."

Rob held up his hands. "I'm only looking out for your welfare."

"I'm sure." Collin sighed. "You and everyone else." She gazed toward the lodge. The few people remaining came and went as if nothing had happened. Or at least they pretended well.

Rob remained silent for several moments. "Do we want to do something for the family? Take up a collection for flowers? Something? Anything?"

Collin nodded. "We'll discuss it with Jeff and Erin when they get back. The company will pay any expenses the family has."

Rob cleared his throat. "Um...what if the police decide it's murder? Then what?"

"We help the remaining family members." Collin held her son in her gaze. "We haven't heard any of them are officially accused of anything at this point." *Beyond Pam's ravings.*

Rob sat forward. "What if? Say one of them is accused. Does the company hire a lawyer to defend them?" He held Collin's eyes. "Knowing what Vy saw, do we still hire a defense lawyer?"

Collin stared at the ground. Stared into her heart. Her mind. Finally looked up. "I don't know. I don't." She drew in a deep breath. "It's not my call to make."

A car pulled into the circle driveway. Collin looked over. Sheriff's car. *Now what?*

Maybe they came for breakfast.

Oh, if it were only so simple.

Sheriff Manning stepped out. He donned his hat, smiled, and joined Collin and Rob. "How is it going?"

"Not bad, Sheriff. What can we do for you?"

"Just wanted to tell you my deputies, members of the Forest Rangers, and the Conservation Corps are all up in the hills looking for whatever your shooters are hiding. We've got drones patrolling where we can't and people everywhere else. We should get some answers today."

"Thank you, sir. I appreciate it, and I know my husband will. When he gets back in from the lake." Collin pointed to the boat in the center of the lake with the tubes behind it. "He's out there entertaining the water lovers." She sighed. "I'd be out there, but I got outvoted."

The sheriff smiled. "I understand. How are you feeling?"

"Stiff. Beyond that, I'm fine."

Rob quipped, "Long as she doesn't go in the water."

Collin threw a jaundiced smile at him. "No one asked you."

Manning smiled. "Well, I only stopped to tell you about my men in the woods. You all have a nice time." He turned to go, and then stopped. "Mrs. Quince will be out to collect her things later this morning. We'll have a deputy with her in case she needs assistance."

Collin's gut twisted. "Sheriff, Pam told us she didn't want an autopsy done. Could she block it?"

"No, I'm afraid not. She couldn't find enough witnesses to support her story her religion prevented it."

Enough witnesses? Who would she find? Collin hesitated. "She also said you were accusing the boys of murdering Tom?" She held up a hand. "I know you can't comment on an active investigation. Can I talk to her while she's here?" Collin stopped. "She's not under arrest, is she?"

Sheriff Manning would have made a world-class poker player. His expression never changed. "No one is under arrest. It might be best if you don't speak with her at this time. She's overwrought." He hesitated. "She blames you for her husband's death. You and your husband. Perhaps it would be better to wait."

Collin ducked her head. "I understand. Thank you for the advice, Sheriff Manning." She looked up. "The invitation is still open for you and your men to join us for meals. Or snacks. Or S'mores. With people leaving early, we have an overabundance of food."

Manning touched the brim of his hat. "I appreciate the offer, Mrs. Farrell. I'll pass it along to my men. Have a good day, folks."

Manning climbed back into his cruiser and left. Collin sighed.

Rob walked over and put his arms around her. "Not your fault, Mom." He gave her a tiny smile. "Not even Zena, the Warrior Princess, could have hauled Tom over the side after being shot in the back."

Collin groaned. "Don't be bringing her up."

Jeff pulled the boat up to the dock. He jumped ashore, and Erin assumed the captain position. The passengers changed, Rob joined them, and the boat headed out once again.

Jeff walked over and hugged Collin. She sensed the lack of tension in him. "So, you had a good time?"

Jeff nodded. "Yes, I did. It felt good." He put his arm gingerly around her shoulders.

"I'm glad. You needed the break." Breathe. In. Out. Smile. No tension. Breathe.

"Was that Sheriff Manning who stopped by?" Jeff led the way to the lodge porch.

"Yeah. He wanted to update us on the crews searching the woods. They've got people sweeping both sides of the lake."

"Good. They came faster than I thought they'd be here."

"Maybe they want to be sure no one tries to destroy evidence."

"Makes sense." He sat in a rocker and pointed to the one beside him. "Sit." Collin complied. "What else did he have to say?"

"Pam will be escorted out to gather their stuff later today. Manning suggested we not try to talk to her. She blames us."

"Still?" Jeff cocked his head to look at her.

"So he says." Collin sighed. "Time and the Lord. It's the only thing to heal her."

Jeff nodded. "Right. Wish we could do more." He rocked slowly beside her.

"Rob asked about taking a collection, maybe for flowers." Collin refused to rock in time with him. No synchronized old people.

"Not a bad idea. The company will provide for everything but donations from individuals might make it more personal." Jeff shielded his hand to peer across the lake.

Collin hesitated. Rob's question hung in her mind. She hesitated. Hesitated. "What if she's accused of murder? Do we pay for a defense lawyer?"

Jeff gazed at the ground. "I don't want to think that far ahead. We take this one day at a time, milady. One hour at a time." He picked up her hand and squeezed it.

"Right."

Jeff smiled at her. "Sit. Relax. Enjoy the sunshine."

Collin let out a long breath. "Right. Trust."

Jeff grinned. "As much as you can." He laid his head back on the top of the chair.

Collin nodded once. "I can do this. See? I'm relaxed." She dropped her shoulders, winced, and then smiled. "Relaxed."

"Liar."

"Truth."

* * *

Near four p.m., a patrol car pulled into the driveway. Collin, Jeff, and Rob stepped out of the house to see what was happening. A deputy got out. The driver proceeded down the path to the cabins, stopping at number twelve.

The deputy nodded to the group. "Mr. and Mrs. Farrell." He looked at Rob.

Collin introduced the young people. "Our son, Rob."

"Deputy Caruthers. I'd like to ask you some questions about what happened yesterday."

Jeff motioned to a picnic table. "Sit."

The group sat. And the questioning began. "Mrs. Farrell, can you tell me about Wednesday morning?"

Collin steeled herself. "I spoke with Sheriff Manning about it."

"I know. But this will be for the official record. I'm sorry to put you through this again."

"I understand." Collin relived the events, filling in details as asked.

"What time?"

"How long were you on the lake?"

"How long did you perform CPR?"

"What did you touch in the boat?"

Collin tried to give only facts. But Caruthers wanted more. "After you dove in the water, did the shooter try to target you again?"

Collin pursed her lips. "They may not have been shooting at me. I honestly don't know who they were shooting at."

"How many shots total?"

"Two?" She shook her head. "I don't know."

"That's fine. And once the firing stopped, did you check on Mr. Quince?"

"No." Collin stared at the ground. "I didn't have the strength to pull myself back into the boat. The best I could do was stay afloat and wait for rescue."

Caruthers turned his attention to Jeff. "What alerted you your wife needed help?"

Jeff's face hardened. "When the shooting started. I knew she had gone out in the kayak. I didn't know if she needed help. I didn't want to wait to find out. I took off immediately to look for her."

"And the shooting…"

"Stopped. I saw Tom's boat and drove over. I saw Collin in the water."

"Did you know then Mr. Quince had died?" Caruthers made notes in his pad.

"Collin told me he'd stopped breathing. I took his pulse. I admit I felt more concern for my wife's condition at the time. I did what I could to stop the bleeding and then headed back to shore."

Caruthers looked at his notebook. "We have the details on the actual investigation of the scene. Who told Mrs. Quince her husband had died?"

"I did."

"How did she react?"

Jeff seethed. "How do you expect? They were horrified. All of them. I brought them to the patio, where a female deputy took care of them. She escorted them into town, I believe."

Caruthers nodded. Read some more. "Mrs. Quince called you from the station. What can you tell me about the conversation?" He sat back to wait for an answer.

Collin watched Jeff's face. Drawn. Angry. Defensive. Backed into a corner. "She wanted our help…determining if our…church doctrine…in any way prohibited a body from being autopsied."

"And you told her?"

Jeff breathed hard. "No. I told her no."

"Did she accept your answer?" More pen scratching.

Jeff looked up. "No. She didn't. It upset her. I can understand not wanting to…to desecrate the body of her loved one."

Caruthers held Jeff's eyes. "I can as well. Unless I wanted to know how my loved one died. Right then, no one had any indication of how he died. Wouldn't you want to know?"

Rob interjected. "Would it bring him back?"

Caruthers turned. "Excuse me?"

"Would knowing bring him back? Maybe that's what she thought. If she thought anything." Rob held the deputy's eyes.

"I appreciate the candor. I have some other questions for you." Caruthers shifted on the bench.

Collin waved him on. "Continue."

"The youngest boy." He looked at his notes. "Sam. What do you know about the trouble he's been in?'

Collin's head jerked. "Trouble? I don't know anything about him being in trouble." *Not "in." Causing trouble, yes.*

"Mrs. Quince said she told you about him attempting to burn the house?" His voice came across as slightly incredulous.

"She told me there were burn marks in the kitchen. He obviously wanted to get attention. He never seriously tried to burn anything down."

"She said the curtain had been totally consumed in flames. And the boy denied doing it. Mrs. Quince claims she found the lighter in Sam's pocket." Caruthers read more of his notes. "Why would she want to have him evaluated by a psychologist?" He looked up, again waiting for an answer. Or explanation.

Collin pursed her lips. "There were things going on. Sam…the boy wanted to spend time with his father. He felt left out. He's a good kid. And he's only nine."

"You had him at your house last weekend. Is that true?"

The boat made a circuit past the dock. People on the raft waved and shouted. Rob waved back.

Collin answered, "He stayed with us, yes." Lord, I don't like where this is going. Help me speak truth. I don't want to leave anything out, but I don't want to add more than they need to know. Help me discern the difference.

Caruthers consulted his notes. "Was there any trouble? Did anything happen which concerned you about his behavior?"

"Like what?" Two crows flew overhead, expressing their opinion of the boaters disturbing their fishing.

The deputy paused, looked down, and then looked at Collin. "Mrs. Quince related her son…acted inappropriately with your daughter. Touched her." He let the implication hang.

Jeff and Collin both sat up hard. Collin slapped the table. "Not true. Never." She gathered herself. "I…" *Watch your words. Choose carefully.* "I found them in the bedroom. Alone. Her brothers were outside the room. I opened the door and told them they were not to be playing any game all four of them couldn't play at the same time. Sam accepted it, and they switched to something else. My daughter said nothing happened. Nothing in her behavior led me to believe otherwise. He did not touch her in any way."

Caruthers made notes. "What about in the backyard? What happened there?"

Collin looked down. Closed her eyes. "Sam suggested they all take their shirts off. My children refused. They've been taught not to take clothes off outside unless Mommy or Daddy tell them it's okay."

"So Sam didn't try to pull your daughter's shirt off? Didn't try to kiss her on the mouth?"

"No! Absolutely not." Collin laid her hands on the table. "Nothing happened. Nothing. Sam is nine years old. Nine. Nothing happened between them. I was there."

"And if you hadn't been?" Caruthers had his pen poised.

Collin sat back in her chair. "I don't play what-ifs. There are a thousand scenarios you can spin. I'm telling you what happened. Nothing." Every muscle in her body screamed. The only ones that didn't were her vocal cords. *Good choice. Right choice.*

Jeff put an arm on Collin's shoulder. "What is all this about,

Deputy Caruthers? Why all the questions about Sam?"

"We're gathering information. Trying to piece together what happened and why." He looked at his notes, and then looked at Jeff. "Did you see anyone tampering with Mr. Quince's boat before he went out Wednesday night?"

Jeff shook his head. "No one tampering with it, no." He stopped, and then admitted, "Brutus filled the tank with kerosene before his father left."

Rob cut in. "That was Tuesday night."

Caruthers wrote something in his book. "Why would he do that?"

Rob shook his head. "Monday night, a bunch of us were talking around the fire, you know? Batting things around. Brutus joked that if the boat broke down, Tom…Mr. Quince…would have to spend time repairing it. And if he did, he could take the time to teach Sam how to use the tools to fix things."

"Was he serious?"

"Maybe. It happened. I can't say Brutus filled the tank on purpose. Maybe he got the cans mixed up. But that was Tuesday night. Tom, my uncle, and Dad all worked and fixed it Wednesday morning. It should have been fine after that."

Caruthers wrote furiously in his notes. "Did Brutus ever threaten to hurt his dad?" Caruthers looked up from his writing.

"No." Rob's voice came across loud and clear. "Never. He loved his dad. He'd get frustrated, yeah. But we all do at some point. We work through it."

Caruthers nodded. "Yes, we do." He looked through the notes. "Tell me about the battery."

Jeff answered this one. "My brother-in-law, Erin Winger, told Brutus about our company's college scholarship program. Tom Quince objected to Erin giving Brutus the information. He accused Erin of interfering with his family. He punched Erin out."

"Did Mr. Winger fight back?"

Collin interjected, "My brother was in his wheelchair at the time. He had no opportunity to fight back."

"Why didn't you report this to our office?" Again, his probing gaze.

Jeff stared at the floor. "Tom is…a valued member of our company. We didn't want to damage his reputation or cause his family strife. We thought we could handle it in-house." He looked across the lake. "Maybe if we had reported it, he'd still be alive."

"I'll want to speak to your brother-in-law."

Collin stood. "I'll get him now." *I will not have Erin accused of murder. Or even have any whispers he could be involved with this.* Her gut burned. Her hands shook. She walked with deliberate steps into the lodge.

Erin and Vy were at the kitchen bar. They looked up as Collin entered. Erin's eyes narrowed. "What's wrong, Cane? I don't like the look in your eyes."

Vy huffed. "When I can see what's in your eyes, you know there's trouble. What is it?"

"There's a Deputy Caruthers asking questions about Tom and all the activities this week. Someone told him about the assault, and now he wants to talk to you." Collin bit the words out.

Erin chuckled. "Relax. It's fine. I have an impeccable alibi with my DEA wife."

Collin's face burned. "I don't like—"

Erin squeezed her shoulder. "Pam is casting around for anything and everything she can. This doesn't surprise me." He rolled his chair around to the front of the room. "If you will open the door, I'll go talk to him."

Vy corrected him. "We will go talk to him."

They exited to the patio.

Erin shook hands with Caruthers. "Deputy. I'm Erin Winger." The bruising on his eye and chin spoke for him.

"Mr. Winger. We're collecting information about Mr. Quince and his activities. Would you tell me about his assault on you and why no one reported it?" He poised his pen.

Erin laid his hands on his lap. "We're family, Deputy. Our company, I mean. We valued Tom as an employee and friend. He punched me out—"

Collin noted Erin didn't use the words "attacked me."

"—because he thought I interfered with his family."

"And it justified attacking you in your wheelchair?" Caruthers cocked his head to the side.

Erin glanced down. "I didn't think so. But he did."

"And you let it go? Didn't think it needed to be reported?"

"We decided as a family not to press charges. We warned him if anything like this happened again, we would. But we forgave him and felt we handled it the best way we could."

"You forgave him. Just 'poof?'" The eyebrows went up again.

Erin smiled. "It's never just 'poof.' But yeah, after sleeping on it, we—I—forgave him. I didn't hold it against him."

Caruthers wrote in his notebook. "So you didn't threaten to 'get even' the next day?"

Vy's eyes widened and then narrowed. She leaned forward, so Caruthers met her eyes. "My husband does not 'get even' Deputy. He allows the Lord to work His will. I can vouch for Erin's whereabouts and actions from Wednesday evening all the way up to now." She sat up a little straighter. "Vy Winger. DEA identification W123F7."

Caruthers nodded his head. "Thank you, ma'am. I'll make a note of that." He turned his head to the side. "You were the one who told the sheriff's office you found empty pill bottles and drug residue in their cabin. Tell me."

Vy kept solid eye contact. And her hands in her lap. "I went to gather up some clothes and things. We thought we would pack them so Pam wouldn't have to."

"Were you at all concerned about contaminating a crime scene?"

"No." Vy's voice carried heat. "I had no idea the cabin might be a crime scene."

"Did you have permission to enter?" Caruthers read his notes, and then looked up at Vy.

"The door was open." Vy laid her hands on the picnic table.

Caruthers looked at his notes. "Interesting. Mrs. Quince says she made sure to close the door." Caruthers met Vy's eyes. "You say it was open?"

Jeff interrupted. "Deputy, when I sat with the family, the youngest boy, Sam, went in and out of the cabin. He didn't close the door behind him."

Caruthers made a note. "I'll add it to the records." He looked back at Vy. "What happened next?"

Vy continued her telling of the events. "When I went in, I saw the bottles on the dresser. There were two of them, and they were empty."

"Did you handle them?"

"No. I saw the labels. Lorazepam. Pam told me Tom mixed his

meds." Vy added, "I didn't think much at the time. But on the table, I saw a white powder and particles of crushed tablets." Her eyes dared the deputy to challenge her. "My training makes me sensitive to those kinds of evidence. I walked out, locked the door, and headed to the lodge. I saw the car hatch partially open. Then I saw the bullet shell on the ground by the tire. I came back here and called your people."

Collin added, "When I climbed in the boat with Tom, a bottle of meds fell out of his pocket. Lorazepam. It had been filled on Friday but looked half-empty. There's no way all those should have been gone."

Caruthers nodded. "We found high concentrations of the drug in several of the empty beer bottles as well."

Jeff's face darkened. "Mixing alcohol and anxiety meds is a recipe for death."

Caruthers nodded. "Which makes this a murder investigation." He stopped, looked down, and then looked back at the group. "I have to tell you after the four of you, Mrs. Quince has pointed the finger at Sam."

A bomb could have gone off, and no one would have reacted. Life drained from Collin's soul. She stared into space. *Sam? Sam? He's nine. He's a baby. Why? How? This can't be happening. It can't be.*

Collin swallowed hard. She looked around the table at the faces. Stunned. Dazed. Bewildered. Overwhelmed. She saw it. She felt it. Collin whispered, "No. No. Never." She cleared her throat, forced volume to it. "Not Sam. He's only nine. He's a baby. She can't be serious. She can't be."

Caruthers ducked his head to the side. "Right now, if we eliminate you four, we still have four suspects. Mrs. Quince, Brutus, Wendy, and Sam. Of the four, Mrs. Quince is leaning towards Sam. She's giving us all the information from his school, the psychologist's evaluation, his time with you." He raised his eyebrows. "She wants us to believe Sam is the killer."

Collin sat back, unfeeling. Why? Why would she? He's her baby. Why isn't she fighting claw and nail to save him? I don't understand. I don't. Lord, help me. Please. Make this make sense. Please.

The deputy rose. "I want to thank you all for your candor. I got what I needed. Can we reach you at these numbers if we have more questions?" He rattled off phone numbers for Jeff, Collin, Erin, Vy, and Rob. Collin nodded. He touched his hat. "Thank you again for your time. I know this is hard. I appreciate your help." He walked to his car, got in, and drove away.

The group didn't move. Water flooded Collin's eyes. Dribbled over the lids. Cascaded down her cheeks. Saturated the front of her shirt. But she didn't move. No one did. No one could.

FRIDAY NIGHT

By the evening, all the other campers departed, leaving the Wingers and Farrells. The sun had gone down. Jeff lit a fire in the pit, which burned to an intense glow. The five sat behind the firepit without talking for several minutes. Jeff pitched an occasional woodchip into the logs. Sparks danced in the air, imitating fireflies. The lodge sat dark and cold and empty.

Collin spoke the question she'd been wrestling with. "How could she accuse Sam? Why not wait and let the police decide?"

Vy joined Jeff in the chip-throwing. "Because he's the logical mark." She leaned forward. "If Brutus or Wendy or even Pam herself is accused—and found guilty—they go to prison. Maybe even death row. But Sam? He's nine. No way is he tried as an adult. No way is he tried, period. With him profiled as a troubled child, the court sends him to a psych hospital. Maybe he stays until he's eighteen. Maybe he gets out earlier. He turns eighteen, his records are sealed, and life goes on. It's the easy choice."

Collin shook her head violently. "No. It's logical, but it's not right. Sam would never kill his dad. Never." She curled her legs into her chair and wrapped her arms around her feet.

"I'm not saying he did. I'm saying Pam would choose to see him accused rather than any of the rest of them. She doesn't lose any of them."

Erin leaned in. "But will the sheriff's office pursue him to the exclusion of anyone else? Will they look at the others?"

Vy nodded. "A good office will look at all the suspects." She grimaced. "Even when one confesses."

Collin's head jerked up. "You don't think she would coerce him into admitting he did it, do you? For the good of the family?" *Lord, please. Don't allow this travesty to happen.*

"Not with someone his age. Only the killer could give him enough details to make a confession work. And a nine-year-old won't remember them. Not in the right order."

Erin turned to his wife. "Okay, Sheriff. Explain to me the shooter in the hills."

"Maybe the shooting is a cover for the murder later. It would establish there were bad guys in the hills. Then if Tom doesn't die from the pills, the killer shoots him, and it looks like the bad guys did it."

Rob tossed a stick into the pit. "Then Wendy or Brutus could have been on the ridge shooting target practice? And making it seem like it was someone else?"

Vy shrugged. "Unless there were hired guns."

Collin snorted. "You really do think of every scenario, don't you?"

Jeff shook his head. "But why? Why kill Tom? Why not divorce him if you're unhappy with him?"

"Because she only gets half of what he has. And child support only for Sam. It's not going to keep her living like she has been."

Collin nudged a burning log. "Except I know Pam. She's not capable of murder."

Vy held up her hand. "We're all capable of murder, pushed hard enough."

A shot pinged a bullet into the fire. Sparks and embers and wood pieces scattered into the air. Erin slid out of his chair onto the ground. Collin, Jeff, Vy, and Rob all dove to the dirt. No one breathed.

* * *

Static. "Who's firing? Who's shooting at the civilians?"

"The ninjas."

Cursing. "My fault. My fault."

"Commander?"

Silence.

"Commander?"

* * *

Erin stage-whispered to Vy, "Someone forgot to tell the hired guns the jig is up."

Vy sneered. Jeff inched his head up.

Nothing.

He crouched higher.

Jeff reached for his phone in his pocket. He entered the number. "Yeah. This is Jeff Farrell. Right. Uh-huh. Same one. There's been another shot fired. It came at us."

Another blast. More sparks flew. Bodies hit the dirt again, aiming for more protected places. Jeff whispered forcefully into the phone, "Did you hear that? They fired again!"

Erin touched Vy's knee. "You think they know we're here? Do we risk turning on a light to let them know?"

She shook her head once. "I don't know. I don't know what they're shooting at."

"Do they?"

And again. And again. And again. A regular barrage of bullets flew at the firepit, chipping away at the stone, brick, mortar, anything solid.

Erin rolled over to protect Vy. She kept her eyes on the darkness. "Two shooters, Jeff. Standing together."

Jeff relayed the information to the 911 operator. "Right. Hurry."

Jeff signaled to Vy. "Retreat?"

"Yeah."

"Collin, Rob, move back to the house."

Collin stayed on her belly and commando-crawled backward to reach the lodge. Rob beat her to it, reached up, and opened the door. She scooted inside, followed by Rob. Vy wormed her way in, followed by Erin and Jeff. The group edged their way behind the bar in the kitchen. It seemed the most solid furniture behind which to shelter.

All five adults lay on the floor, waiting for the firing to stop. Erin pulled himself up to a sitting position. Jeff assisted him. Rob reached over to help Vy. Collin rose on her own.

They stayed crouched. Left the lights off. Waited.

The shooting stopped.

Five minutes passed.

Jeff straightened. "I think they're done." The group stood. Gingerly took steps away from the kitchen bar. The only light was the glow of the fire outside. Best to keep it that way. *Don't give them anything else to hit.*

Vy looked around. "You have anything that can reach them?"

"No. There are no firearms in this house."

"Bow and arrow?" Jeff frowned. Vy ducked her head. "Just a thought."

Erin slid beside the window and peered out. "They really don't like your firepit. Who designed it?" He carefully inched the curtains back.

Collin hissed, "Very funny." She stayed in the area closest to the kitchen. Pots and pans might act as a shield. Some of the cast iron ones, anyhow.

"No, I mean it. Everything hit the firepit."

Jeff's voice questioned Vy. "Was it all they could see?"

"Maybe. All the bullets did hit the same target."

"Which means what?"

Erin repeated, "They don't like the firepit. They're design snobs."

Jeff groaned. "Erin! If you can't be helpful, hush." Vy sank into a wingback chair. Jeff's face darkened. "I hope the sheriff's men can figure it out."

Erin remained standing by the window, leaning against the wall. "So maybe the shooters and Tom's death have nothing to do with each other."

Jeff held up his hand. "Good question to ask the sheriff. More important, what do we do now?" Jeff joined Erin at the window. "What happens if we leave?"

Erin chuckled. "Now there's an idea. Why didn't I think of it?"

Vy stared at the front door. "One way to find out. Except..." She looked around. "Who wants to be the first out the door?"

Jeff waved off Erin's raised hand. "I'll go. But I've got an idea." Collin raised her eyebrows at him. "I stay low. Start the engine without actually getting in the car. Crawl along beside it. See what happens. Circle the driveway and pick the rest of you up. Then we take off and drive to town."

Erin shook his head. "Let me do it."

Four voices echoed sharply, "No."

Vy touched his hand. "Your stealth days are over, my love. I'm the most qualified."

"But you're preggers. And I'm not risking you and our children."

Jeff cleared his throat. "We can argue who's the most expendable until the cows come home. I suggested it. I'm going. End of story."

Collin eyed him. "Stay low." She kissed him…

…as Rob slid out the door. Four voices hissed at him, but he ignored them. Collin joined Jeff at the window and watched. She held her breath and prayed. *Lord…please. Your will, but please.*

* * *

Static. "Report!"

"We've got people in position around them. Do you want us to neutralize them?"

"We can't. It compromises our presence."

"What do you want us to do?"

"Monitor the situation. Hope local law enforcement can take them out. Then we don't have to get involved."

"If they can't?"

Silence. "I'm going to recon the area. Stay sharp."

"Yes, ma'am."

* * *

Rob made it to the car, dodging behind chairs and tables and the remains of the firepit. Without climbing into the vehicle, he started the engine.

No shots. No opposition. Collin held her breath as Rob "walked" the car halfway around the circle to the point where he would be on the same side as the shooters. Then he put the car in reverse and backed up to the door. He pushed the buttons to open the back passenger doors. "Come on. Let's go."

Vy ducked low and complied. She sheltered behind the door. Erin and Jeff followed. Jeff supported his brother-in-law as Erin climbed in the back seat, followed by Vy. Collin slid in the third row behind them. Finally, Jeff crawled into the front seat. Everyone kept their heads down, exposing as few body parts as possible.

Rob gunned the engine. "Let's go."

The vehicle jumped to speed and raced toward the main road.

Gunfire erupted. Nothing hit the car, however. Bullets flew above, ahead, and behind the car, but nothing struck the vehicle. Poor aim? God's protection? Collin had the feeling she knew the answer.

Jeff handed her his phone. "Alert the sheriff's office about what we're doing."

"I would if I knew." She took the phone and called the operator. "Yes, it's the Farrells. We are attempting to leave the property to see if it makes a difference. Right. Yes, they're firing at us. No, we're not trying to provoke them." *Intentionally. More like baiting them to see what they'll do next.*

Collin listened. "Yes, we still need the sheriff to come out. Meet us on Road 27. Nearest the camp. We'll be waiting out the storm."

Rob stopped once they were clear of the camp and presumably out of range of the shooters. He kept a field of trees between them and the lake. Jeff glanced at all the passengers. "Suggestions? Theories? Ideas?"

Erin grumbled, "Wish I had something to give you. I got nothing."

Vy pursed her lips. "I have to agree with Erin. I got nothing, either."

Rob quipped, "Well, don't look at me. If the professional doesn't know, the street rat certainly doesn't."

Jeff eyed Collin. "Anything?"

"Nothing. Not a clue."

"Then we wait for the police and see what they have to say." He paused. "Wonder what the sweep of the woods found?"

"I'm sure it'll be brought up." Collin wished she felt more conviction about her statement.

In his usual supportive fashion, Erin quipped, "I'm not."

The group climbed out of the van and huddled on the side nearest the trees, watching for gun flashes. Whoever was on the ridge had ammunition to burn. And no sense of aim. Bullets sprayed in and around and near the lodge.

Collin saw the lights but heard no sirens. The cavalry arrived. Such as it would be. Two sheriff's cruisers pulled off the road beside Jeff's stopped car. Deputy Caruthers exited one car, a female partner with him. Two male officers climbed from the second car.

Caruthers took charge. "Mr. Farrell. Sorry to meet you again like this."

"Yeah, me too." Jeff motioned over his shoulder to the camp. "I'd much rather be there sleeping or eating or doing anything but this."

Caruthers nodded. "It's been quite the week, hasn't it?"

"You could call it that."

Vy nodded to the deputy. "Sir. Can you tell me what your sweep of the forest grounds came up with?"

Rob added, "And what it has to do with us being considered target practice?"

Caruthers raised one eyebrow. "Not very good shots if you were the targets."

Rob sneered. "We should be grateful, I suppose."

Caruthers motioned to one of his officers. "Deputy Trevant, what did the sweep find?"

"The sweep came up with nothing. Nothing illegal growing. No stills, no manufacturing areas, no mushroom fields. According to the sheriff, there's nothing in the hills anyone would want to hide."

Erin snorted. "Bigfoot has a rifle."

Trevant swallowed a grin. "We didn't find any tracks of anything but wildlife you'd expect to see." She shook her head. "Nothing. We found nothing."

Jeff threw his hands in the air. "Someone is shooting at us. Maybe they're getting some fun out of it, but we're certainly not."

Caruthers asked, "No lights on at the camp?"

"Nothing. They're shooting at shadows and motion at worst."

Caruthers nodded. "Good. We're going to leave you here and move into position at the camp. Drive to town and stay there. We'll get in contact with you."

Caruthers and his people loaded back into their vehicles and turned down the cut-off to the camp.

* * *

Static. "Local mounties have arrived, Commander."

Silence.

"Commander?"

Nothing.

"Commander?"

* * *

The new motion caught the attention of the shooters. Gunfire erupted.

And was returned. Instantly the exchange became intense. Jeff ordered, "Everyone in, now."

The group piled in. Erin wedged in the back between Vy and Rob. Erin asked, "Which way are we going?"

Vy argued, "Back to the lodge. There are law enforcement officers under fire. There may be casualties. They're going to need your EMT skills, Jeff. We'll stay well back, out of the way, and wait it out. But I can't leave my people to face this alone."

We're "your people" too! What about us? Jeff gritted his teeth and eased the van forward just shy of the entrance to the camp. The bullets still flew. Flashes in the hills gave away the positions of the bad guys. And there were three of them, not two.

Caruthers and his team hunkered down in defensive positions behind whatever solid cover they could find. Some of it didn't look too solid. A voice cried out in pain. Caruthers yelled, "Trevant's hit."

The moon rose enough to give the faintest of light to the area. Enough so Collin could make out the shapes of her family. Erin and Vy climbed out of the van and huddled their heads together. Collin heard her brother say, "I make it five hundred yards to the shooters."

Vy agreed. "Five hundred and just. Too far even for a good sniper."

"With the right skip, I could make it."

Vy cleared her throat. Erin murmured, "I've done it, Vy. Robert made me practice shots like this before he'd let me come in the house at night. Spent a lot of time living in the backyard before I could hit it consistently. But I learned."

Collin closed her eyes. Robert Winger. Our blood father. I wonder how his life sentence in prison is going?

Vy kept her voice low. "I believe you could make it. If we had a gun. But we don't, so it's a bit academic right now."

A throat cleared.

In slow motion, everyone turned to see who had materialized in their midst.

A shadow figure in black camo stood outlined in the partial

moonlight. They had a rifle on their shoulder, a mask across their face. No one moved.

The figure cleared their throat again. "I like your thinking. You sure you can make that shot?"

Erin stared at the figure. Collin closed her eyes. She knew his answer. But was this the time?

"I can make it." Collin dropped her head and opened her eyes. *He thinks it's the time.*

"How often?" The figure took a step forward.

"Nine times out of ten." Erin's head turned from the figure to Vy, and then back again.

"No brag, just facts?" There was a lilt of humor in the voice.

Erin chuckled. "No brag."

The figure handed the rifle to Erin. "Make it."

Erin motioned to Vy. "I need to be up."

Vy helped him to a standing position, leaning against a tree. The shadow moved on his opposite side. "I saw three flashes."

Collin breathed in and out slowly, mirroring what she knew Erin would do. Calm. Calm the muscles, the nerves, the thoughts. Nothing mattered but the angle. Did he see it?

Erin glanced at the rifle, asked, "Which way does it pull?"

"A shade to the left."

"How wide is your shade?"

"Two degrees."

Erin nodded. Collin joined him in the calculation. Two degrees over five hundred yards, augmented by the angle of deflection off the water… Breathe out. Breathe in. Let half of it out. Hold. Pull through the trigger…

The rifle popped. A voice in the woods screamed. Erin fired a second time. Another voice cursed and howled. The shooting stopped.

The figure patted Erin on the shoulder. "Very nice. I might need to look you up next time I need a sniper." The person took the rifle from Erin, stood, laid it in the bushes, and then said, "Thank you for your service." The next moment, they disappeared into the darkness.

Rob's eyes were saucers in the dim light. He glanced all around the circle. "What just happened? Someone?"

Erin leaned against Vy. Collin heard the tremor in his voice even as he joked, "Friends of Bigfoot. They take their forests seriously."

He lay his head back against the tree.

Vy's voice trembled as well. "There were three shooters."

"Someone got a free pass home." Erin sighed. "That nightscope was impressive. Some people get all the cool toys."

Vy laughed, but Collin still heard the tension in her voice. "I've got some toys you can play with." She leaned forward and kissed him. Their silhouettes disappeared in the shadows.

Collin covered Rob's eyes. "Not in front of the children."

He groaned at her. "Mom!"

Jeff motioned to the van. "Everyone in. I know they've got people who need help. At least I can do something useful."

* * *

Static. "Commander?"

"Gather the troops and return over the west ridge. I believe our presence is no longer required here."

"Yes, ma'am."

"You did keep those transcripts, correct?"

"Yes, ma'am."

"Send them to me. I know where they'll be needed most."

"Are you rejoining us, ma'am?"

"I will. Three-day pass to the unit who spots me first."

"Very good, ma'am. When should we look for you?"

"That would be telling, now, wouldn't it?"

"Yes, ma'am."

"Goodnight, Lieutenant."

"Night, ma'am."

* * *

The five loaded into the van and smoked dirt back to the lodge. Jeff stopped far enough away to yell, "Sheriff! I'm here to help the wounded."

Caruthers's voice yelled back, "Come on in. We're going to need you. Deputy Trevant took one in the arm."

The five joined the law enforcement contingent. Jeff pointed across the lake. "Take my boat if you want to gather the other wounded. If you think it's safe."

"We'll let them know help is coming. If they want it, they'll let us approach. If they start firing again, well, they can sit there 'til morning."

Jeff ran into the lodge, grabbed his paramedic gear, turned on the lights, and then tended to Deputy Trevant's wounds. Two deputies climbed in Jeff's boat and took off across the lake to retrieve the wounded. Their spotlights bounced off the trees, illuminating the spaces between.

Rob and Vy supported Erin to the patio and parked him in the chair with the fewest holes. Vy folded on the ground beside him; Rob mirrored her on the other side of his uncle. Caruthers glanced at the group around him. "Who fired the shots?"

Collin drew in a small breath. Would Erin confess?

Of course, he would. Erin held up his hand. Wearily. "I did."

Caruthers nodded once. "Nice shooting. Where'd you get the rifle?"

Erin paused. "I'm going to give you two scenarios. One, I found it in the bushes. Two, a shadow figure stepped out of the forest and handed it to me. I'll let you choose which one you want to believe."

There wasn't enough light to see Caruthers's face. Collin imagined it instead. There would be questions later. Lots of questions. For now, let everyone breathe. And appreciate being alive.

The deputies returned with the two wounded. Neither man looked familiar. Jeff patched and bandaged what he could. Collin assisted him as he needed.

Caruthers's commented, "No ID. Figures." The bad guys were loaded into the sheriff's cruiser and escorted to town. Law enforcement loaded into the other and followed, promising to return after daylight for the "mop up." Caruthers made sure to collect the mystery rifle from the bushes.

Collin and Jeff joined Vy and Rob on the ground. Collin leaned against the lodge deck. Crickets and frogs chirruped and croaked, singing songs to the stars above. An owl hooted. A soothing breeze played across the lake, lapping little waves on the shoreline.

No one moved. No one spoke. They let the silence heal the landscape and their souls.

Until Rob broke the silence. "I get first shower."

"Rob!" Collin looked for something to throw at him. *We do not throw things at people because we disagree with them.*

Yes, Mommy.

Jeff grumbled, "That's why we put in all those point-of-use water tanks. So everyone could have hot water at the same time."

"It's not the hot water I want. It's the water pressure. Three showers going at one time is two too many. I'm going first."

Vy got in the fray. "Shouldn't it be women first?" She stood. Rob copied her motion. Together they lifted Erin to his feet.

Rob corrected her. "Women and children. I'm the child of this group. Besides, you women always defer to your husbands, and I still end up last."

Jeff extended his hand to Collin. They stood and followed Erin, Vy, and Rob inside. Rob asserted, "So I get the first shower."

A throat cleared. "Actually, I got the first shower. And it was wonderful."

* * *

A figure in one of the long white lodge robes sat at the kitchen bar. She had her hair wrapped up in a towel. She wore glasses and face paint designed to obscure her identity. But she smiled as she wrapped her arm around in front of her. "These robes are beautiful. You do pamper your guests, don't you?"

Collin's brain whirled. "We try." It sounded lame, but it was all she could think of.

The woman held her hands up to show they were empty. "No weapons. Nothing. I left mine in the bushes, if you remember."

"Your weapon." Erin motioned Vy to let him down on a stool opposite their visitor. "I see. Well, I appreciate the use of it. The sheriff didn't exactly buy my explanation of where it came from. I'm sure I'll hear about it more tomorrow." He glanced at the refrigerator. "Do we have any leftovers?"

Collin groaned. "Erin Winger!" Jeff sank into a wing-backed chair closest to the kitchen. Vy perched next to her husband. Rob found a spot midway between the two groups. Collin sat on the arm of the chair Jeff had chosen.

Erin quoted, "'If your enemy is hungry, feed him.' Least we can do, right?" He motioned to the refrigerator. "You got a shower. Did you get anything to eat?"

The woman chewed on the side of her mouth, tilted her head.

"No, but I wouldn't turn anything down." She corrected herself. "I wouldn't turn much down. K-rations, I'd refuse. And I hope we're not enemies. We are on the same side."

Jeff's eyes narrowed as he stared at her. "Are we?"

"Would I support your local sheriff if we weren't?"

Jeff shrugged. Collin slipped her hand on his shoulder and squeezed. Vy began pulling out leftover cold cuts, salads, condiments… Collin raised her eyebrows at Jeff. He shook his head. She thought a moment, and then moved to the bar and fixed a sandwich. As she turned back to the common room, she noted the expression in Jeff's eyes. She sighed, made a second sandwich, and carried both plates to where they sat. Vy fixed a dish to share with Erin. She curled up on the floor beside him, her feet out in front of her.

Rob joined the munch-bunch. Only after everyone had something to eat and drink did he raise his hand. "Are you going to tell us what's been going on? Who the shooters were?"

Erin suggested, "Start with a name we can call you. Always helps."

The woman glanced off to the side. "Bertie. Call me Bertie. And I'll tell you all I can. Which isn't going to be all you want, but it'll have to do." She looked at Vy. "You know what it's like to be undercover." Bertie winked at Vy.

Vy startled. "Why do you say that?" She shifted to the side.

Rob chortled and hooted. "Because you carry yourself like a cop, Aunt Vy. I've told you before. You can't shake it."

Vy glared at her nephew. Bertie tried to cover a smile. "Straighten out the relationships here for me." She motioned to Jeff and Collin. "You're a couple." She pointed to Vy and Erin. "You're a couple." She looked sideways at Rob. "You called her aunt, and you've called her Mom." She indicated Collin. "Adoption?"

"Yeah. When I was eighteen."

"I see. Very nice. You must have been a special child."

Collin grumbled, "He's been a pain in my *cadenza* since he was fourteen. I figured I'd get even and be one in his the rest of his life." She smiled at her son. "Love you, Rob."

Jeff cleared his throat. "Okay, I can't get past the weirdness of this. We're sitting here eating like old friends, cracking jokes and laughing. And I have no clue what's going on."

Bertie sat back. "You're right, Mr. Farrell. Okay, here's what I can tell you." She lined the food on her plate into a landscape. "My unit—and no, I can't tell you what unit—dropped over the ridge to do training for a designated period. I had scouts check out your lake, which, according to our records, should have been unoccupied."

She squirmed. "Obviously, our records were wrong. But being the resourceful unit we are, we decided to take the opportunity to train in a real-world situation. Practicing cover and stealth, among other skills. The idea would be for your people to never see or hear my people. Which we accomplished. For a time." She took a bite of her sandwich and smoothed out the ridges on her plate.

Jeff scowled. "Until your people started target practice in the hills."

Bertie leaned forward. She tapped the bar top. "Those were not my people. My people were under strictest orders not to fire under any circumstances." She sat back. "We put eyes on the shooters. The first group had two kids, teens. A boy and a girl, both close in age."

Collin glanced at Jeff. "Brutus and Wendy?"

Bertie nodded. "I believe those are the two. We kept tabs on them. I couldn't afford for there to be civilian casualties with my unit looking on and doing nothing." She looked at the floor. "Maybe another commander would have withdrawn forces and let you fend for yourselves." She shook her head. "But I'm not that person." More of the sandwich disappeared.

Erin offered, "And we appreciate it."

Bertie shrugged. "The kids were up in the woods a couple of times. Mostly pot-shotting. No heart in it. We didn't think it would come to much." Her voice hardened. "Until Wednesday night. When a second group shows up." Her eyes narrowed. "Bad guys. All dressed in black like they were playing ninjas. High-tech ninjas. Carrying rifles like they meant business. And business wasn't good."

Bertie drew a breath. "We watched them meet up with a hiker from the camp."

Jeff jerked up. "My camp? I mean, our camp?"

"Yeah. And I had resources close enough to listen to what they said." She held up her cell phone. "Give me a number to send it to."

Vy beat Jeff to the draw. "555-578-5112."

Bertie typed the number in. "Sending you the files now." She looked around the room at the group. "She kept saying, 'He'll drink the beer.' I didn't know what she meant."

Collin stared at the floor. *The beer Pam spiked with Tom's drugs. She meant to kill him. This wasn't about abuse, was it, Pam?* Collin sat back. She breathed out and then lowered her eyes.

Bertie ducked her head. "I'm sorry. It gets worse."

Jeff squeezed Collin's shoulder. She slipped to the floor beside him drawing her knees up to her chest. "Go on."

"Thursday morning. One shooter is staking out the point where the boat has run aground. Just watching. Then you"—Bertie pointed to Collin with the remains of her sandwich—"show up and start CPR on the victim. The shooter fires on you. Knocks you out of the boat and fires again. Presumably to make sure you were dead."

Collin breathed in, breathed out. *Lord? Thank You for protecting me. Again.*

Bertie hadn't finished. "Then the shooter throws the weapon in the lake and hightails it back to the camp. And to cabin twelve."

Jeff gripped the arms of the chair. His voice came out cold and hard. "Which explains why she asked me if you were okay. Why she worried about you. No one told her you'd been shot. But she knew." Jeff seethed. "She knew because she tried to kill you. She thought she had."

The implications descended on the room like a shroud. No one spoke. No one moved.

Rob broke the silence. "Are you going to report this?"

"No." Bertie shook her head. "We can't."

"She tried to murder my mom!"

Erin spoke. "The sheriff has enough to nail her for Tom's murder, I'm sure. He should be able to put her away for life."

Jeff scoffed. "Maybe. But if she blames it on Sam, actually gets him to confess, she walks away free."

Erin faced Bertie. "Which still leaves the mystery of what the three shooters were up to, and why they chose us for target practice." He snorted. "Which they needed, but I'm not complaining. Commenting. Not complaining."

Vy bopped him gently on the head. He looked up at her. "Objection withdrawn."

Bertie nodded. "You're right, it doesn't." She finished her sandwich, downed her drink. "Some things need to remain a mystery." Her eyes narrowed, and she focused on Vy. "But you and I need to have a discussion in private."

Vy gave Bertie the side-eye. "We do, hmm?" Curiosity tinged her voice.

"Yes. It's a business concern. Can we move to one of these splendid rooms you have here and talk for a bit?"

Vy rolled to her feet. "Certainly." She waved a hand to Bertie. "The billiard room is always open. None of us play billiards."

Bertie gave her a quizzical look. "Why do you have one?"

Erin chuckled. "It seemed like the thing to have."

"Uh-huh." Bertie followed Vy to the designated room off the side of the common area.

Rob watched until the door closed and then turned around. He kept his voice low. "Drugs. It's about drugs. But how did Bertie know Aunt Vy is with the DEA? I only said she's a cop."

Jeff's face scrunched into disapproval. "If her unit"—his tone expressed displeasure, with a hint of disgust—"is who I think it is, then they were probably listening to everything everyone said this week. I don't like it."

Collin reviewed Bertie's words and actions from the evening. She laid her hand on Jeff's arm. "Don't judge too quickly. She might be giving Vy information to help convict Pam of murder. Premeditated murder. And she may have saved our lives tonight."

Erin nodded. "Stepping out of the shadows when she did? I've never thought of angels as wearing face paint, but I must have been wrong." He shifted.

Sitting too long in one position hurt him. Collin asked, "You want your crutches?"

Erin shook his head and then nodded. "Yeah. Good idea."

Rob stood. He gathered the empty plates, carried them to the kitchen, and set them in the sink. Then he disappeared into Vy and Erin's suite, coming back with Erin's arm crutches. Together they brought Erin to his feet. Her brother took several steps around the room, stretching and straightening, curling and uncurling his back. He looked up at Collin and grinned. "I need the trio to walk on me."

Jeff humphed. Collin watched his eyes. They held almost a twinkle. Almost. "Individually or all at once?"

"Yes." He moved around the area, staying away from the billiard room. No chance of being accused of listening in. Discretion.

Collin noticed the laps he walked took him closer to the kitchen. She waved a finger at him. "No more food. Vy would not approve."

Erin lifted his head in disdain. "*Moi?* Never." He looked at the kitchen clock. "Not until midnight, anyhow."

He continued walking for several more minutes, and then found a wall to lean against. He hunched his shoulders, flattened them against the wall, and did slow slides up and down. A foot, maybe more, maybe less. Enough to straighten out the kinks.

Collin watched him, almost envious. Nothing kept her from joining her brother except the need to keep her world in control. Tight control. *Pam killed Tom. She tried to kill me. Was the money so important to her? She couldn't leave and be happy? I don't understand.*

She's going to let her baby take the rap for what she did. Going to send him away for years to be raised by doctors and psychologists and psychiatrists and social workers. All so she can have Tom's money?

Resolve hardened her heart. *Not if I have anything to say about it. Trinity Builders will never pay her one dime…*

She pulled up short. Did the company have the option? "Innocent until proven guilty." Yes, Bertie had the evidence to prove Pam guilty. But couldn't present it in a court of law. And without a guilty verdict, Trinity would have no choice. Pam would receive everything any other grieving widow or widower would receive. Salaries. Pensions. She could even choose to go to college, and Trinity Builders would pay for it.

Collin lowered her head to her knees and closed her eyes. *Lord, this is so hard. Let me see justice.* Her mind created the scenario of the Lord standing in front of her.

"Justice? Justice is humankind receiving the consequences for their own actions. Guilty before Me. Deserving the death penalty. All of you. Every single soul since Adam.

"But then there's Grace. Grace is getting what you don't deserve because SomeOne Else took the penalty. He suffered and died, so you wouldn't. Which do you prefer?"

"But she's guilty. She killed a man."

Jesus stood before her, holding out His hands. Pointing to His feet. Showing her His side.

Tears blurred her eyes. "I'm sorry. I'm so sorry. Forgive me. As

I forgive her. I hear You. I will. It's hard. Help me. "

"*Justice is Mine. Love is yours.* "

Collin raised her head. She wiped her cheeks against the knees of her jeans. Jeff gazed at her. She nodded, and then leaned her head against his seat. And waited.

Vy emerged once to retrieve her cell phone, and then disappeared again. After another forty minutes, Vy and Bertie came out together. Both women wore poker faces. Collin knew better than to ask.

No one else asked, either. Erin walked across the room to meet his wife. Erin looked deep into Vy's eyes. She looked into his.

Rob groaned. "Jedi mind tricks. I knew it."

Bertie grinned. "You're a fun bunch to be around in a crisis. It's almost like it's natural for you."

Jeff grumbled. "Not natural. Frequent, but not natural." He sat forward. "I take it you two reached an agreement about something?"

Vy nodded. "Yes. That's all you need to know."

He snorted. "I knew you were going to say that."

Erin chuckled. "Welcome to my world."

Rob asked, "So, are we done now? For tonight, anyhow? The police will be back in the morning to wrap things up, I'm sure." His eyes narrowed slightly. "And you'll be long gone, right?"

Bertie grinned slightly. "I don't know about long gone." She turned to Jeff. "I'd love to try one of your bedroom suites. Just for the night? Or part of it, anyhow? May I?"

Jeff lifted his hands into the air. "Oh, why not? We've got room."

Collin offered, "I've got pajamas you can borrow."

Bertie laughed. "Now you're spoiling me."

"No, I've got an impressionable son I have to protect."

Rob groaned. "Mom!"

MONDAY

Sheriff Manning shook hands with public defender Benjamin Duvall. "Thanks for coming, Mr. Duvall. I have a difficult case which needs your delicate touch." He pointed to the wooden chair beside his desk. "Have a seat."

Mr. Duvall took the chair. He laid his portfolio folder on a corner of the desk, pushing aside yesterday's coffee. "What do you have?"

"Nine-year-old who wants to confess to murdering his father." Manning floated the information over the stack of files on his desk to Duvall.

Duvall's head jerked. "What? Where's his mother? Family?" The attorney twisted his head around as if looking for someone who wasn't present.

"She's the one prompting the confession. Says he's a troubled child. She showed me the transcripts of his psych eval. Also told me of an incident with a friend's four-year-old daughter." Manning shook his head. "All of which the parents of the girl deny."

"Who do you believe?" Duvall scanned the document Manning gave him.

The sheriff laid his hands on the desk. "Listen for yourself, and you tell me. I want to talk to the boy, but I need you present."

"Is this a formal interrogation?"

"With a nine-year-old? Not a chance. It's a fact-finding session." Manning held Duvall's gaze. "I know what we're going to hear. I need someone to advocate for the boy." The sheriff shook his head. "Mostly, I need a witness."

"You're not seriously going to prosecute a boy for this, right?"

"Listen. We'll talk after." Manning stood.

Duvall followed, carrying his notepad. The men walked down

the hall to a smaller office. Sheriff Manning opened the door.

The office had no windows. A TV screen, hooked to a game console, hung on the wall. A square table with chairs placed at the other end. Milk crates of toys, a bookcase with various levels of reading material, and child-size chairs rounded out the sparse furnishings. Sam Quince sat on a couch facing the TV, furiously zapping space invaders. Deputy Barnes, in plain clothes, sat beside the boy. Competitor or teammate Manning didn't know. Both players looked up as Manning and Duvall entered.

Sam acknowledged their entrance but immediately went back to his game. Barnes stood and shook hands with Mr. Duvall. "Ben."

"Jason."

Manning motioned to the table. "Let's talk."

Jason touched Sam's shoulder. "Sam, I want you to meet Benjamin Duvall. He's going to sit with you while Sheriff Manning asks you some questions."

Duvall held out his hand. "Hello, Sam."

Sam lowered his eyes. "Hello. Are you my lawyer?" The boy didn't return the handshake. Duvall put his hand down but looked over at Manning. Manning raised an eyebrow but said nothing.

Duvall sat on the couch. "Maybe. Do you need a lawyer?"

Sam shrugged. "The sheriff said he would get me one. Mom told him I didn't need one, but he said it was the law."

Duvall smiled. "Well, Sheriff Manning is right. You should have a lawyer with you." He motioned to the table behind them. "The sheriff wants to talk to you. Let's go sit and let him ask you questions."

Sam shrugged. "Okay." He lay the controller down, got up, and followed Duvall to the back of the room. The boy took a seat across from Manning; Duvall sat beside Sam. Deputy Barnes stood beside the door.

Sheriff Manning pulled out a recording device and laid it on the table. He smiled at Sam. "I'm going to record what we say, so no one can accuse us of trying to trick you into saying something or lie about what you said. Is that okay?"

Sam looked at Duvall. Duvall nodded. Sam shrugged. "Yeah. I guess."

Manning cringed inwardly. He drew a breath and began. "What's your name? Your full name?"

"Samuel Thomas Quince."

"Thomas. Thomas is your dad's name, isn't it?"

Sam nodded. "Yeah. Brutus got it for his name first, but I got it for the middle." Sam laughed. "He said he would have put it in Wendy's name, too, if Mom would let him. She didn't."

"Brutus. He's your older brother?"

"Yeah. He's nineteen. Wendy's eighteen. Then I came along." He looked at the floor.

"I see." Manning kept his voice gentle and conversational. "Why are you here, Sam?"

"Huh?" Sam looked up, confusion on his face.

"You came in to tell us something. What is it?" Manning leaned forward, his arms crossed across the table.

The boy picked at his thumb. "I'm supposed to tell you I did it."

"Did what?" Manning raised his eyebrows.

"I put the medicine in Dad's drink."

"Who told you to tell us?" Manning kept his voice gentle.

"Mom. She said I needed to tell you what I did. I put the medicines in his drinks."

"What medicine? Your mom said he took lots of medicines." He looked at Duvall and nodded.

"The ones from her purse." Sam drew figures on the table with his fingernail.

"Do you know what they were?"

Sam shrugged and shook his head. "No." He looked up. "No, sir."

Duvall smiled at Sam. "You're fine." He patted the boy on the shoulder.

Manning looked at Duvall, and then back to the boy. "What did it look like?"

"Huh?" Again, the confused look.

"The medicine. What color was it?" Duvall shook his head, his lips drawn.

The boy rubbed his thumb. "Um…white. I think."

"How big were the pills?"

"I don't know. They were just pills." Sam looked up. "They were the ones Dad asked me to get him when he has a headache and wants to take a nap. Sometimes when he didn't want to go somewhere, he would take them, too."

"I see." Manning smiled. "Did he take them when he went fishing?"

"No. Dad likes fishing. He likes it a lot." The boy's face lit up.

"Did you like going fishing with him?"

Sam bit his thumb on the side. "He doesn't like taking me. He says I never can sit still long enough." The light went out as quickly as it appeared.

"Uh-huh." Manning sat back slightly. "So you put medicine in your dad's drink. How much medicine?"

"I don't know. A bunch of pills." The boy shrugged. He'd obviously lost interest in the questioning.

"How many is a bunch? Five? Ten?"

Sam stared at the table, and then looked at the Sheriff. "Maybe ten?"

"You think you put ten pills in his drinks?" Duvall made notes in his portfolio.

"Yeah." The boy nodded. "Maybe ten."

"Which drinks did you put them in?" Manning's gut tightened. *Hard. So hard.*

"His beer. Dad likes beer."

Manning frowned. "How did you do it?"

Sam's eyes flared. Duvall shifted in his chair. Sam shrugged. "I pulled the caps off the top."

"Did you have a bottle opener?" *One question at a time. Slowly.*

"Uh…yeah. I did. Mom had it in the drawer in the kitchen place."

"Okay, then what did you do?"

"I put the medicine in."

"Did you pour it in?" *He has no clue.* Manning shifted in his seat.

"Huh?" Sam looked over his shoulder at the video game.

"The pills. Did you drop them in one by one or pour them in all at once?"

Sam looked at the table again. "Uh…yeah. I poured them in."

Duvall's eyes narrowed, and his face hardened. He glared at Manning but smiled at Sam. "You're doing just fine, Sam."

Manning smiled as well. "Just a couple more questions, Sam. How many bottles did you put medicine in?"

"Huh?"

"Did you put medicine in more than one bottle?" *He's nine. He's just nine.*

Sam studied the floor. He looked up. "I don't know. I can't remember."

"How did you put the lids back on the bottles?"

Sam looked up at Manning. "Put the lids on the bottles?"

"Yeah. How did you get them to stay on the top?" *Especially so your dad didn't notice.*

Sam's eyes flared again. He glanced from the table to the floor and back to the table. "I don't know. I just stuck them on, I guess."

"Okay. Where was your mom when you did all this?"

"Um…out talking to Aunt Collin." Sam's eyes brightened. "She's not really my aunt. She's married to Jeff. Dad works for Jeff. I call him Uncle Jeff." Suddenly the boy became animated. "Uncle Jeff took me to the Bounce Palace! We had the best time. It was really cool. I want to go again." He became quiet. "I wish Dad would take me places." He looked at Duvall. "Maybe he will when we get back to town. He said he would spend more time with me. Maybe he'll take me there."

Manning exchanged glances with Duvall. He lowered his voice. "Sam. Your dad is dead. The medicine you put in the bottles killed him."

Sam looked up. "He's not dead. He's not. It's one of his jokes. He's always joking. He's not dead."

Duvall laid a hand on Sam's arm. "Sam, your father is dead. The pills killed him."

Sam jumped to his feet, crashing the chair to the floor. He screamed, "No! He's not dead! He can't be dead!" The boy attacked the table with his fists. Duvall tried to take hold of him, but Sam turned his attack on the attorney. "No! No! He's not dead!" He lashed with his fists, kicked with his feet, pounded with his head. Duvall held on to him, corralling him in his arms.

Manning held Duvall's eyes. The attorney gazed back, shaking his head slightly. Manning nodded. The sheriff stood, touched Barnes on the shoulder, and exited the room. He walked back to his office, sank into his chair. "Some days, I hate this job." He closed his eyes against the moisture building in their corners.

MONDAY

Life in Oakton returned to normal. At least with the triplets. Collin and Jeff made sure the trio knew none of the events after leaving the lake with Grandma and Grandpa. They did have to sit down on Monday and explain about Tom.

Collin had them come into the living room after breakfast. Jeff stayed home long enough to help her work through it with them. The bubbies all sat on their bottoms on the floor, looking wide-eyed and expectant. Collin sat in front of them on the couch. Jeff sat beside her. Collin kept her voice gentle. "Sam's daddy, Tom, went home to be with Jesus. Sam is very sad, and we need to be very helpful to him when we see him."

Caleb cocked his head. "Mr. Tom went to be with Jesus? Why?"

Collin looked at Jeff. She said softly, "Your turn."

Jeff touched Caleb's chest. "Do you remember the caterpillar we found in the spring?" Nods. Joshua crowed, "I found it! I found it on the sidewalk."

Not to be outdone, Caleb raised his hand, palm up. "I held it. It felt squiggly."

"I touched it. It felt soft." Tee's remembrance.

Jeff nodded. "Right. And what did we do with it?"

"We got a jar from Mommy's cabinet, and we put it in the jar!" "We poked holes in the lid for it to have air to breathe." "Daddy poked the holes. We're not supposed to play with nails." "And we put sticks and leafs and dirt in the jar."

The excitement of the lesson bubbled up through the children, and they all talked at once. Jeff waited and said, "Then what happened to the caterpillar?"

The trio looked at each other for several moments. Tee's face became very solemn. "It went to sleep."

Joshua bounced. "It spit stuff out of its mouth and wrapped up in a blanket."

"A cocoon. Right. Then what happened?" Jeff leaned forward to be at eye level with his children.

Again, faces looked at each other for the right memory.

Collin prompted, "What came out of the cocoon?"

Caleb jumped up and spread his arms wide. "A butterfly!" He raced around the room, flapping his wings.

Tee joined him. "It flew! We opened the jar, and it flew away. It looked so pretty."

Joshua held up his palm. "It landed on my hand. It felt tickly."

Jeff asked, "Where did the caterpillar's body go?"

Deep thinking. Tee said, "It stayed in the jar. It was all empty and gone."

Jeff continued gently. "What happened to Mr. Tom is kind of like that. He left his body here, but the Tom part went to be with Jesus. Like the caterpillar changed, we change."

Caleb's eyes grew wide. "Do we get wings?"

Joshua began flying around the room. "We get to fly!"

The trio flew around the room for a few moments until Collin called them in for a landing. "Okay, okay. Sit down again."

They sat. Tee looked pensive. "Mommy, if Mr. Tom is with Jesus, why is Sam sad?"

Collin drew a breath. *Help me with this, Lord.* She said gently, "Can we see Jesus?"

Joshua nodded. Caleb and Tee shook their heads. Joshua changed to shaking his head. Tee said, "No, 'cause He's divisible."

Collin kept from laughing. Jeff had to turn his head. "He's invisible, honey. We know He's always here with us, but we can't see Him, right?"

Caleb nodded emphatically. "Right."

"Mr. Tom is with Jesus. We can't see Mr. Tom, either. And that makes Sam sad."

Tee asked, "Can we talk to him like we do Jesus?"

"No, honey. When people go to be with Jesus, they stay with Him where He is. And we don't see them or hear them until we go to be with Jesus ourselves."

Tee's lip began to tremble. "But I want to talk to Mr. Tom."

Collin pulled the little girl into her arms. "I know, baby girl. Which is why Sam is sad. He's happy his daddy is with Jesus. But he's sad because he's going to miss him."

Joshua nodded. "I will miss him, too." Collin saw no genuine comprehension in her son's eyes. She looked to Caleb. His face scrunched into deep thought, but what the conclusion might be, she didn't know. He nodded because Joshua nodded.

Joshua had one last question. "Can we see Mr. Tom in his cocoon?"

"No, baby. We don't get a cocoon. We're not exactly like the butterfly." She stopped and dug out the tried and true, "When you're bigger, you will understand more."

Which put an end to questions. At least for the time. Collin smiled. "Everyone kiss Daddy goodbye so he can go to work."

Everyone vied to be first. Collin waited until they were done to get her embrace. She hugged him. "Try to have a good day, my love."

"It's going to feel strange. And I'll have to tell the ones who weren't there." He shook his head. "And straighten out the stories of the ones who were." He sighed. "I'll see you tonight." He picked up his pink pony lunch box and walked out.

Collin swooshed the trio off to play. They disappeared to the back. Collin picked up her Bible, sat on the couch, and whispered, "Speak, Lord." Tears filled her eyes. "Oh, Father. Please. Make it make sense." She opened the Book to Psalms and began reading.

* * *

Later in the afternoon, Jeff's phone rang. He looked at the caller ID on his desk phone. Pam. He drew in a long breath, exhaled a longer prayer, and then picked up the call. "Pam. How are the kids doing?"

"Like you'd expect. They're still both torn up about this whole thing. Losing their father, and now this murder investigation. It's terrible. They want to grieve in peace, but they can't." Pam strained with the words. "It hurts so much."

Jeff swallowed his base instincts. "I don't know what to say, Pam. I'm praying for all of you. We all are."

"I appreciate it. We do."

"How is Sam?"

Pam choked. "I haven't seen my baby since Friday. The sheriff's office kept him. They have him in some facility for juveniles with psychological issues."

"I don't understand." Truth. *Why?*

"He attacked the sheriff. Sam told me he wanted to talk to the sheriff about his dad. My poor baby wanted to know how Tom died. He wouldn't believe me when I told him. He had to talk to the sheriff. I left him with Sheriff Manning and went back to be with Wendy and Brutus. The sheriff called me and told me Sam claimed he put the medicine in Tom's beer. He confessed to the whole thing. Then he lost it and attacked the sheriff."

Jeff's gut burned. Again. "Why would you leave him there?" He didn't care if it had been an accusation, not a question. He'd passed the point of choosing his words carefully.

Pam cried. "What did you want me to do? He insisted! He begged me to let him talk to the sheriff alone."

Bitterness filled his tone. "He's nine, Pam. Nine years old. You're his mother. You're supposed to protect him."

Pam snarled, "You don't think I tried? I'm hurting, too, Jeff. Tom was my husband, my life. My whole world died with him. You don't think I cared about him? I loved that man."

The declaration sickened Jeff. He swallowed bile. Closed his eyes. Gripped the edges of his desk. *God! Help me. Fill me with You.*

Calm seeped in. He cleared his throat. "I'm sorry, Pam. I didn't mean to judge. It's hard for all of us who love your family." Jeff drew in another breath. "What can I help you with right now?"

Pam's voice evened out. "I need to know if the company will keep paying Tom's salary. I still have to support Brutus and Wendy and pay the bills. When Taylor's husband died, she said you paid off her mortgage. Will you do the same for us?"

And the hits keep coming. Lord, speak for me. I can't do this. I can't. "Pam, I've got another call I have to take. I'll call you back as soon as I can." Jeff hung up, and then sat back in his chair. He leaned forward, crossed his arms on the desk, and then dropped his head. "God, please. Please. Talk to me. Help me."

Justice belongs to Me. The time will come when every idle word will be judged. How much more will actions be measured?

Tears burned in Jeff's eyes. "She murdered him. Cold-blooded murder. And she's blaming it on her baby. How? How can she be so twisted? We love her. She watched the triplets. How? How could we not see her for who she is?"

She is My child. A Good Father disciplines His children. I will repay.

Jeff swallowed. Swallowed. Wiped his eyes on his shirt sleeves. Sat up. Breathed. Then called Pam back. "Sorry for the interruption."

"I know you have a business to run. I'm sorry to bother you."

"No, it's fine, Pam. It is." Jeff summoned all the grace he could muster. "I will talk to Human Resources and see what our policies are. I'm sure we will help you all we can."

Pam's tone shifted to anguish. "That's Erin's department, isn't it? You don't think he'll hold what Tom did against us? He won't think we don't deserve help, will he? Jeff, we need the money. My job won't hold us over—"

"Pam, Erin will do what is right." *Even when it galls him, and you don't deserve a dime, you murdering—*

He cut off the thought. "Erin loves your family. He'll make sure you're taken care of."

Pam sighed. "I'm so relieved. It takes one burden off." She hesitated. "I have to arrange for Tom's burial. I don't know where to go."

Jeff closed his eyes. "Talk to the church. They can help you more than I can."

"I hadn't thought of the church. Thank you. I'll call them." She paused. "How are the triplets? Did you tell them about Tom? Do you think they understand?"

"As much as any four-year-old can, I guess. They know he's with Jesus. Beyond that, I can't say." *Don't ask about Collin. You wanted to murder her, too. Don't ask. Don't ask. Don't...*

"How is Collin doing? Is her back going to be okay? Maybe I could come over and help her out with the trio."

Jeff swallowed hard. "She's fine. She's tough. The bubbies are being gentle with her and helping her out. We'll be fine. You concentrate on yourself and your family. You have enough."

Pam sighed. "You're right. I feel so helpless. The house is empty. I keep looking at his couch, expecting to see him lying there." She choked. "I miss him so much."

Jeff's jaw tightened. "I'm sure you do. I have to go, Pam. I'll check in on you later."

"Bye, Jeff."

He disconnected the call. He stood, rocketing his chair against the wall. His body shook. Jeff drew in a breath, walked around the desk, opened his door, and strode to Erin's office. He didn't knock. Stalked in, closed the door behind him.

Erin looked up from his desk. "What's up?" He locked eyes on Jeff's face and immediately climbed to his feet.

Through clenched teeth, Jeff demanded, "Get me out of here."

Erin grabbed his arm crutches. He punched a number on the intercom.

Rob's voice came on. "Yeah, Erin. What's up?"

"Take over. I'm outta here for a while."

"How long?"

"Until I get back."

"Riiight. Gotcha."

Jeff led the way out of the office in front of his brother-in-law. The two men walked to the service elevator at the rear of the hallway. They passed no one. Erin hit the button for the garage. Neither man spoke a word. Jeff caught Erin glancing at him, but the younger man asked no questions.

They climbed in Erin's car. Erin put it in motion and headed for the freeway onramp. A short drive through mid-morning traffic dumped them onto the beltway. Jeff lay his seat back, closed his eyes and breathed. His jaws remained locked.

Erin said nothing. He navigated the long, looping drive around the city of Oakton. Thirty- five miles, or forty minutes. Depending on how fast you wanted to go or how lucky you felt.

Twenty minutes in, Jeff lifted the seat. He breathed easier. His jaws relaxed, as did the rest of his body. He shook out his shoulders.

Erin glanced over. "Better? Alive again?"

"Yeah. Thanks."

"No problem. You want to tell me about it now or later at the Monday night meeting of the senior partners?" Meaning Jeff, Collin, Erin, Vy, and Rob.

Jeff chuckled. "During all the confusion? The triplets create more chaos than it's worth."

"Okay, the junior partners are less well-behaved, but they add life to the proceedings. Besides, Vy made a casserole and salad. I'm not eating it by myself." Erin evaded a blue sedan running up on his rear end.

Jeff glanced over. "Vy's a good cook. Why would you complain?"

"Because she's trying to get me to eat healthy. The casserole's bound to be full of broccoli and cauliflower and other vegetables I won't like. I'll eat it, but I don't want to eat it all week." A slow-moving box truck pulled onto the freeway from the shoulder, and Erin swerved to avoid it. He muttered, "A blinker would be nice. Jesus would use His blinker."

Jeff laughed. "Okay, bro. We'll have the meeting."

Erin nodded. "But you'll tell me now what precipitated the need to escape. And observe the bucolic landscape of our fair city. You didn't notice, but Varner's farm has new cows."

"I appreciate the escape. No, I didn't see the cows. Angus?"

"Holstein. Nice ones. Probably heifers." Erin loved cows.

Jeff lowered his eyes. "Pam called. She wants us to pay off her mortgage and ensure Tom's salary continues to get paid."

Erin pulled over on the shoulder and stopped. Jeff eyed him, unsure why. Erin threw the car in park. "You drive." His voice came down dry and hard.

Jeff patted the seat. "No. You drive. I'm good again."

Erin threw the car into gear, checked the mirrors, and then pulled out onto the freeway again. "What did you tell her?"

"I told her I'd check with Human Resources and let her know our company policies."

Erin dipped his head. "Nice dodge. Now, what are you going to do?"

"Check with Human Resources about company policy. I don't know if we have one specifically stating what we will do. I know we've done it, but I don't think there's a written policy."

"Hmm."

"She brought up when Billy died, we paid Taylor's mortgage." Jeff looked out the side window as they passed the Marvel Bakery. The aroma of fresh bread permeated the air.

Erin asked, "Does that create a legal precedence saying we have to for everyone?" He dodged a slow-moving truck hauling soybeans, and then pointed the car to the Billings Street off-ramp.

185

Jeff questioned, "Why are you stopping?"

"I want an ice cream."

Jeff groaned. "You are bad! What is it with you?"

"I'm having all Vy's cravings, I tell you. There's a drive-through with chocolate soft-serve. Only place in town I can get one. I'm stopping."

Erin turned off the freeway, made a left and two rights, and pulled into the drive-through. He ordered two large cones, handed one to Jeff, paid, and drove back to the freeway.

Jeff protested, "I didn't want one."

"No, but I can't eat two before they melt. Help a brother out."

Jeff growled but began licking the ice cream. Something about the child-like pleasure of eating ice cream in the car sapped the last of the anger from his soul. He relaxed muscles he didn't know were still on full alert. By the time they reached the exit for the office and downtown, Jeff had calmed down. He fist-bumped Erin. "Thanks, man. I knew there's a reason I like you."

Erin grinned, lopsided. "I take you to all the finest places." He motioned with his head. "You need to do another lap?"

"Nah, I'm good."

Erin used his key card at the garage, drove in, parked, and the two men climbed out of the car. They walked to the main elevator in the lobby and took it back to the seventh floor and their offices. Erin tapped fists with Jeff before heading to his own space. "Relax. We got this."

Jeff nodded. "I'll go talk to Abbott and then to legal. Find out what my options are."

"If we don't pay Pam's mortgage, what excuse are you going to give her?"

"I'll have to think about it. I'll let you know."

"Good."

Rob stepped into the hall. "Where'd you two go?"

Erin motioned to Jeff. "Big guy wanted ice cream. Cravings are terrible things."

"So he's getting Vy's cravings now, too?"

Erin shrugged. "Ask him." He entered his office and closed the door.

Rob eyed Jeff. "Dad?"

Jeff grinned. "Never mind. Is Abbott in his office?"

"No, he's in mine. I went to Erin's office, and Abbott went to mine. What's up?"

Jeff shook his head. "We'll talk tonight." He put his arm around Rob's shoulder. "Let's get you back to work in your own space."

"Thanks."

THREE MONTHS LATER

Vy stared at the note again. *Noon. Slatterly's. Get a booth.* The message held a signature: Bertie. What did the secretive commando want? What information did she have? It seemed so out of place for a legal secretary and mother to be transporting drugs. Why? Money? It was the usual easy answer. But there had to be more. She knew Pam. They all knew Pam. And for her to be passing drugs made no sense.

Vy had been tracking leads, and they all went nowhere. The two men who had been shot at the lake lawyered up and refused to talk. Strange they would rather go to jail than flip on a source. Which meant they were more afraid of their chain than of going to prison. This had to be a significant, powerful organization.

She walked into Slatterly's ten minutes before noon. The young woman at the podium talked excitedly to one of the servers. Both wore black pants, white button-down shirts, and blue-and-white striped ties. "You wouldn't believe how sick I got last night. We partied until three this morning. I had the worst time getting out of bed."

The female server laughed. "I'd believe it. You were dancing on the tables with every guy there. And some of the girls. I've never seen you so drunk."

Vy waited politely while the two girls talked. After five minutes of chatter, Vy leaned forward. "Excuse me?"

The young woman looked at her as if seeing her for the first time. "Yes? How many?"

"Two. And a booth, please."

The maître d' picked up two menus and handed them to the server. "Table five."

The server walked to a booth directly across from the podium. The moveable benches were covered in patched vinyl. Silverware for two graced the table, wrapped in paper napkins. The server asked, "Do you want to order before your friend gets here?"

"I'll wait. May I have a glass of water, please?"

"Lemon?"

"No, thank you."

"Sure." The girl walked back to the podium to continue the conversation.

Vy sighed. A second server brought Vy a glass of water with lemon and set it in front of her. "Hi. I'm Aria. I'll be your server today. Can I get you anything?"

Vy smiled. "No, I'll wait until my friend comes. But thank you."

She nodded. "I'll keep an eye out for her. What does she look like?"

Which posed a good question. Vy didn't know how Bertie would appear. She smiled. "It's hard to know what she'll be wearing. And she likes to surprise me with different hair colors. But she'll find me."

Aria laughed. "Oh, one of those friends. I have a few like that. You never know what they're going to change next. I had one once who—"

A manager walking by interrupted her story. "Aria, table fifteen is wondering why their order is taking so long. Will you check on it, please?"

Aria nodded. "Yes, sir." She left immediately for the back.

Vy pulled out her phone and checked her messages.

A rush of people flooded the front of the restaurant. Ten, maybe fifteen men and women in suits and ties and skirts and slacks and jackets all mobbed the podium. It looked like a stereotypical lawyer's office had come for a luncheon meeting. The group jostled and crowded and elbowed and shouldered to be first to the table. The voices were loud, raucous, and obnoxious.

Out of the crowd, an older, much older, woman stepped. She looked like she'd been run over by the mob at the front. Breathless, she leaned against Vy's table. She had tightly curled gray hair ringing her lined face. The glasses she wore had been knocked askew. Her matronly dress twisted around her. She wore an expression of weariness and embarrassment. "I am so sorry, my dear. May I sit down for just a moment and straighten out my shoes? I'm afraid they were stepped on, and I've nearly lost one."

Vy nodded. "Of course. Sit. I'm waiting for a friend, but take your time."

The woman sat down with an audible sigh. She took several moments to regain her composure and put things back where they belonged. All the while, she chattered, "It's terrible, the incivility of people these days. I remember when men would stand back and let a lady pass in front of them. When being a senior made you respected. It's terrible, I tell you. Terrible."

Vy swallowed a smile. "Yes, it is sometimes."

The woman leaned back in the booth, placing her withered hands on the surface. "Sometimes? It's all the time anymore. You can't walk across the city without getting run over. The lights at crosswalks don't stay lit long enough to make it from one side to another. When you're as old as I am, it takes longer. But no one wants to make allowances for old people. We're supposed to get out of the way and let the young people pass." Her voice cracked. She sighed again.

Vy kept her tone even and light. "What brings you out today?"

"Oh, I'm meeting my book club for lunch. We meet here every Thursday." She looked proud. "Ten years we've been coming here, meeting to discuss the latest books." The woman sighed. "Hardly anyone reads real books anymore. All they want to do is look at their phones."

Vy eyed the woman with pity. "You meet on Thursday?"

"Yes. It's getting harder and harder to make it here, but I keep coming. I must change buses three times, but I wouldn't miss coming for the world." She leaned in. "It's the only time I get out of the house since Edgar died. Twelve years in December."

"I'm sorry to hear about your loss. But today is Tuesday."

The woman's eyes opened wide. "Tuesday? Are you sure? It's Tuesday?"

Vy nodded. "Yes, I'm afraid it is."

The woman seemed to wilt. Vy wanted to reach over and hug her, but she refrained. She did pat the woman's hand. "I'm so sorry you came all this way."

The woman sat up and smiled at Vy. "Well, I suppose since I'm here, I should have lunch. Would you mind a companion? I'll pay for myself. I just miss having people to talk to."

Trapped. Now what? Maybe Bertie would stay longer than the elderly woman, and Vy and Bertie would still be able to have their talk? Vy didn't want to tell the frail woman to go away. Not after all the difficulties she'd endured to get here. Vy smiled. "Of course, you're welcome to stay." She extended her hand. "I'm Vy."

The woman smiled. "My friends call me Bertie." She winked at Vy.

Vy's eyes flared. She ordered the rest of her features not to respond. She ducked her head slightly. "Bertie. A very good name."

The woman smiled. "I like it. It's convenient. Not pompous or snooty."

"No, it's a good name. For a good woman."

"Why, thank you, Vy."

Aria came back to the table. She looked from Bertie to Vy, and then asked Vy, "Is this the friend you were waiting for?"

Vy laughed. "No. But this delightful woman and I are going to have lunch together anyhow."

Bertie picked up the menu, looked at it, and then handed it to Aria. "I'll have the senior lunch platter. But no lettuce on the burger, please. My teeth won't hold to chew lettuce. And I'll have a diet soda. I have to be so careful with my sugar. My ankles swell something awful these days."

Aria's eyes opened slightly. "Uh, okay. No lettuce. And diet soda." She looked at Vy. "What will you have?"

Vy handed the menu to Aria as well. "The tomato soup. Crackers, too, please. And the fruit bowl."

Bertie sighed. "I remember when I could eat all those crunchy fruits. I do miss them. It's hard being limited to applesauce or pureed pears."

Aria ignored Bertie's comments. "What would you like to drink?"

"Water is fine, thank you."

Aria backed away. "I'll put your orders in right away."

Vy leaned closer to her companion and lowered her voice. "You're making quite the impression."

Bertie grinned. "There's the idea. Everyone will remember the complaining old woman with the bad dentures." She pointed to Vy's belly. "How is the pregnancy going?"

"It's going. Twins. I'll be out of the field after this case."

"Good for you."

"What have you got for me?"

Bertie picked up the knife and used the reflection as a mirror to check the surroundings. "I received permission to put some people in the hills at the lake. Seems our mark makes regular trips out there. Those pillows are very popular."

Vy frowned. "I don't get it. Her running contraband doesn't make sense. She's not the type."

"Have you checked her office?"

A chill swept through Vy. "Her office? Poe, Lyman, and Wolery? They're one of the top legal firms in town."

Bertie ducked her head. "I'm only saying you might look. Mr. Wolery has a decided interest south of the border. These cheerleader pillows are all the rage down there."

"What does he have on her to get her involved?"

"That's your job to find out. My guess? He wanted the pillows made. She started making them, and then she got suspicious of the numbers and called him on it. He either threatened her, or she threatened him."

A food runner arrived with their meals. Aria followed and asked, "Does everything look right?"

Bertie smiled. "Oh, yes, thank you, dear. I will need a box for half of this. It can be my dinner tonight."

Aria smiled. "Of course, ma'am. I'll bring it with the check." She walked away.

Vy snickered. "You have this character down pat. The wrinkles are a work of art."

Bertie smirked. "Practice. Lots of practice." She cut her burger in half. "How did the murder investigation go?"

"Sam confessed."

Bertie looked up in horror. "No. They didn't pin it on him, did they?"

"The case is still open. He's in a medical facility right now. I hope they can help him get straightened round. Losing his dad has really hit him hard."

Bertie snorted. "And having your mom tell you it's your fault? Kids always think they're to blame anyhow. But to actually be blamed…" She trailed off. "Horrendous." She chewed on a mouthful of burger. "Why hasn't the sheriff's office gone after her?"

"The way I see it, they're afraid they don't have enough for a conviction. There are fingerprints from every family member on the bottles. Pam made sure everyone handled the pill bottles and beer at some time." Vy grimaced. "Our best hope is nailing her on the drug trafficking charges." Her eyes darkened. "Of course, if she turns state's evidence, she could walk with probation."

Bertie picked up a French fry. "The recordings I gave you won't help?"

"Not without being able to say how and by who they were made. Too much exposure for your unit." Vy crumbled her crackers in her soup and spooned a mouthful. "I hate it, but it's reality in this business."

Bertie chewed her sandwich. She finished the half and then worked on the fries. "Unacceptable. It is."

"It's life, Bertie. What are we going to do?"

Bertie shook her head. "I don't know. But I will do something." She winked, and her eyes twinkled. "I may have to invent a wood sprite to testify in court." She winked at Vy. "Maybe your husband's Bigfoot."

Vy chuckled. "I can almost see you in court. Good luck with it."

Bertie lost her smile. "I can't let a murderer walk. I can't. Not when I know the truth." She stared at the table. "Maybe I lose an operative. I'll have to figure out something."

They finished lunch. Aria brought the bills and the box. Vy took the receipts. "Ms. Bertie, you had such a far way to come, and you still have to get back. Let me treat you to lunch."

"Oh, I couldn't let you, young woman. I insist on paying my own way. It's what my Edgar wanted. He told me before he died, 'Bertie, I'm leaving you enough to keep you comfortable. You should never have to worry about anything.'" She sighed. "Of course, he based his idea of comfort on the economy twelve years ago. Things are so much more expensive now."

Vy swallowed the smirk. "And why I am going to pay for this lunch. I know how much things cost these days."

"Why, thank you, my dear. This has been the best day. Meeting a new friend. It's like someone planned this. I just love when stuff like this happens."

Vy nodded, her face still and solemn. "I do, too." She handed her card to Aria, who ran it at the podium and then returned it to Vy with the paper to sign.

Bertie looked in her purse. "Oh, please, let me get the tip." She pulled out a wallet, carefully took out two crisp dollars, and handed them to Aria. "Thank you so much for your wonderful service, child. You've been a delightful waitress."

Vy wrote in a tip, signed, and then handed the top copy back to Aria. "Thank you."

Aria nodded to both women. "Have a good day, ladies. Come back soon."

The women stood. Vy eyed Bertie. "Can I give you a lift anywhere?" They walked out the door into the heat and humidity. Vy extended her arm to Bertie to keep her steps steady.

Bertie smiled. "Oh, that would be such a blessing. If you could take me back to the bus stop, I would so appreciate it." They stepped off the curb into the parking area.

Vy suggested, "I could take you home. It's not a problem." Vy kept an eye out for anyone in a rush to get their food from the drive-up window.

"How sweet of you, young woman. But I live all the way across town. I wouldn't want to put you to so much trouble." Bertie took a foldable cane from her purse and locked it into shape.

"It's no trouble. Really." Vy waited for a signal from her enigmatic friend.

Bertie murmured, "My car is parked over on Rally, near the stop and rob."

Vy smiled. "I'm parked right over here." She waved to her silver van. "Let me take you."

"You are so kind, my dear. This world needs more people like you." Bertie held to Vy's arm as they crossed the parking lot, unlocked the van, and climbed in. Only after the doors were closed, locked, and the van put in motion did Bertie relax. "Whew! It's tough being old."

Vy laughed. "At least you'll have practice for later."

"Truth."

A RANDOM THURSDAY NIGHT

Rob knocked on the door of the Fields' house at seven. He wiped his palms on his jeans and ran Collin's mantras for calm in his mind. *Breathe. Relax. Breathe. Relax. Breathe. You are a child of God. You are accepted. You are loved. You are enough. Smile. Breathe.*

Rob breathed and smiled. The "relax" part took more effort. But he straightened his shoulders, lifted his head, and knocked a second time.

Selma opened the door. She wore a pullover sweater and a midi skirt and had a frozen smile. "Rob. Welcome. Come in."

He dipped his head. "Thank you, Mrs. Fields. I appreciate your hospitality letting Gabby and me work on her scholarship application."

Selma stepped back to admit Rob. "Well, she seems to need all the help she can get. I'm not sure she's ready for college."

Gabby swooped in from the hall and grabbed Rob's hand. "Hey, handsome. I'm glad you made it." Gabby dressed in sweats, casual and comfortable. If a bit sloppy.

The doorway opened into a large living room. There were overstuffed recliners, rockers, and couches lining every inch of the walls. A once-colorful but now well-worn area rug covered the wall-to-wall carpeting. Past the living room was the dining room with its fifties-era metal table. Six chairs, all with dark green seats, surrounded the table. Gabby's laptop occupied one end. She had shoved back the mountain of catalogs, papers, and notebooks, filling the rest of the table.

Gabby pulled him to the table and indicated a chair directly in front of the laptop. "Sit here. You can enter the information."

Mindful of Selma's eyes on them, Rob declined. "I'll sit beside you, and you can enter it."

"I'm not good on the computer. I'm better on the phone. Except when I have to set something up. Then it gets tedious."

"It'll go fast."

Gabby sighed. "Fine." She sat down with a thump. "Let's do this."

Rob wanted a drink of water, something to do with his hands. But Selma didn't offer, and Gabby didn't either. He put the thought away and focused on the task. "Go to Trinity's website." She typed it in. "Okay, enter your dad's department number."

Gabby looked at her mom. "What's his department number?" Selma moved to the opposite end of the table and sat down with a catalog. She didn't answer her daughter. Did she not hear?

But the simple question caught Rob off guard. "You don't know it?"

"I don't pay attention to that kind of stuff. Dad's work, not mine."

"He's never told you?" Rob kept the incredulity from his voice. Abbott had been working for Trinity nearly six years, since its inception almost.

"Maybe. I don't remember."

"Okay, then type in his department."

Gabby raised her voice. "Mom?"

Selma looked up from her shopping. "What?" Annoyance permeated her voice.

Gabby huffed. "What department does Daddy work for?" She tapped her hand on the table.

Selma looked down at her pages. "Human Resources."

Gabby typed in the information. Rob motioned to the screen. "You can fill in the rest of this screen."

Gabby typed for a few moments, and then asked, "What college?"

Rob cocked his head to one side. "What do you mean?"

"It asks me what college I'm going to."

"And?"

"Well, I don't know. I haven't made up my mind."

Rob sat back. "You need to apply to colleges you want to attend before getting the scholarship."

"That's stupid. Why can't I get the money first, and then decide?"

"Gabby, how much you get depends on where you go. If you sign up for, say, Delaware Seminary, it will cost more than St. Mary College."

"I don't want to go to a Christian college. They're too restrictive."

Selma's head came up. Her eyes burned at her daughter. Gabby noticed and shrugged. "Mom, I'm not going to Christian college. All they do is push women to become teachers, and it's not what I want to do with my life."

Selma's voice hardened. "What's wrong with teaching as a career?"

"Nothing. Except I know how much Christian schools pay, and it's nothing. I want a career where I can earn real money."

This is not Gabby Fields from the young adult group at church. This is Gabby Fields, revealed. Lord, give me wisdom.

Rob kept his thoughts to himself. "Let me tell you how the process works. I knew what I wanted to do for a career." He smiled. "I wanted to be a social worker like Mom. I knew I wanted to stay local, so I researched which schools in this state had the best programs for social studies. Found out OSU is tops around." He laughed. "Imagine. Go, Bucs." Selma rolled her eyes. *Michigan fan, right?* He continued, "And while I was in my first year, I discovered I could do more for people by switching to urban planning. Which I did." He stopped. "And all beside the point. I applied to OSU, found out what it would cost, and then applied for the scholarship."

Selma's voice carried a snide tone. "Didn't hurt Jeff and Collin adopted you, either."

Rob kept his tone even. "No, it didn't. But I didn't know they planned to until after I started college." He met Selma's gaze. "The scholarships I applied for and earned on my own."

His eyes narrowed, but only as slightly as he could. *Calm. Stay calm.*

Selma sniffed. "Affirmative Action. If Gabby were a person of color, she'd be eligible for those scholarships as well."

Rob felt his gut tighten. He countered politely. "Neither the college admission nor the scholarship forms made any reference to nationality, race, or color, Mrs. Fields. We all get in on equal footing."

Selma remained unimpressed. "I'm sure they get around those rules. They have quotas to fill."

"Racial quotas were outlawed, Mrs. Fields. The Supreme Court upheld they are unconstitutional. Race may be considered, but it can't be the determining factor." He turned from Selma to Gabby. "Do you have your high school transcript?"

She looked to Selma. "Mom? Do I?"

"If you applied to get it like I told you to, you do."

"When?"

"Just after you graduated. The school gave you a website to contact." Selma returned to thumbing through her catalog.

Gabby waved it off. "Oh, well, I can just download it."

Rob tried to swallow away the dryness in his throat. "You'll need it to fill out the college applications."

"This sounds like a lot of hassle." Gabby rolled her eyes.

Rob tried to smile. "It's how the system works."

Gabby closed her computer. "What if I don't want to go to college? What if I want a career?"

"Careers take some education. They have specialized schools for nursing, pilot training, mechanics..." Rob smiled to let her know he was joking.

Gabby laughed. "Yeah, I could see me as a grease monkey."

Rob lost his smile. "Gabby, that term is offensive to a lot of people."

She looked surprised. "Why?" Her voice held a note of incredulity.

"Because in its original use, it referred to people of color climbing around like monkeys. They meant it to be demeaning and derogatory."

"Well, I didn't mean it to be an insult. I hear it all the time."

"I'm sure people don't usually mean it, but it doesn't make it less offensive."

Selma laid her catalog down. "People today are so sensitive to every word anyone says. I can't hardly speak without offending someone about something. You people need to get over yourselves."

Think before you speak. Think long and hard. You're better than this. Choose your words carefully. Think of Abbott. Remember Whose you are.

Rob ran a thousand scenarios through his mind in a moment's time. "It'll be easier to get 'over ourselves' when people stop thinking of others as 'you people.'" He swallowed. "You're fond of saying 'God separated the nations,' and He did. But He referred to nations, not races. Keep reading the text because the verse says, 'We are all His children.' No second-class citizens. We're all His."

Selma's nose lifted ten degrees in the air. Rob ignored her and turned to Gabby. "When you know what it is you want to do, what you want to study, I can help you with the submissions. Until then, we're spinning our wheels."

The front door opened, and Abbott walked in. He saw Rob. "Hey! I know you. We had lunch together."

Rob smiled. "Yeah, we did. Worst diner in the world."

Abbott chuckled. "Absolutely right. I almost went home sick." He walked over and gave Gabby a kiss on the cheek, gave Selma a kiss on the lips, then hugged Rob. "How's it going?"

Rob looked over at Gabby. She shrugged. "It's going. I guess I need to do some work before he can help me."

"Like?" Abbott moved toward the kitchen. He looked at Rob, and then at the table, and then at Rob. "You want something to drink? We've got sodas. And water. And juice. Though I'm not sure how safe it is. I thought I saw it moving this morning."

He smiled at Selma. Her eyes continued to be narrowed. Abbott looked from Selma to Rob. "Uh, let me get those sodas. Then you can tell me what really happened."

Selma snipped. "Rob was insulted by something I said in innocence, and then accused us of being racially 'uneducated.'"

Rob didn't try to correct Selma's portrayal of the facts. He waited until Abbott returned with two glasses of ice and two cans of soda. He handed a glass and a soda to Rob. Abbott set his on the table, pulled out a chair, and then motioned for Rob to sit as well. Rob sat back down next to Gabby. He copied Abbott's pouring of the soda into the ice.

Both men took a long swig. Rob's mouth moistened. Amazing how dry it had become.

Abbott gazed at his wife for several moments. He turned to Rob. "Would you like to dispute the facts as presented, Counselor?"

Rob swallowed his smile. "Yes, sir. Gabby used the slang term, 'grease monkey.' I told her it's an offensive term and where it originated. Mrs. Fields took umbrage to the correction."

He looked at Selma. "What did you say in return?"

Selma eyed Rob with malice. "I said people were too sensitive these days."

Abbott prompted, "And?"

"That was all."

Abbott sighed. "No, it wasn't. You went on, Selma. I know you. You made some comment about 'you people,' didn't you?"

Selma turned her head away. Abbott looked at Rob. He raised his eyebrow.

Rob admitted, "I told her it would be easier to get 'over ourselves' if others didn't think of as us 'you people.'" He looked down, and then added, "I also mentioned God separated the nations, not the races."

"Ah hah! You know the verse." Abbot grinned. "Then I suppose you also know the verses that follow about us all being God's children, right?"

Rob nodded. "I may have mentioned it, yes, sir."

Abbott drained his drink, refilled the glass. "I apologize for my wife, Rob."

Selma sat up straight. "I have nothing to apologize for."

Abbott raised both eyebrows and stared at her. "You didn't offer him anything to drink, did you? I see none of your baked goods on the table like you'd put out for any of your friends." Abbott added, "Your non-'people of color' friends."

Gabby stood. "If you and Mom are going to fight, I'm going to my room."

Abbott shook his head. "No, Gabby. This will concern you, too. If you and Rob are serious about dating, you better get used to it. You can't hide in your room every time it gets heated. Or ugly. And it will."

Gabby gave an exaggerated sigh and sat back down. Abbott held Rob's eyes for several moments. He turned to Selma. "Remember Jesus and the Pharisee? 'You gave me no water for my feet, you gave me no oil for my head...' The one who loved was the one He commended. You can pretend you're doing all this in His Name, but you're liable to find yourself with the goats wondering, 'Didn't we do all these amazing things for you?' And He will say what, Selma? What's the rest of the verse?"

She glared at him but refused to answer. Abbott waited, and then finished the parable. "'Depart from me. I never knew you.' You can't love God and hate the children of God. All the children of God. Every tribe, tongue, people, and nation."

Rob watched Gabby's body language. The young woman was bored. Bored, bored, bored. Not listening. And she didn't care.

You wanted an answer. Do you see it?

Rob stood. "I think I should leave now." He held his hand out to Abbott. "Thanks, sir. I appreciate the drink and the time." He smiled with his eyes alone. "And the defense. I'll see you at work tomorrow."

Abbott stood and hugged Rob. "Bright and early."

Rob turned. "Mrs. Fields. Gabby, I'll talk to you after church Sunday night, if that's okay?"

She nodded. "Yeah." She jumped to her feet and hugged him. "You don't have to leave because of them."

"I'm not." *Trust me.* He hugged her in return, and then escaped out the door. After he climbed into the car and headed home, he laughed. "Okay, Lord. You gave me about as obvious a sign as I needed. No, Gabby and I are not compatible. Not 'cuz of her mom. Gabby's so different at church. Sunday Christians. How can people leave You at the door? I don't think I'll ever understand it." Scripture floated to mind. *He who is forgiven much loves much. He who is forgiven little loves little.* Rob nodded. "Yeah. I know what I am without You. And I don't ever want to be that person again."

He drove the rest of the way home singing.

* * *

Sunday evening the young adult group had a guest speaker. Pastor Gregor and his wife, Zelena. They were missionaries to "closed" countries, countries where the Gospel of Jesus is forbidden to be taught.

Gregor smiled and pulled up videos. Gabby sat next to Rob and muttered, "Great. Home movies." Rob shifted in his seat. *Lord, give me the words.*

Gregor pointed to the screen. "We draw a crowd. We have musicians who will set up on a street corner. Nothing illegal about music. Then our dancers will step in." Young men and women, younger than many in the young adult group, stepped out in unison on the screen. Folk dance. Break dance. Gymnastic dance.

The crowd around them grew. On the side of the road, an artist began painting a picture. But one of those upside-down pictures you can't really see what it is until it's finished. High-flying acrobats came next. And still, no one in the group spoke. The audience on screen became enthralled. And involved. Cheering. Clapping.

Gregor nodded. "Yes. We draw them in. Our musicians take a break, and we talk to them about God." He looked around the room. "Not about Jesus. We cannot use His Name. But we can share what God has done for us. We use our gifts from God, and we speak of Him."

Basketball players came out in the street. Gabby sat forward. Rob watched her out of the corner of his eye. Something caught her attention. A remarkable display of dribbling, passing, shooting...the ball popped and sang and flew. All in synchronized rhythm. Gabby's eyes widened. She whispered, "That's amazing. Watch!"

She turned to him. Rob saw a spark of life in Gabby he'd not seen before. *She does have passion. Lord, use it. Your will, Father. You've used less, I know.*

Gregor pointed out individuals passing around in the crowd. "You see these men?"

Someone quipped. "Taking up a collection?"

Gabby turned and glared at the speaker. "Not funny, Craig."

Gregor shook his head. "Secret police. They come to make sure we do nothing subversive like mention Jesus. They check our literature to ensure we have no contraband Bibles or pamphlets. We cannot publicly speak His Name."

He smiled. "But we can invite anyone interested in learning more to a picnic in the hills the next day." He nodded. "There, outside of the city, we can share freely. From a crowd of a hundred like this"—he pointed to the watching audience—"we may have twenty or thirty come to the picnic. And of those twenty, we may have two or three who ask to learn more about Jesus."

A girl gasped. "Two or three?"

Gregor nodded. "Sometimes none. Then, like the disciples, we pack up and move on to the next town."

"All that, for two people?"

"Who pays for all this?"

"How long do you go out?"

"Where do all your people come from?"

"What happens if they catch you with a Bible?"

Questions were thrown from all sides. Gregor waved the group down. "One at a time. I will answer all I can. Who pays for this? We do. The performers. The people on the tour. Each one pays for his or her own expenses. They have to raise funds to be able to go."

"What does a hotel cost?"

"Hotel? We don't stay in hotels. We sleep in our vans. Sometimes churches, where churches are still allowed, will open and let us sleep on their floors. But we live on the road."

"We go out for several weeks at a time. We will plot a route on a map with towns close together. Sometimes we have contacts in the towns who will give us information. Sometimes we go in faith the Lord wants us in a certain place."

Rob raised his hand. "What happens if you're found with contraband? Or the authorities decide they don't like your message?"

"Most often, we get shut down and told to leave town. We've been arrested and given twenty-four hours to leave the region." Gregor smiled. "Sometimes we're driven to the border."

He pulled up a photo on his PowerPoint. A fierce-eyed man glared from the screen. He looked massive. "This is the mayor of a town we visited last summer. He did not approve of our show." Gregor's eyes twinkled. "He shut our power down and told us to leave town."

He pulled up another picture. A uniformed man, badges on his chest. A white band across his shoulders. "This is the police chief. He told us we could set up in the park outside of town. And he would run the electricity from the police station."

Gregor tapped the projector. "If God wants our show to go on, nothing and no one will stop it. 'If God is for us, who can be against us?' Many are. But His will prevails."

More questions. More answers. And finally, the question, "Why? Why do you do all this for one or two people?"

Gregor looked around the room. "Think back to when you first learned about Jesus. Where would you be if the person who spoke to you thought, 'It's only one person. They aren't important. I'll go where I can have a large audience and reach more.'" Gregor moved his finger back and forth through the air. "Where would you be if the one never spoke to you?"

Silence filled the room. Gregor nodded. "That is why we go. One person is as precious to the Lord as a hundred. He left the ninety-nine, remember?"

Pastor Jamison broke up the meeting. "We have snacks and beverages in the back. I'm sure Gregor and Zelena would love to meet you individually if you have the time."

The group dissipated, separating off into twos and threes. Gabby pulled on Rob's sleeve. "I want to talk to Gregor."

Rob nodded. "Sure."

They had to wait about twenty minutes, but Gabby refused to leave. She stood in line, shifting from foot to foot, waiting her turn. Gabby stepped forward when the young man in front of her finally moved away. She clasped hands with the missionary. "Thank you for coming. Thank you for showing us those pictures. The basketball demonstration. I've never seen anyone use sports...or the arts...as outreach. It's so amazing." She stopped. "Do you have people from this country in your troupe? Or is it only people from Europe and Asia? From the closed countries?"

Gregor's face grew serious. "We welcome people from everywhere. It is more difficult for an American because of the language barrier. Most of our people come from different countries and diverse regions, but there is usually a common 'base' language they can make sense of. And most Europeans can speak more than one language." He smiled. "But it doesn't disqualify anyone. If you believe the Lord is calling you to the field, pray about it. Then contact me." He handed her a card. "And we can always use prayer warriors. Some people go by staying behind."

Zelena laid her hand on her husband's arm. "You would stay and talk all night. But we must be going, dear. Thank you for coming." She shook hands with Gabby and Rob, and then led her spouse off.

Gabby and Rob drifted towards the patio and the firepit. Gabby pointed to two chairs away from the usual group. "Let's sit over there."

They pulled two chairs close together so they could talk. Rob eyed Gabby closely. Her eyes were guarded. He touched her hand. "What is it, Gabby? Something is bothering you."

She looked off to the side of the patio into the dark. "I can't date you, Rob." She looked up and held his eyes. "I can't. It's not right."

Rob's gut checked. "What do you mean?" *Listen. Hear.*

Gabby stared into the dark again. "Daddy had a long talk with Mom and me after you left the other night. All about where our allegiance lies." She shrugged. "Mom's is to her prejudice. The things she'd been taught all her life. She picked them up without ever examining if they were true or not."

Gabby turned to look Rob in the eyes. "I sat right there, piling on her. Yea, Daddy, you're right. Mom never thought about what she believed. She just believed it because someone told her to." She made a fist and passed it in front of her chest. "Go, Daddy."

Gabby hung her head. She leaned forward. "Then he got to me." Gabby went wide-eyed. "Me? What did he mean? I'm not like Mom."

The young woman shook her head. "Or am I? You challenged me about it one time. The things I said in church weren't the things I said at home. I said things because that's what I was taught to say."

She stared at the ground. "Things like, 'I'd follow Jesus anywhere.' 'I give Him control of my life.' 'He's my everything.' All those wonderful platitudes. And I didn't mean any of them."

She looked at Rob. "I said them. I believed I meant them. But I didn't. Not deep inside." A tear dribbled down her cheek. Rob brushed it away. Gabby continued. "I know Daddy's faith is real. I see Jesus in Him. He lives it. He breathes it. But I passed it off as 'extreme.' I figured you didn't have to be fanatical about it."

She shook her head again. "Then I spent the week at the lake with you and saw it in your family, too. Funny thing, though, you guys never talked about it like it was something special. I mean, Mom always makes it seem like she's something special because she reads her Bible or goes to church. Like the Lord owes her something because of it. But your family…"

Her face lost expression. "When your uncle got punched out, all of you were more concerned about what Jesus would do than you were anything else. I mean, who even thinks that way?" She touched his hand. "Collin gets shot, and your dad is broken up but is still trying to follow what would Jesus do? I kept thinking, 'Who are you people?'"

Rob started to speak but stopped. *Listen.*

"The real question I should have asked is, who is this Jesus? I realized I don't know Him. Not like you do. Not like your folks do. Not even like my dad does."

She gazed off again. "I need to know Him. I need Him to live down in my soul, in my heart and head, like He does in you. Until I do, we can't date. It's not right, and it's not fair to you."

Rob picked up Gabby's hand. "I've liked you, Gabby. You're bright and smart and beautiful." He paused, gathering in thoughts. "It takes a wise person to admit they don't know something. I'm proud…" He stopped. "That's not the word I want, but I can't think what it is." He grinned at her. "I'm not happy you don't love Jesus. But I'm happy you realize you need to. And want to."

He leaned in and kissed her cheek. "Anything I can do to help you in your search, I'll be there."

Gabby kissed him on the cheek back. "Wait for me."

"Always." Rob looked around, saw the coast clear, and leaned in for one full-mouth kiss. Gabby returned it.

He sat back. "I need to go home." He stood, pulled her to her feet. "So do you. I won't bug you. I'll wait for you to call me."

She nodded. "I think that's best." She hesitated. "I love you, Rob."

"I love you, Gabby."

They walked away, holding hands until neither could touch the other any longer.

A FRIDAY AFTERNOON

"Vy, report to my office."

Vy rolled her eyes. 4:55 p.m. on Friday afternoon? Really? Anytime Deputy Director Varner summoned someone to the office at that time meant nothing good. She stacked the papers on her desk neatly, shoved them into her top drawer, and locked it. Vy pushed back from her computer and looked down at her swollen ankles. She whispered, "Hang in there. We've got two more weeks, and then you can stay elevated for the duration. I promise."

Vy stood, straightened her tunic, and walked to the director's office. She knocked.

"Enter."

Vy entered, and then stopped at the director's desk. "You called, ma'am?"

"Sit, Agent Johnson."

Vy shifted her weight. "Ma'am, will this be a more-than-a-minute-or-two meeting? Because if it's not, I prefer to stand. Getting up and down can be more trouble than it's worth."

Director Julia Varner smiled, and then swallowed it. "Understood. Trust me." She motioned to the chair. "You'll want to sit for this one, Vy. You're not going to like what I have to say. It'd be better for you to take it sitting."

Vy's eyes narrowed. She sat. This would not be good. "What is it, director?"

"The case you're pursuing? With Attorney Wolery?"

"Yes…" Vy drew it out. She had a bad feeling about this. Besides the hardness of the chair and the protests of the babies in her womb. They definitely had opinions when she sat.

Varner locked eyes with Vy. "You will immediately cease all

investigations into the matter. The case is closed."

Vy sat back. Stunned. She took a moment. "Is there a why to this?"

"Beyond orders? No. Except they didn't come from this office."

"Or this department?" Bile rose in Vy's gut.

"You could safely assume that, yes." Varner continued to keep her eyes locked on Vy.

Vy lowered her eyes and pulled herself together. She nodded to Varner. "Very good, ma'am. I'll inform my team." She swallowed the bitterness. "We were so close."

Varner's tone softened. "I know you were. Which is why this call came down." She shook her head. "There is no consolation, I know. Start maternity leave early. Today. You deserve it."

Vy stood. "Thank you, Director." It did no good to rage or argue. The director didn't make these decisions. They had to come from someone much higher up the food chain. Someone with a reputation—or ally—to protect. Vy shook hands with her boss, turned, and walked out the door. She went back to her desk. Vy gathered her purse, jacket, and her carryall.

She shared the down elevator with a crowd of agents headed home for the weekend. The conversation kept her from focusing on what had just happened and its implications. Once in her car, Vy pounded the steering wheel. "No! Lord Jesus, no!" Pam would walk free.

Vy pulled out her phone and texted, *Case terminated. No consequences.*

Five minutes later, the reply came through. *Lunch. Tomorrow. Same same.*

Heard. Vy put the car in gear and headed home.

* * *

Noon at Slaterly's on a Saturday proved little different than a weekday. Vy smiled at the thought of how Bertie might appear. *She could look like herself, and I wouldn't know.*

Faces could change, but height and weight were more difficult to fake. Vy eyed each new customer with a critical eye, trying to guess which one would approach her booth. No one fit the bill.

Until an old gentleman in a shabby suit shuffled over. He had gray hair falling in wisps below his hat. His face had deep lines and dark age spots. He looked at Vy. Or looked at the booth. When he saw Vy, his face wrinkled in sorrow. Tears trickled from the corner of his eyes. He hobbled to her table. His voice trembled. "Excuse me…I'm so sorry. May I sit for a minute? I won't bother you. It's…" He sobbed a moment. "This was our place. Every Saturday at noon, we'd come here."

Vy moved to stand. "I can find another table."

He waved her frantically down. "No, no. Please. I just want to sit here for a moment. Honestly. It helps keep my memory clear. I never want to forget Tom."

Vy sat back down. "Please, sit. Tell me about Tom." *You are good, woman. I need to learn your secrets. After I get past being a whale.*

The gentleman carefully worked his way into the booth, grunting and moaning as he settled across from Vy. He took off his hat, revealing a half-bald head. He reached out his hand.

It was callused, hard, and dry. "I'm Robert."

"Nice to meet you, Robert. I'm Vy."

"Thank you for indulging a sentimental old man."

A server came to the table. "I'm Taggart. I'll be your server today. What can I get started for you?"

Vy smiled at Robert. "What did you and Tom have?"

Robert teared up again. "He always had the fish. Tom loved fish." He looked down, wiped his eyes. "I had the BLT." He looked up at the server. "I'll have the fish and chips."

Vy nodded. "In honor of Tom." She sighed. "Too much grease. I'll have the penne pasta."

"And to drink?"

Robert said, "Lemonade."

"Just a water is fine." Taggert left.

Robert sat back slightly. "Should I ask?"

Vy scowled. "We got too close to someone with pull. Shut the case down cold."

Robert let out a disgusted sigh. "I hate politics." He stared out the window several moments. "I hate letting a murderer walk even more." He turned to face Vy. "I have to live with myself. I can't let this go."

"What are you going to do?"

Robert raised his eyebrows. "Talk to the sheriff. See what we can work out for testimony. If he doesn't have enough to get a conviction, written testimony may not help, either. Someone will have to appear in court and swear to what we heard."

"You'd lose an operative."

"Or career. I've been thinking about early retirement as it is."

Vy sat back. "You'd do that?"

Lunch arrived. After the plates had been set down and accepted as "Everything looks fine," Robert lifted a piece of breaded fish. He saluted Vy. "To Tom."

Vy lifted a fork covered in penne. "To Tom."

Both chewed silently. Patrons mingled in the aisle, waiting to be seated. College football filled the big-screen TVs turned to be viewed from any angle. Voices cheered or booed from the bar, depending on the play's outcome. Servers walked past with trays laden with beer and other beverages.

Robert swallowed. "Wouldn't you?"

Vy dipped her head to the side. "If it came to it, yes. I love what I do, but…"

Robert nodded. "But you have to make a stand. This is the hill I'll die on, I guess."

Vy chuckled. "You can always get a job as a make-up artist in Hollywood. You'd be a natural."

Robert smiled. "Possibly."

Vy added, "We're always on the lookout for good operatives."

"I think my government days are over."

"Trinity Builders would hire you."

"For what?" Robert chuckled. "I'm not exactly a carpenter."

"We'd hire you because you're an honest individual with principles." Vy smiled. "And you know how to negotiate difficult terrain."

"I hear the benefits package is sweet." Robert grinned.

"It is." Vy consumed more of the pasta. The twins didn't seem to mind the tomato sauce. At least they weren't objecting. Yet.

Robert started in on the fries. "They have the best fries in the city, I think."

"You come here for the fries?"

"Why else? They recognize my cast of characters, so they don't think anything about me coming. And they're central to all my escape routes. It works."

Vy swallowed her water. "If you do retire, will we get to meet the person behind the mask?"

"You'd want to? I'm not part of your church set."

"So? We have non-church friends. We're sort of equal-opportunity folks. We like to accept people for who they are."

"You're definitely an equal opportunity crowd, I'll give you that."

Vy chuckled. "Well, family is as family does. We hang together as a bunch."

"It shows." Robert finished his meal. "I hate to eat and run, but if I'm going to do this, I need to get with Manning before he does something stupid or foolish or official. Whatever."

Vy nodded. "Understood. I'll get the check." She chuckled. "Loved the two-dollar tip. So perfect for your character."

"Older people. You gotta love 'em." Robert slipped three twenties out of his jacket pocket. "Leave him the rest. He's got kids at home."

Vy smiled. "You're a good man, Robert."

He slipped back into character. "Thank you for humoring me. I truly enjoyed today. Almost as much as if Tom had been here." Tears moistened his eyes again. "He would have loved talking with you. I'm so sorry you never got the chance to know him."

Vy patted Robert's hand. "I am, too. You have a good rest of your day, sir."

He put his hat on, tipped it to her, and then slowly crawled out of the booth and trudged out of the restaurant. Vy watched him come around the corner and pass by the windows. He continued his slow shuffle down the street, crossed with the light, and then disappeared into the crowd of walkers.

Vy finished her pasta. Taggart came back by. "Is there anything else I can get you?"

"No, thank you. It was delicious."

The server looked around. "Did Robert leave already?"

"Yes, he had another appointment."

Taggart nodded. "The cemetery. He always goes after he comes here. Makes his visit to the city complete, he says." The server nodded. "It's nice to see such devotion in a couple."

Vy lifted her chin a bit. "Yes, it is. They must have had a special relationship."

"I guess."

Vy handed him the money. "Robert said to leave this for you. He said you have children at home."

Taggart shook his head and stuck the money in his server's book. "He always leaves me a generous tip. And he rarely orders anything. He's a great old man."

"Agreed." Vy stood. "Have a good day, Taggart."

"You too, ma'am."

Vy walked out.

A FEW MONTHS LATER

Collin moved the sheet cake around the white-covered table to ensure it sat centered. The OSU motif with the representation of the "Shoe" in the center seemed off-kilter. Punch bowl to the left, pretzel, nut, cracker bowl to the right. Plates on the end. Napkins and forks at the other end. Accessible from both sides. Did she need a candle? Flowers?

They're going to college. Not a birthday. Not a wedding. Keep it simple.

Collin sighed. It had to look right. Like someone cared. Like someone loved Wendy and Brutus and was proud of them for deciding to attend college. Pam had opposed the idea. Their mother felt they should wait another year. Maybe two. It would give them all time to adjust to life without Tom. It would help her heal from his loss. She needed this time with them.

Except they had waited. Waited out the fall/winter semester. It had been six months since Tom's death—murder—and Pam wasn't ready to move on. Wendy and Brutus were.

Jeff stomped in from shoveling snow off the sidewalk. He brushed the sleet and ice off his shoulders in the kitchen. Collin scolded, "Not in here. Go out in the garage and do that."

Her husband retreated, grumbling, "But it's cold out in the garage."

"You'll live. I don't want people sliding on the wet spots."

Jeff's voice floated in through the door. "I'd wipe it up."

Talitha danced in from her bedroom. "Is the party ready? Can we have cake?" Gretchen, the German Shepherd, danced along with her.

"Not yet. Not until everyone gets here."

Caleb and Joshua raced in. "I beat!" "Uh-uh. I did."

"Mom? Who beated who?" The boys wrapped themselves around her legs, waiting for her decision.

"You tied. You both won." Collin untangled her offspring from her feet.

Joshua muttered, "I won first."

Collin eyed her son. "Excuse me? A tie means you both arrived at the same time. There is no 'first.'"

He hung his head. "Yes, Mommy."

Caleb pointed to the cake. "See the cake, Joshua? See it? It looks like the shirt Daddy has on."

Talitha examined the dessert carefully. "Where does it say 'Go Bucs,' Mommy?"

Collin pointed to the lettering around the sides of the cake. "Right there. See? 'G-O' spells Go."

Joshua pointed to the next word. "And that says Brutus."

Collin smiled. "No, honey. It says 'Buckeyes.' Then it says Brutus and Wendy."

Tee sat on the floor. "Do they have to go far away to college?"

"No, honey. Ohio State is across town. We drive past it whenever we go see your aunts and cousins in Indiana."

Caleb nodded deep. "Right. We see the Shoe, don't we, Mommy?

"We see the stadium, yes."

Gretchen sniffed at the table. Collin caught the dog's eye. "You do, you die, dog. Go lay down." Gretchen huffed, but lay down in the kitchen on her dog bed.

Jeff walked back into the family room. "I don't know why I bothered shoveling the walk. It's still snowing. It's gonna be ice tonight."

"You can put out salt later." Collin shifted the cake one last time. She hoped. She looked at the clock. "You think Vy and Erin will really come? Bringing the babies out in the cold like this?"

Jeff kissed Collin. "Erin will be a wreck, but Vy will insist. She's wanted the trio to meet their newest cousins."

Caleb looked up sharply. "Cousins? We get to meet the babies? Uncle Erin's babies?"

Collin cleared her throat. "I think Aunt Vy had something to do with those babies, too."

Tee laughed. "They're Uncle Erin's babies during the day, and they're Aunt Vy's at night."

Collin narrowed her eyes. "Did Uncle Erin say that?"

Tee nodded. "Yes." Her face became serious. "Why did Uncle Erin say not to tell Aunt Vy?"

Jeff chortled and picked up his youngest. He kissed the girl. "Uncle Erin says things he thinks are funny, but Aunt Vy might not think so."

Tee held her daddy's face between her hands. "Will she be mad at him?"

Collin carried a punch ladle out from the kitchen. "She'll pretend she's mad, but she won't really be."

Joshua jumped in front of his father. "Pick me up, Daddy."

Jeff set Tee on the floor and picked up his son. "There. Now you're up. What are you going to do about it?"

Collin pointed away from the table. "Roughhouse over there. I don't want anything knocked over."

Jeff dropped Joshua's head down while holding on to his legs. Joshua squealed, "I'm upside down!"

"Do me, Daddy!" "Do me, Daddy!" Gretchen bounded into the family room to supervise the play. And make sure none of her babies got hurt.

Collin left the commotion to finish setting out the galvanized tubs with ice and sodas. A second bowl with chips joined the table. *Dip. Don't forget the dip.*

What else? What am I forgetting?

Presents. The presents. They'll need their hoodies. Can't start school without the hoodies.

Or the lunch boxes. Again, gifts chosen by the trio. Collin had supervised the selection. She did not want Wendy and Brutus embarrassed on their first day of school. The boys selected a box shaped like a football. Tee found a soccer ball lunch bag for Wendy. The trio had been so happy with their choices. Hopefully, Wendy and Brutus would be just as happy. Or at least act like it.

The backdoor opened. Erin and Vy walked in carrying a baby carrier apiece. The trio immediately left their father and stormed the rear entrance. "Uncle Erin!" "Aunt Vy!" "Did you bring the babies?"

Erin had one arm crutch and struggled to get in the door. Jeff swooped in, took the baby carriers from Erin and Vy, and expertly set them on the table. Blankets covered the contents. The trio stood back, eyes wide, waiting to see what their aunt and uncle brought.

Collin hugged her brother as soon as he stabilized in the kitchen. He grinned. "I've been replaced in their affection." Gretchen slipped in and stuck her nose in his hand. He patted her head. "At least the dog still loves me."

"Once the newness wears off, they'll go back to you. Or if someone starts crying." Collin turned and kissed Vy. Her sister-in-law looked happy. Tired but happy. "How is it going, Vy?"

Vy sank onto a kitchen stool at the center bar. "It's going. I don't know how you did it with three."

"I had help, remember? Erin and Jeff were here."

Vy snorted. "Erin's with me, too, but still...." She smiled. "I'm blessed. They're not bad babies. They're just busy babies. Awake babies."

Collin hugged her. "Those are the worst kind, I know." She held out her arms. "Coats?"

Vy shrugged out of hers. Erin followed suit. Collin took them, and then handed them to Jeff. "Spare room."

Jeff bowed. "Yes, ma'am. Of course, ma'am." He called over his shoulder, "Don't unwrap anything 'til I get back. I want to see the unveiling."

Having made her rounds, Gretchen returned to her bed to keep an eye on everyone.

Tee tugged on Erin's sweater. "Uncle Erin, did you bring the babies?"

Erin looked at Vy, horror on his face. "Vy? Did we forget to bring the babies?"

Vy played along. "I thought you brought them."

"No, I thought you brought them!"

Tee's eyes clouded, and her lip stuck out. "No one brought the babies?"

A squeak sounded from under the blanket. All three triplets spun around to stare wide-eyed at the baby carriers. One of the blankets moved. A weak cry protested from the second seat. Gretchen's ears perked up.

Jeff raced back into the room. He had his phone out, ready to take pictures. Erin leaned the first seat forward. "Bubbies, meet your cousin Geoffrey-with-a-G George Winger." He pulled the cover off.

Three faces froze in awe. Three voices all exclaimed, "Ooooo…" "He's so little." "Can we touch him?" Erin picked the boy up. Collin held her hands out, wagging her fingers. "Give me, give me, give me." Erin passed the infant to his sister.

Collin cuddled the infant to her shoulder and hugged him. "Hey, little one." She bounced him up and down slowly in the peculiar mother's dance to soothe a child.

Erin pulled the cover from the second carrier. "And this is Caitlin Evelyn."

Again the absolute awe from the triplets. Erin passed her to Jeff. The trio whispered derivatives of "Can we hold them?"

Jeff instructed, "Go sit on the couch."

A mad stampede followed, and three bodies jumped onto the couch and sat perfectly still with their legs straight out in front of them.

"Sit quietly. I'll put them in your laps. You may touch their hands, but not their heads. I don't want your hands up around their eyes. Got it?"

Three nods. Three voices echoed, "Yes, Daddy."

Jeff and Collin placed the twins in the triplets' laps. The twins wiggled and stretched. The triplets watched on in wonderment. Geoffrey yawned. Tee laughed. "He yawned, Daddy!"

Caitlin opened her eyes. Caleb whispered, "She sees me." He looked at his father. "Can she see me?"

"She sees you. She doesn't know what you are, but she sees your shape."

Joshua—bold, fearless Joshua—held Geoffrey's hand. Tears ran down his face. Collin's son looked at her. His voice warbled as he sobbed, "He's so tiny. How can he be so tiny?"

Gretchen came to investigate. She sniffed each infant, and then retreated to the kitchen. Apparently, they smelled like babies. And she had enough practice to know.

Jeff got one picture before one of the twins interrupted the beautiful moment with a loud passing of gas and probably more. The triplets giggled. "One of them farted!"

Erin got up. "Might be my son." He picked up the infant, held him in the air, and sniffed the baby's rear. "Yep, this one."

He carried the offending party to the kitchen table, laid out a changing cushion and blanket. He turned. "Anyone mind?"

Jeff waved him on. "Go right ahead."

Caitlin decided she didn't want to be left out of the changing party. Again the triplets giggled. Tee held her nose. "Mommy, she smells bad!"

Vy started to climb to her feet, but Collin waved her off. "I'll get this one. You rest."

"I am not going to argue with you." Vy sank back down on the stool.

A knock sounded on the door. Jeff called, "Come on in!"

Abbott, Selma, and Gabby Fields entered. Selma saw the twins and cooed. "Oh, babies!" She looked at Vy. "May I hold one of them?"

Erin chuckled. "When we get one clean, you can have it."

With her superior experience, Collin beat her brother to the finish. She handed the infant girl to Selma. "This is Caitlin."

Selma kissed the infant on top of her head. "You are just the most precious thing." She held the baby back to look at her. "Yes, you are. You're beautiful. You know that?"

Collin watched Erin and Vy exchange proud, knowing looks. Erin shrugged. "For a mixed-race baby, she's okay. Maybe if she looked more like me..."

Selma cut him off. "You hush. This baby is beautiful as she is. If she needs to look more like one of you, it should be her mother. There's the real beauty in the family."

Vy smiled. "Why, Selma. Thank you."

Selma ducked her head slightly. "I'm a fool, but I can admit I'm wrong." She looked at Vy. "Forgive me."

"Forgiven."

"Good, because I hope someday, if I ever have a grandchild, it will look as beautiful as these two."

Abbott looked around. "Where is Rob?"

Jeff said, "He called. He's on his way." The Fields family went into the family room and made themselves comfortable on the various couches and chairs available for sitting. Jeff handed sodas around, and then looked outside. "Speaking of, here he is now."

The overhead garage door opened. Collin waited until she heard the kitchen door open to call, "Brush the snow off outside."

Rob called back, "Yes, ma'am. Yes, ma'am. I ain't never come in this house out of the snow before."

Collin kissed his cheek as he entered. "Hush you. Don't backtalk your mother."

"Never." He kissed her in return. "I saw the Quinces pulling up. They'll be in in a minute." Gretchen stretched and rose from her bed. She trotted over to Rob's side. He reached in his pocket and pulled out a chew bone. "Here you go, girl. Glad to see you, too." The shepherd returned to her bed with her prize.

Collin chuckled. "Good. The triplets have been eyeing the cake all afternoon."

Rob looked around. "Where's the ice cream? What's a party without ice cream?"

Caleb and Joshua raced in. "Rob!" "Rob!" He swung one up, and then the other. "Hey, bubbies. What's going on?"

Tee joined them, and all three chattered at once. "We saw the babies!" "They're so little!" "They pooped their diapers." "Uncle Erin had to change one of them." Tee held her nose. "It smelled bad."

Rob chuckled. "That's what babies are like." He walked over to fist-bump his uncle Erin. And take Geoffrey-with-a-G off his hands. He took the baby into the family room and acknowledged Abbott and Selma with a smile. He sat beside Gabby and grinned. "I got one."

Gabby hip-checked him. "I'll get the other one when Mom gives her up."

The front door opened. Brutus stuck his head in. "Is there a party going on here?"

Jeff called, "There is now. Come on in."

Brutus and Wendy made their way in and passed hugs to all present. Moments later, Pam walked in. Collin read her eyes. She wore a trapped look in them, one that said, *"I don't want to be here, and I'm not happy, but I'll pretend I am. Unless I can make a scene. And I might."* Collin moved to her and smiled. "I'm glad you came, Pam. It means a lot to Brutus and Wendy to have you here."

Pam almost sneered but avoided it by a hair. "What could I do? Stay home? My children are going to college. This should be the best time of their lives. You think I'd ruin it for them?"

Well, since you mention it, yes. If you could. But they're adults and doing what adults do. Making their own decisions.

Wendy moved deeper into the room and saw the decorated table. She squealed. "Mom! Look at this cake!" Her eyes shone with joy. "It's perfect! Aunt Collin, where did you find someone to do this?" She turned to face Collin.

Collin smiled broadly. "I'm glad you like it. I called around." *And around and around. Until I found the* one *bakery that could do it right.*

Wendy grabbed Brutus's arm. "You have to look at this. It's the Shoe! It's perfect!"

Brutus hugged Collin, his face undecided between tears and smiles. Smiles won. "Thank you, Aunt Collin. You don't know what this means."

I think I do. I really think I do.

The trio bounced around, talking to everyone, hugging everyone, chattering, and laughing. Tee asked Brutus, "Where is Sam? Did he come, too?"

Brutus kneeled down. "No, Tee. Sam is still at the special school. He came home at Christmas for a while, but he had to go back to school. Just for a little bit longer."

Tee hung her head. "I miss Sam."

Brutus hugged her. "I do too, Talitha." He patted her head. "He really loves those letters and pictures you send him. They make him happy."

She brightened. "I'll make him some more. And I have some for you and Wendy when you go to school."

Caleb bounced beside his sister. "You want to see what we got you? Joshua and I picked it out special just for you."

He started to drag Brutus from the room, but Jeff caught the little boy's hand first. "Whoa, there, Caleb. No giving away the presents. We're going to talk first, and then we'll get out the presents."

"And have cake?" Tee had a one-worry mind.

"Yes, darling. And we'll have cake. Come on." Jeff led the littles back to the family room and the couch. Everyone else moved to the family room and found seats.

Rob passed Caitlin to Gabby for a snuggle. Geoffrey was lateralled to Pam. She kissed him, and then handed him back to Erin. Collin intercepted the infant. "Mine."

Jeff held up his hand. "Everyone have punch or a soda?" Cups were lifted. "We invited you all here to share in the joy of Brutus and Wendy starting school next week." He smiled at the Quince teens. "I'm proud of you two. It's been a tough six months. You're turning a new leaf—"

Erin quipped, "A Buckeye leaf."

"—a Buckeye leaf on your lives. Brutus, what is your major as it stands now? And no, we won't hold you to it for the next four years."

General chuckles. Abbott leaned over and murmured to Collin, "I had five of them the first year."

Selma laughed. "And three more the second."

"Never let it be said I wasn't a man who knew my own mind."

Brutus smiled. "After careful consideration"—he grinned at Erin—"and two out of three throws of a dart, I've narrowed it to marine biology."

Applause. Joshua looked up at him. "What's that?"

"I'll study what's in the ocean."

Caleb said brightly, "Sharks!" He bounced on his bottom. "Baby shark, do do do do do…"

Jeff interrupted before a full-blown chorus could begin. "We get the idea. There are more things in the ocean than sharks."

He held up his hand to prevent a recitation of other creatures under the sea. "Wendy, what about you?"

She chewed her lip. "I can't decide. I'll do general studies until I can make up my mind."

Pam spoke quickly. "You could as easily wait out the year until you know. Then you wouldn't waste all these classes."

Collin kept her voice gentle. "They won't be wasted, Pam. She'll have to take them sooner—"

Pam raised her eyebrows. "I'm addressing my daughter."

"You were. I'm sorry." Collin settled back on the couch and patted Geoffrey's back.

Wendy picked up Collin's defense. "I have to take them some time, Mother. If I get them done now, it will take less time to get my degree once I decide what to study."

Pam held her daughter's eyes. Wendy smiled. And smiled. Pam turned away. "Sam will be disappointed he's missed seeing you. You could have both waited until he got home permanently."

Wendy raised her eyebrows. She looked at her brother, and then at her mother. "And we would have. Except you told the doctors you didn't think he would be ready to come home for another six months to a year." She motioned to her brother. "We both thought he was doing fine."

Pam's eyes narrowed. "This isn't the time or place to be discussing Sam."

Brutus leaned forward. "We're all family here, Mom. We all know what's happening."

He turned to Abbott. "Uncle Abbott, would you pray for Wendy and me?"

The older gentleman nodded. "Of course. Lord, we ask You to watch over Brutus and Wendy as they start school next week. Hold them in your hands."

Tapping at the door interrupted him. Collin shoveled Geoffrey over to Jeff and got up to see who knocked at the door.

José stood shivering in the falling snow. Collin opened the door. "Get in here! I didn't know you were coming."

He nodded. "Wendy invited me. Am I interrupting?"

"Never. Come on in. Give me your coat."

He passed it to her. "You'll give it back?"

"Unless I like it better than mine."

José grabbed something from the pocket, and then walked to the family room. Collin yelled, "José's here!" Gretchen stuck her head in the family room to make sure this wasn't a stranger or burglar or other nefarious creature needing to be challenged. Nope, just José. The dog trotted back out of sight.

Cheers echoed from the younger set. More polite calls sounded from the adults. Collin chucked the coat and hustled to join the party. She had a feeling she didn't want to miss something important. The parcel José grabbed had a familiar size to it.

José sat on the floor beside Wendy's chair. She rested her hand on his shoulder. Pam glared at both of them. Abbott cleared his throat. "I believe I had begun praying for Brutus and Wendy."

José held up his hand. "I'd like to interrupt first."

Erin chuckled. "You already did."

"Then I'll do it again." José twisted around to be on his knees, facing Wendy. He held her eyes. "Wendy, I need to ask you. Will you be my wife?" He glanced at Brutus, and then back to Wendy. "And yes, I have your brother's permission to ask."

Wendy caught José in an excited embrace. "Yes! Yes!"

Pam exploded. "Absolutely not! I forbid this. Your father—" She jumped to her feet.

Brutus kept his voice even. "Our father isn't here, Mom. Wendy is an adult. She can make her own decision."

"Not while she lives in my house! Six months, and you're disrespecting everything your father stood for and believed. How could you be so ungrateful?" Pam's body shook. Her face burned with anger. Her fists clenched and unclenched.

Brutus let heat tinge his words. "Ungrateful? Where would we learn that? It's time to drop the act. We know you were the one pulling the strings. Oh, Dad was no saint. But you manipulated him. You played the victim well. We felt sorry for you. Everyone did. Your life was so miserable...so you said. It was always you who told us what Dad said, or did, or thought. But you were the one who didn't want Sam around, not Dad. Sam interrupted your career. He took away your future. Then this trip comes, and it's the perfect opportunity for you to kill two birds with one stone. Someone murders Dad, and Sam gets the rap."

Pam lashed, "Your brother—"

"Is innocent. He didn't kill Dad."

Pam sniffed. "The sheriff determined—"

Brutus's eyes narrowed, and he cut her off. "In the preliminary report. But there's been a further development. A witness came forward. Someone heard you discussing Dad drinking the beer before he died."

Pam whirled around. "What witness? Where?"

A knock—a heavy knock—sounded at the door. Again. Collin went and opened it. Police stood on the porch.

"Is there a Pam Quince here?"

The unknown voices brought Gretchen into the room. She stared at the newcomers but didn't approach or bark. She gave them the doggy stare-down as if saying, "Behave, and we'll get along fine. Touch my people, and we'll have words."

Collin waved them in. They entered the room. Pam's eyes widened in panic and shock. She jumped to her feet. The first man stepped forward. "Mrs. Pam Quince? We have a warrant for your arrest for the murder of Tom Quince. You have the right to remain silent..."

They handcuffed her. Pam did not give up her right to remain silent but cursed roundly the entire way out the door.

Brutus looked at Collin. "I'm sorry, Aunt Collin. I didn't mean to interrupt the party, but I thought she'd take off if she got word about the witness."

Collin walked over and hugged Brutus. "It's okay," she whispered in his ear. "I'm so proud of you." She kissed his cheek.

Brutus looked at his sister, still clinging to José. "Sorry I couldn't warn you, Wenders."

Her face drew into solemn lines. She nodded to her brother. "It's okay. I love you, Bub."

Brutus turned back to Abbott. "You keep being interrupted. Would you please pray for all of us?"

Abbott stood to his feet. "I am honored." He bowed his head. "Lord, thank You for these young people. Thank You for the love between Wendy and José. Bless their union with Your grace and peace. Watch over Brutus and Wendy as they begin their studies and José as he completes his. Hold all these in Your arms. Lead them, guide them, direct them in Your paths. We ask this in Jesus' Name, amen."

Collin's heart tugged. "What about Sam? What happens to him?"

Brutus ducked his head. "He's going to stay with Aunt Polly and Uncle Matt. They're Dad's family. The psychologists want time to work with him about not coming home to Mom. They think he should be ready to leave in another two weeks." He motioned to Wendy. "He'll go back to regular school and stay with them during the week. Wenders and I will take care of him on the weekends."

José slipped his arm around Wendy's waist. "He can come live with us after we get married." He smiled at her. "We might even adopt him."

Collin hugged and kissed the young couple. Again. "I think that is a wonderful idea. Sam will be in great hands."

Tee bounced on her bottom. "Cake. Cake. Cake."

Collin grinned at her. "Hush, child."

Her face fell, and her lower lip extended. Erin murmured, "Cake. Cake. Cake." Tee's eyes light back up. Collin scowled at her brother.

Cake was cut, finally. Gretchen hung around in case any messes needed to be cleaned up. Presents were given. Love shared. The Fields departed (with cake). Brutus, Wendy, and José left (also with cake). Collin, Jeff, Rob, Erin, Vy, and the five children remained. And still, cake remained. The twins were placed in their carriers, sleeping peacefully. The triplets lay on the floor watching a movie. The adults relaxed in the quiet.

A knock came at the front door. A gentle knock. Tentative, even. Jeff started to his feet. Collin waved him off. "I got all the others. I'll get this one."

She opened the door. A thirty-something woman huddled against the cold. She smiled at Collin. She had shoulder-length brown hair pulled back in a ponytail. She wore an OSU Alumni jacket, black jeans, and a silver and red toboggan. Collin recognized the height and weight, if not the face. The woman held out her hand. "Hello, Collin."

She eyed her sideways. "Bertie?"

"May I come in?"

Collin caught the woman by the sleeve and pulled her in. "Of course! Come in where it's warm." She turned around. "Hey! It's Bertie!"

Gretchen came in to check out the newest addition to the household. She sniffed Bertie over carefully, and then licked her hand, pronouncing her safe to remain. The shepherd decided the kitchen was too far for all this coming and going, so she lay in the family room.

Vy, Jeff, and Erin stood to their feet. Gently, so as not to wake the babies, they all broke into applause.

Bertie curtsied and bowed. "Knock it off."

Collin hugged the woman. "I'll take the jacket and hat."

"I can't stay long. The storm is building, and I've got slick tires. But I wanted to come over and introduce the real me."

Erin held out his hand. "Welcome, real me. Name?"

"It's technically AnnaBertrand Meriweather Doule. I have always preferred Bertie."

Jeff grinned. "I can see why." He motioned her to the couch. "Sit. At least for a little while."

The triplets climbed to their feet to meet this new person. They introduced themselves, told her how old they were (now five) and they would start school in the fall but not full-time. Not until next year. Right, Mommy?

Caleb, probably hoping for seconds, offered, "We had a party.

Do you want cake?"

Tee bounced up and down on her toes. "It's really good cake."

Joshua added, "But there isn't any ice cream. Mommy said it wasn't an ice cream kind of party."

Bertie's eyes sparkled with all the attention. She addressed the trio as a whole. "Thank you. I'll have a little piece. And it's okay there's no ice cream. I could step outside and put snow on it if I wanted ice cream."

Collin served Bertie. The former commander eyed Vy. "You're thinner." She grinned at Erin. "You're not."

He humphed at her. "I'm keeping up my strength."

Bertie tried to lean around the corner. "Babies in the nursery?"

Vy motioned to the kitchen. "They're in there. I'll introduce you when you're done with the cake."

Jeff sat on the floor with his children. He leaned toward Bertie. "I appreciate what you've done. And what it's cost you."

Bertie shrugged. "What's a career compared to doing what's right?"

Erin's tone darkened. "You're one of the very few who would make that exchange."

Bertie slid a bite of cake into her mouth, savored it. "I have to live with myself. And my maker." She dipped her head. "I hear he's kind of strict about those things."

Collin smiled gently. "He's mostly One Who loves you."

Bertie looked down. "Maybe." She looked up. "Maybe someday you can tell me all about Him." She finished her cake. "Let's see those bebes."

Vy stood with Bertie. Collin decided another look at the sleeping twins wouldn't hurt. The three walked into the kitchen. Vy lifted the covers. Bertie stood back and stared, her face as awed as the trios'. Moisture collected in the woman's eyes. She brushed it away roughly and lowered her head. After a moment, she whispered, "May I?"

Vy nodded and lifted Caitlin out of the carrier. She cradled her child a moment, and then handed her to Bertie. "Meet Caitlin Evelyn Winger."

Bertie snuggled the infant into her arms. Wonder filled her face. She turned away from Collin and Vy, danced slowly to a barstool, and sat down. She touched the tiny fingers, which curled around her own. Bertie leaned forward and kissed the little hand. She whispered, "Hello, littlest one. You are so beautiful."

Bertie kept her back to Collin and Vy. There were whispered words only Bertie and Caitlin shared. Vy and Collin exchanged glances. Collin's heart hurt. What had this woman given up? First for her professional life, and now the career itself? Who was this principled person?

After five minutes of conversation, Bertie turned back to Collin and Vy. Her face streaked with tears, but she smiled through them. She stood and handed Caitlin back to Vy. Collin handed Bertie a tissue, and then whispered, "Unless you want Gretchen to clean you up. She'd be more than happy, I know."

"Um. Dog kisses." Bertie laughed. "I've missed those, too."

Vy reinserted Caitlin in her carrier, and then the three women walked back to the family room. Jeff had gone to the back to put the triplets to bed.

Rob stepped outside a moment, and then came back covered in ice pellets. He shook his head. "Nope. Icing out. No one's going anywhere." He raised his brows at Bertie. "Especially if you have slick tires. And why would you leave those in winter?"

Bertie shrugged. "I've been a little busy. I haven't had time for proper vehicle maintenance."

Jeff walked in from the back. "What's this about slick tires?"

Bertie grimaced. "Never mind."

Collin shook her head. "You can't be driving out in ice. We just got to meet you. I don't want to risk losing a friend so soon."

Erin nodded. He looked at Vy. "We'll spend the night. I've got good tires, but nothing holds in ice. I'm not chancing it."

Jeff held Bertie's eyes. "We have plenty of rooms. Not like the lodge, of course, but you won't have to sleep with a triplet."

Collin grinned. "And I've got pajamas you can use. I still have an impressionable son."

"MOM!"

If you enjoyed *Reckoning*, sign up for Colleen Snyder's newsletter to stay up with new books and new projects. It will also give you a place to talk to the author directly. And she loves to talk to her readers. Trust me!
Emails will NOT be sold, shared, or used for any other purpose. Promise.
Go to: colleensnyderauthor.com and leave your email to sign up. Read on to learn more about Colleen's other books in the series.

Did you miss the first book in the Collin Walker series?

VERDICT AT THE RIVER'S EDGE

What terrifies you?

In the dark recesses of your soul, what is it that you've managed to avoid, to hide, to bury deep, never to be faced? And what if the Lord asked you to face that fear for no other reason than, "Because I'm asking?" What would you do?

Welcome to Collin Walker's world.

Collin Walker, a social worker from the inner city of Oakton, Ohio, comes to Camp Grace for what is billed as "an extreme sports camp." Her single purpose: to show her ward, Rob Sider, that there is more to life than the streets "...show you can be strong and still love, win without cheating, and succeed in life without all the bells and whistles...." Collin has no way of knowing that God has other plans for her week: facing a lifelong terror of rushing rivers, and perhaps her greatest fear of all, the possibility of real love.

Available now on Amazon: Verdict at the River's Edge

Also available: Book Two in the Collin Walker Series:

INHERITANCE

Three hundred MILLION dollars. Your inheritance. Buy anything you want, go anywhere you want, do anything you want. All yours. Except…

You're a social worker. How do you maintain "street cred" with the kids you've devoted your life to?

How will that kind of money affect the man you love?

And then there's your birth family. The ones that abandoned you to die at fourteen. The ones you suspect even now are trying to have you killed over the money. How do you share with them? Or do you?

What would Jesus do? What would He want you to do? Would you do it?

Welcome back to Collin Walker's world

Collin's life has been both turned upside down and inside out. With her grandfather's passing, Collin has been forced into a position she never wanted. Her inheritance of millions comes with baggage. Her father and his brothers have been fighting for it since before she was born. It is the very heart of the reason she's been estranged from her family the past twelve years.

But now, with the will coming into effect, Collin must revisit all the old relationships and all the old traumas. She thought she had made peace with her past through the Lord. But when the past becomes the present, will she still forgive? Even if it's her family that wants her dead?

Join her and find out.

Available now on Amazon: Inheritance

Also available: Book Three in the Collin Walker/Farrell Series

ACCUSATIONS

When was the last time you lied? Do you lie to keep a secret? Or do you keep a secret to hide a lie?

Collin Farrell has a secret, and she can't wait to tell her husband.

Jeff Farrell has a secret, too, one he's been hiding from Collin since before they married.

Collin's brother, Erin, has a girlfriend with a secret she won't tell.

Vy Johnson is a DEA agent who knows all about lies and secrets.

What happens when Secrets and Lies collide?

Cars get crushed (with the drivers inside.)

Homes explode.

Marriages implode.

Careers—and lives—are jeopardized.

Can God work even this together for the good of all involved and still get the glory from it?

Available Now on Amazon: Accusations

Also available: Book Four in the Collin Walker/Farrell Series

DESPAIR

"Choose. One lives. One dies."
What do you do when hope is all you have?
Is it really all you need?
Where is God when every choice looks dark?
Erin Winger's fiancée and his infant niece have been violently kidnapped. . The kidnappers don't want money. They want revenge. And not against Erin or the baby's mother. No, the kidnappers want revenge against Erin's father. The father Erin and his sister put in prison three years ago. A cold-hearted man who has no interest in saving anyone.

Bound, gagged, and imprisoned in an abandoned shack in the deep of winter, can Erin's fiancée and the baby survive? In the race between hypothermia and life, can they both endure the sub-freezing temperatures long enough for help to reach them?

Available now on Amazon: Despair

DECEPTION

"One man in a thousand, Solomon says, will stick more close than a brother...But the thousandth man will stand by your side, to the gallows' feet and after." Rudyard Kipling

Who is your "thousandth man?" The friend with who you can share your heart and soul? The one who knows your triumphs, your loves, your weakness, your fears?

What if they betray you?

Someone is trying to destroy Collin Farrell by tormenting her with reminders of the past. They are planting letters in the house—while she's home—threatening her and her children. The same someone has let loose lies and rumors that can destroy Collin's reputation and character.

Only a friend would be close enough to pull it off. But which one? Who hates her? Who wants to drive her away from the church? Destroy her family? Can she distinguish between who loves her and who is merely pretending? Can you?

<u>**Available now on Amazon: Despair**</u>

Look for *Twisted*, a novella coming soon:

"So, what do you think?"

Walker kneeled in the ruined church and stared at the burn marks on the floor. She traced the patterns with her hand. Lifted her fingers to her nose and sniffed. Walked around the remains of the sanctuary and eyed the charred studs. After a moment, she looked at Pastor Mars. "This wasn't from a lightning strike. This was arson."

Wait for it. Wait for it. Watch his eyes.

Pastor Mars's eyes widened, then returned to normal. His cheeks reddened. His hands twitched. He pulled them together and held them at his waist. He stammered, then pulled himself together. "Why would you say such a thing? How can you know?"

The voices in her head joined Pastor Mars in his accusation. *Yeah, how? You're an eighteen-year-old girl. You don't know anything.*

You're trying to get attention.

You're showing off.

Did you really believe he wanted to know what you thought when he asked you? You have any idea what the term 'rhetorical question' means?

Walker pointed out the signs. "The fire started in four different spots. You can see the burn patterns on the floor. I can smell the accelerant." She pointed to the walls. "All these caught at once." She stared hard at the middle-aged man. "You should call someone to investigate."

Mars pulled his suitcoat into place. He settled his shoulders. Raised his head. "I'll call the fire department. The fire chief can make that determination if he thinks there's enough evidence." He looked at Ron Jennings, the leader of the relief group. "Does this mean you won't start the teardown? That's what you came for, isn't it? To help us rebuild?"

Ron shook his head. "We'll have to wait for the fire chief." He nodded to Walker. "She's got the good eye. And the background." He smiled at her. "Such as it is."

Walker didn't smile back. *Yes, I have myriad skills. None of which I ever wanted. But that wasn't a choice I was given.*

Ron, being Ron, tried to be diplomatic. "Once we get the okay, we'll tear this thing down in a day. In the meantime, I'm sure there are other places we can be of service. And yes, that is why we came. To help this town rebuild."

The category three tornado that tore through Rallins, Indiana, devastated the farming community. From the rise where the small country church stood, Walker could see a row of houses without roofs.

Trees lay across porches. One old oak had smashed through a garage door. Another had been uprooted and dropped into a front room. Bushes, tree limbs, and debris from homes, littered the streets. And those were the ones she could see.

Walker hiked back to the army barracks tent in the field behind the church. It sat below the hill where the church had stood. Mars apologized profusely for the accommodations or lack thereof. With the devastation in the little town, the congregation had nowhere to put the relief team from Oakton, the capital of Ohio. Cots were set up with a canvas curtain to divide the men's living quarters from the women's.

Her twenty-five college mates sat on top of and at the two picnic tables provided for their use. Ten women, plus Walker, and thirteen men, plus Ron Jennings, made up the all-volunteer team. Walker was the youngest, Ron the oldest. He'd delayed his college career two years before starting a major in English. Now in his fourth year, he was the "old man" of the team at twenty-four. Everyone else fit in between.

Racially, they were more diverse. Like the Sunday School song sang, "Red and yellow, black and white," and every hue in between. Ron's dark skin contrasted with Walker's pale white Anglo-Saxon background. Two of the women were of Latino descent. Maybe they weren't quite "every tongue, tribe, and nation," but they were close. Their most common denominator was they'd all been homeless.

Walker slipped into the table where the females sat. Maria, with dark hair, beautiful eyes, and a perfect complexion, glared at her in mock anger. "What did you say? Pastor Mars looked happy until you started talking."

"He asked me what I thought about the condition of the church. I told him it burned because of arson."

Maria sighed. "Of course you did. And his response was?"

Walker stared at the table. "How could I possibly know that? I'm a kid. What would I know?" She didn't bother keeping the bitterness from her voice.

"Is that what he said? Or how you interpreted it?" Maria's voice lilted in jest.

Ignore her. She doesn't know you. No one takes you seriously.
You are loved.
Ignore that. He doesn't know you.

Walker repeated the Pastor's words verbatim. "'How can you know?' I'm a kid."

Maria's eyes twinkled. "Maybe if you let your hair grow long instead of bobbing it, and maybe if you wore a little make-up, and maybe chose some decent shoes instead of those hightops, people wouldn't assume you're a kid. They'd recognize you for the sophomore in college that you are. Even if you are only eighteen."

Walker breathed slowly. Maria tapped the table lightly. "Passing as a boy worked for you on the streets, Walker. I understand. I do. But you've been off the streets for two years now. Think about putting it away. You have a new life. You're a new creation. Appreciate it."

Walker lowered her eyes and stared at the ground. She closed her eyes. "It wasn't the streets, Maria. It's what came before." She looked up into her friend's eyes. "God may forget my past, but I can't. There are too many reminders."

She chewed her lip, then admitted. "We're in Indiana. I was told if I ever set foot in this state again, I'd be found and killed." Walker snorted. "Not something you forget."

Maria shifted on the bench. "Does it still have power over you?"

"I'm here, aren't I? I came on this trip. No, it doesn't hold power over me. But so many seeds were planted in my life...." Walker trailed off. She shook her head. Raised her eyebrows. "I'm a work in progress that may never be done."

Maria smiled gently. "We're all works in progress, Walker. We can only live it one day at a time."

From the men's table, Jun, the math major from India, yelled, "Hey, Walker. Get your basketball. Let's play."

Before Walker could rise, Ron rejoined them. "I talked with Pastor Mars, and since we can't start on the church, we can go door-to-door and ask people if they want help. Some might be waiting for their insurance companies to come out. Some could be ready and would love the muscle. We'll start in the morning. Everyone down with that?"

Nine heads nodded. Jun pointed to Walker. "We're going to get a game going. You want to play?"

Ron shrugged. "Why not?" He looked back up the hill. "I don't think the pastor can see us enough to object to a co-ed competition."

Jun chuckled. "Especially since it will be nine against one." He grinned at Walker. "And you will still beat us."

Walker shook her head in mock anger. "No, I won't. I'm a team player."

Maria laughed. "Yeah. She's on the girls' team. Four against six. And with her, we will beat you."

Walker ignored the trash talk and hustled to her bunk. She retrieved her ball from under the cot. The feel of the hard rubber stilled her soul. Her love, her passion. The only time she felt fully alive was on the court. Pine floor or asphalt, it didn't matter. She could be herself. And it was the only time the inner voices were silenced.

The young people moved to the mostly abandoned basketball court. There were hoops but no nets. Free throw lines remained in evidence, but the center line had been scuffed out. Sidelines were non-existent. Contrary to Maria's claims, the teams were split three and two, men to women. Maria threw the ball up, and play began.

Walker's mind went into game mode. Nothing existed except the ball, the basket, and the players in between. Run, run, run. Pass. Run. Pass. Block. Shoot. Pass. Block. Run. Run. Run. Shoot.

She had no idea what the score was, who was ahead, or by how much. If there were observers, she didn't see them. Nothing mattered but the precise movement of the ball to the goal. Her passes sang. Her shots dived through the hoop. Her blocks were clean and with passion. Walker lived and breathed on the court for the love of the game.

Only when someone—Ron, maybe?—called, "Game!" did she return to awareness of the world around her. Everyone breathed hard, hands on their knees, bent over double to catch oxygen for their lungs. Adrenaline surged through Walker. Her face hurt from smiling. She looked from player to player. "Who won?"

Maria gasped, "Do you really care?"

Walker grinned. "No. Was it a good game?"

Ron put his arm around her shoulders. "Yes, yes, it was."

Walker froze. Life drained from her, sucked into a black hole in her being. Her eyes lost focus. Nightmare memories engulfed her. She stood stock still, twitching almost imperceptibly as remembered blows assailed her body. Over and over and over....

A voice broke into the emptiness. Gentle. Quiet. Soothing. "Walker. Walker. You're okay. Listen to me. Listen to my voice. You're here at the church. You're with friends. Your brothers and sisters in the Lord. We're all here for you. You're in an illusion. It's past. It's gone. Over and done. Not real. You're safe. You're loved. Come back, Walker."

The sound reached into the desolation. Seeped through the walls. Became light in the blackness. A trail to follow out of the long ago back to the now. Walker's eyes closed. She took a deep breath, let it out slowly, then opened her eyes.

Maria stood in front of her, eyeing her closely. "Are you with us?"

Walker nodded. She bit the inside of her mouth and looked around. Her classmates stood in a semi-circle around her, watching her, waiting for some sign, some signal she was okay. She smiled and ducked her head to the side. "Kinda lost it there."

Jun snorted. "I guess so."

Ron's face was pale. "I'm sorry, Walker. I didn't know. I..."

Walker interrupted his apologies. "Stop. I didn't know, either." She shook her head. "Fight or flight. My brain went to flight. Nothing to fight with." She took a deep breath. "It's over now. I'm back, I'm fine, and I still want to know how the game went."

Jun laughed. "You don't know? Your team won, of course." His eyes sparkled. "You even switched sides for a bit to help us out, but it wasn't enough."

Walker stepped back. "I what?"

Ron laughed as well. "Yeah. You told me you wanted it not to be a blowout, so you swapped sides midway through the last quarter. Made it close, I'll tell you that."

Walker snapped a look at Maria. "I did what?"

Maria grinned and pointed at Jun. "What he said. You did. You don't remember?"

Walker shook her head. "I don't remember anything when I'm playing. It's all a blur."

"So were you. Woman, you play the meanest game of roundball I've ever seen. Why aren't you on the team at college?"

Walker's joy drained from her. She shrugged. "No time. Work. School. Volunteering. I don't have time for team sports."

Jun nodded. "When we are in Brother Matt's work-for-college program, there is not a lot of free time."

Walker added, "If I were majoring in sports, it would be different. My major is Social Work. That way, I can be useful when I'm done."

Maria eyed her. "You're useful now, Walker. God is using you in everything you do."

Using you? You're worthless. No one needs you.

I don't know. She's good for a laugh every now and then.

Yeah, when she tries to do something intelligent. That's always hilarious.

Walker bowed her head slightly and walked her demons back to the tent. Reality returned.